D0540436

FLIGHT

Also by Victoria Glendinning

NON-FICTION

Trollope

Rebecca West: A Life

Vita: The Life of Vita Sackville-West

Edith Sitwell: A Unicorn Among Lions

Elizabeth Bowen: Portrait of a Writer

Jonathan Swift

A Suppressed Cry

Hertfordshire

Sons and Mothers (ed., with Mathew Glendinning)

FICTION

The Grown-Ups

Electricity

FLIGHT

—— ◄o► ——

Victoria Glendinning

First published in Great Britain by Scribner, 2002
An imprint of Simon & Schuster UK Ltd
A Viacom Company

1 3 5 7 9 10 8 6 4 2

Simon & Schuster UK Ltd
Africa House
64–78 Kingsway
London WC2B 6AH

www.simonsays.co.uk

Simon & Schuster Australia
Sydney

A CIP catalogue record for this book is available
from the British Library

Hardback ISBN 0–7432–2028–5
Trade Paperback ISBN 0–7432–3128–7

Typeset by Palimpsest Book Production Limited,
Polmont, Stirlingshire
Printed and bound in Great Britain by
Omnia Books Limited, Glasgow

For Deborah Singmaster

ARRIVALS

When did it begin to go wrong, for Martagon? At what precise point did he step off the main path? It seemed that at last he had everything. He was at the top of his profession. He had found the love of his life.

June 24, 2000. The sun rises over Provence, drenching the countryside with light and colour from the lavender fields. The undulating ridges of purple stretch away into the haze, flanked by fields of vines in full fresh leaf, dancing in lines over the curve of the land. Sprinklers are already sprinkling, spraying the air with refracted light. The poplars do not stir. There is no wind, and no sound except the hissing of the sprinklers and the drone of bees already busy in the lavender.

It is going to be a perfect day.

An earth track runs along the edge of this lavender field and cuts through the vines. The track joins two villages, and intersects with the narrow road leading to the Château de Bonplaisir. Or, rather, it used to. Now, the track is going nowhere, its trajectory abruptly halted three kilometres on by a perimeter fence of heavy-duty steel mesh, three metres high. Tractors have already made a new path, turning sharply aside at the fence and working round it. In a generation or two, no one will know about the old track, or remember the château as it was before it became the airport hotel.

Martagon first went to the Château de Bonplaisir in the early summer of 1999, just after the contractors moved in to transform it into a hotel. He happened to be in Provence, making a site visit to the new airport under construction. He agreed, unwillingly, to meet the ex-owner of the château and check the inventories of the garden furniture, ornaments and statues, which had been overlooked.

Thus it was pure chance he met Marina de Cabrières at all.

It was meant, they said. We were waiting for each other.

That first meeting was more than a year ago. Today, the perfect day, is the grand opening of Bonplaisir, the new airport for Provence. It was planned to open 'on time, on budget', as a millennium event. The official reason for the five months' delay was the danger of Y2K complications. The real reason is more shameful, and it concerns Martagon.

Martagon had heard something about Marina de Cabrières before he met her. Glamorous, people said. Capricious. She worked in film in Paris, in a dilettante kind of way. That was all he knew. He didn't realize that he had actually already seen her – until the glittering day when he stood with his briefcase, wearing a freshly pressed linen suit, in the shade of the archway that led into the great courtyard of Bonplaisir.

He had seen her a couple of months earlier, when he

was sitting alone with a beer in the Madeleine café in Aix-en-Provence on market day, enjoying the scents from the spice stall outside the café and reading the *Herald Tribune*. She was with a group at the next table. He found he could not stop staring. Wherever he looked, his gaze returned to this red-haired, white-skinned young woman in a sleeveless yellow dress. He saw when she turned her head that there was a yellow silk flower in the knot of hair at the back. Her hair was drawn tightly back from her high forehead and her eyes were heavy-lidded and huge. He wondered how old she was. Early thirties, perhaps. It was hard to tell. She wasn't talking much. She seemed preoccupied.

Martagon stared.

When she got up with the rest of the group to leave, he saw how tall she was. She stood looking across the table at him for a long moment with a denim jacket slung over one shoulder and a blue string bag full of fruit dangling from her hand. It was Martagon who looked away first.

Women often looked at Martagon in public places and on the street. He was well used to that. This woman was different.

As she walked away he noticed that she did not have the slender, elegant legs he was expecting. Her ankles were not exactly thick, but they were . . . ordinary.

The man who loves this extraordinary woman, he said to himself, would love with particular tenderness her unremarkable, serviceable, rather disappointing legs.

He had never given her another conscious thought. But her image appeared, every now and then, unsummoned, in his mind's eye.

The sun has risen higher over the lavender fields, and

the temperature has risen too. Inside the perimeter fence hundreds of people are frantically busy. The main runway glistens with fresh tarmac. On the apron, private jets and short-haul planes in bright liveries stand ready, like toys waiting to be played with. Workers – *les arabes* – who have been up all night pushing polishers round the translucent glass floors of the concourse are exhaustedly going over the same ground yet again.

From New York's JFK, American francophiles and pleasure-seekers, who have paid twenty thousand dollars per head, have already taken off on the inaugural flight of an Air France 747 to the new airport. Included in the ticket is a grand dinner at the Château de Bonplaisir. Limos will ferry the guests from the airport to the hotel along a new road lined with white oleanders and young olive trees. The passengers on the 747 are looking forward to what the publicity pack calls five-star grand-luxe accommodation in large high rooms furnished with museum-quality eighteenth-century beds and armoires and *toile de Jouy* bed-curtains and drapes. They sip their complimentary drinks, thirty-three thousand feet above the Atlantic.

In the late afternoon, the drone of the bees over the lavender merges with the whine of the 747 coming in to land. The event is beginning.

Giles Harper, chairman of Harper Cox, the main consulting engineers to the project, is already at the Château de Bonplaisir, waiting for his wife Amanda to finish dressing and doing her face. Giles sits on the edge of their giant bed looking out into the gardens through a window framed by elaborate pink and white drapes. He has given up smoking; and he is smoking, using a gilded floral Limoges dish from the bedside table as an ashtray. This is, or should be, a great day for Giles. The name Harper Cox is up there with the names of the other main players on an electronic roll of honour unfurling continuously in the departures hall.

He is anxious. He can see on his laptop, open on the console table between the high windows, the e-mail message from marteau@blink.com.

'Not coming. Something terrible has happened. Martagon.'

Giles is past being surprised by anything Martagon does. It was the 'something terrible' that exercised him. Could it be something Martagon now knew, or suspected, about the glass flooring? He knew from his chairman that there was a last-minute query. The site engineer had been anxious and attempting to contact Martagon.

Giles has quite enough imagination to envisage the first running crack, to hear the gun-shot sound, and to anticipate the screaming panic as the floor of the arrivals hall collapses in lethal shards and cubes, tipping hundreds of people down to bloody injury and, for some, death on the floor below, which in its turn . . . But his thoughts tend to the pragmatic. If anything at all goes wrong with the complex glass structure, Martagon's special responsibility, it will bring disgrace on Harper Cox. It will be the end of Harper Cox.

Much more likely, Giles thinks, that something has happened to Martagon himself. Whatever else Martagon is, he's not a coward.

'Martagon's a shit,' says Amanda, coming into the bedroom from her bathroom. She is pregnant, and has bought for the occasion a shimmery floating dress of mixed blues and greens. Her blonde hair is held back from her forehead with a blue velvet Alice band.

'You look really nice,' says Giles. He remembers Marina's sultry, mocking voice saying to Martagon in the hall in the Fulham house, after that awful dinner party, 'No one over the age of twenty-two should be *allowed* to wear an Alice band.'

'Martagon's not a shit,' says Giles.

'I'm only thinking about how often he's let you down. Not to mention your sister.'

Giles's sister Julie is not coming to the opening of the airport. No one knows where she is at this moment.

Giles puts his head in his hands. He is a hard man, except where his sister Julie is concerned.

'So he's not a shit,' says Amanda. 'He's just weak, arrogant, dishonourable, you name it. Marina's the shit, is that it? It's always the woman's fault, is that what you really think?'

'Marina is . . . Marina is something that just happened to Martagon. The most serious thing that has ever happened to him.'

'Like a disease. Well, she'll be here this evening, I don't doubt, all dolled up like the Queen of Sheba.'

It was not such a perfect day after all. Suddenly, in the late afternoon, there was a thunderstorm. But it passed.

Marina will not be at the airport opening. And thirty miles away from Bonplaisir, Martagon Foley has been lying on his back all afternoon in the long grass under an olive tree in the garden of Marina's farmhouse outside Cabrières d'Aigues.

It's no good asking questions unless you are going to get some answers. Martagon doesn't even know what the right questions are. He will stay there as the day declines, trying to think. He is in shock. All he knows for sure is that he has lost his love, and maybe his honour and his reputation as well.

ONE

Martagon the singleton, and Giles and Amanda Harper the married couple, go back a long way.

Martagon was a reader, though not a writer. He had his mother's love of stories and pictures, and also her way of describing things in terms of something else, as part of an oblique mission to explain.

Amanda Harper found him annoying at times: 'I never know what to make of you, I never know where you're really at. Can you ever see anything straight?'

'I'm completely transparent. What you see is what you get.'

'But I don't get you,' said Amanda.

Martagon liked Amanda a lot but did not fancy her in the least, and she knew it. In that sense she had indeed not 'got' him, and it needled her. Once when she complained about Martagon to Giles, he had replied, unperturbed, 'Martagon's a law unto himself. He's an original.'

'He'll come a cropper one of these days,' said Amanda.

His mother had wanted him to be a teacher. She wanted him to be a 'good person', and she said he would make a good teacher. The idea filled him with gloom. He did not want to be a 'good teacher' even though he did, profoundly, want to be a good person, even though he wasn't sure, as a boy, what that meant. Being a good person seemed to involve courage, endurance, honesty, generosity – old-world virtues, the very words a little quaint.

He also wanted adventure, and risk. Having failed to be accepted to study architecture, he settled for engineering – a way of making and doing not unlike the way of a creative artist, and not incompatible either with being a good person or with making a good income. His hope was to live on the edge, and to work on the boundaries between engineering, architecture and fine art.

When he was doing his degree course, engineering students in British universities were, axiomatically, nerds in anoraks. His mother didn't know about anoraks. But she said, 'Will you be coming home from work in blue overalls with spanners sticking out of the top pocket?'

Martagon explained to her the difference between a mechanic and an engineer.

He fought back by cultivating his appearance. He dressed in black from head to foot when it became the arty norm. He made a name for himself as an actor in the most experimental of the student theatre groups. He never lost sight of his aspiration to be an artist-engineer, and was determined to prove that an engineer could be as prestigious and high profile as he knew they always had been in continental Europe. He didn't fit in anywhere, in the England of his youth. If there was some tribe to which he belonged, it was scattered everywhere. He hadn't found it.

He decided that he would work largely overseas, and make an international name for himself. England, to Martagon, carried overtones of separation from parents, boarding-school, rain, adolescent depression. When he was young he conflated his first term at the English school with his father's death, as if the one had caused the other. The shadow of this notion, no longer consciously formulated, still lingered.

Martagon worked hard and was successful, helped along by new developments in the industry – especially in glass technology. Martagon, by the time Giles Harper approached him about the Bonplaisir airport project, was one of a small cluster of international stars who were changing the image of the profession and extending its boundaries.

The fact that Giles came to him at all was a measure of Martagon's value. The two had quarrelled five years previously, and gone their separate ways. Before that, they were great friends. Between them, they orchestrated the merging of Harper's with Cox & Co., and formed the new and profitable entity: Harper Cox.

Martagon was taken aback, just recently, when he mentioned to a younger colleague that he himself had had the good fortune to be trained by Arthur Cox – and realized that the name meant nothing at all. The firm Harper Cox was universally known in the construction industry. But Arthur himself was completely forgotten.

When, in the early 1980s, Martagon took his first job with what was then Cox & Co., it had already been one of the most respected British engineering firms for decades. Arthur Cox had been given a knighthood in Mrs Thatcher's first Honours List. But Arthur never changed. He was still Arthur Cox, and legendary in the industry. He was a bear of a man with a big baggy body and a big creased face under a shock of dry wiry hair, its brown fading to grey. He had a voice like a foghorn. He was austere, teetotal, dedicated, and ran the firm as if he were the father of a family.

That, as time passed and business practices changed, was the trouble. Arthur did not go in for participatory management. He could seem insensitive and reactionary.

He had no notion of power-sharing. Yet his impulses were generous; he was not bent on making a private fortune. As the firm's profits rose on the back of overseas contracts, he set up the Cox Foundation, which funded, as it still famously does, libraries and cultural centres in emerging countries. Martagon is one of the trustees.

Arthur gave Martagon his first job and was unfailingly supportive of his work. After a very few years – scandalously few, some old-timers thought – Martagon had a seat on the main board. Martagon, in return, felt a fierce, filial loyalty to Arthur. All Arthur's people were loyal to him, for that matter, even those who worried about the way things were going.

Martagon still goes through bouts of guilt about the merger, especially at four o'clock in the morning when he cannot sleep. He has only himself to blame. But there was more to it than that. He could never say to anyone, 'I was steam-rollered by Giles Harper.'

It would in any case have been more true to say, 'I was seduced by Giles Harper.'

For Cox & Co., the merger was a disaster. All these years later, the old Cox people who remain do not really mesh with old Harper people. The culture is different. In his heart Martagon is for ever a Cox person, even though the Harper ethos turned out to have the edge, and even though he quit a couple of years after the merger. Martagon, telling the story, could never convey to anyone the personal drama, or the pain of betrayal.

It was Harpers who approached the Cox partnership, suggesting a merger. Giles Harper and Martagon, each representing his firm as CEO, met for the first time over an informal lunch at the Caprice. They found one another exciting. They were both young – early thirty-somethings, with Giles just a few years the elder – and alike in ways that they both found flattering. Or was it just Giles who was flattering Martagon? Who was wooing whom?

To look at, they were chalk and cheese. Giles's grey suit had a sheen on it. His emerald green tie had an even higher sheen. He wore a gold bracelet and a signet ring. When he smiled, he revealed half a gold tooth. He was stocky and muscular, already carrying a tad too much weight for his height. With his south London voice, and in working gear – hard hat, neon jacket and steel-toed boots – he could merge perfectly with the workforce on a construction site.

Martagon, in the same situation, was far more intimately engaged with the problems at ground level than Giles ever was. Yet he looked like an actor cast for the part by a self-indulgent director.

The differences in their self-presentation added a glint of razor-wire to their immediate rapport. They agreed they were both risk-takers. They liked living on the edge, moving around, feeling at ease wherever they found themselves. Harpers' main business was in the UK. Cox & Co. had their long-established international business, which Giles coveted. A merger between the two firms, with the emphasis on overseas expansion, could be a winner.

What both young men also knew – though neither referred to it directly – was that the Cox partnership, for the first time in its history, was losing money overseas. Martagon knew some of the reasons why. Emerging countries were beginning to produce their own engineers, and their governments to insist on local professionals forming part of the team. Sustainability, local opinion, local culture and long-term local needs had to be factored in to proposals and bids from outside firms.

Arthur Cox saw his mission as a 'civilizing' one. Arthur thought he knew what was best for developing countries, which generally meant the inculcation of northern European values and attitudes – everything that spelt 'civil society' to Arthur – as well as what was best for the business.

Cox & Co. were beginning to be seen at best as paternalist, at worst imperialist. They were continuing to tender, but failing to win contracts. Within the firm, only the chief planner, Tom Scree, was vociferous about the need for a change of ethos. Tom Scree was not one of Arthur's favourites. The board should have been undertaking a major rethink, and identifying new markets. Arthur resisted change. Arthur was as he was.

Giles Harper impressed on Martagon that the way ahead lay not only in identifying new markets but in reconfiguring existing ones. They should be going for contracts funded by international aid and development programmes, and co-operate with whichever of the proliferating NGOs (non-governmental organizations, which Arthur, as Martagon told Giles, still called 'charities') were operating in the different areas.

'Making our profit by milking overseas aid, you mean?'

'Look at it another way,' said Giles. 'We'd be putting our expertise at the service of the aid programmes. The poor and disadvantaged in emerging countries don't need naïve idealists swarming all over them, with no practical skills and a load of theoretical bullshit. Emerging countries need bridges, dams, access roads. And for us, it is opportunity.'

Giles made the word 'opportunity' sound sexy. Every new contact, every incoming call, was a possible opportunity, for him. Opportunity was what turned Giles on and opportunity was what kept him going. Martagon only learned later how many irons in the fire Giles had at any one time, and how little he worried about getting his fingers burned. Once Martagon saw a personal bank statement of Giles's, lying openly on a table. If Martagon had been in debt to that amount he would have been a nervous wreck. Giles didn't give a damn. He saved his energies for the next opportunity.

'I'm not interested in money for its own sake,' he told Martagon at lunch, 'only for what it can do. I want the power that money gives me.'

Even at that first lunch Martagon deduced that Giles had business interests on his own account, quite separate from the firm. Giles told a story about the great feeling he had, waiting alone at a deserted Stansted airport at three o'clock in the morning, with no sound other than the whine of distant floor-polishers, and he himself straining his eyes into the darkness for the lights of a private plane bringing him a load of bullion from Eastern Europe.

'The romance of commerce!' said Giles, running his fingers through his curly brown hair so that it stood on end. 'Am I very ridiculous?'

'You're not ridiculous.' Martagon, in return, told Giles about the time he stood on the quay at Lagos beside a man, a complete stranger, on a day when the skyline was speckled with incoming vessels. The stranger was raking the horizon with his eyes in a fret of anticipation. He told Martagon, in a strong Glaswegian accent, that he was expecting a cargo of car tyres.

'Why car tyres?' Martagon asked.

The Glaswegian replied with a single sufficient word: 'Shorrtage.'

Shortage of something, for someone, means opportunity for someone else. That is the market. It is, in Giles's phrase, the romance of commerce.

'I worked out early on,' said Giles, 'that there were adults who did things or made things on their own account, and marketed them. I'd call them the self-employed, now. Then there were adults who did things or made things for a boss, in return for a wage or salary. Then there was the boss, who didn't make things and I wasn't sure what he actually did, either. But in the movies I saw he always had sexy secretaries, and talked on the phone a lot, and had a big empty desk, and people came into his office to be told what to do, or to be slagged off, or sacked.'

'So you wanted to be him.'

'I didn't know how to get to be him. I just knew I didn't want to work for anyone else. In that situation, the only thing left is to deal, to sell something for more than you bought it for. Like your "shortage" thing. It could be tyres, or a goat, or a load of firewood, or a bunch of bananas, or a bunch of power-stations in Venezuela.'

'Why Venezuela?'

'It's just something that I – oh, don't ask.'

'You're one of nature's dealers. A trader.' Martagon drained his glass of Chablis. Giles, who was not drinking, sipped his mineral water. Giles's weaknesses were his sweet tooth, and nicotine. He ordered a *crème brûlée* and lit a Marlboro Light.

'I'm a dreamer, too,' he said. 'And you?'

'Oh, I'm a dreamer. But I'm not a dealer. I'm an investor, figuratively speaking.'

'Meaning?'

'I get involved. I need to see a complex project through from beginning to end. I have trouble disengaging. Maybe because I don't have too much in my life apart from my work. I don't have a family, a particular person, to invest myself in.'

'You must meet Amanda, my wife. And my sister Julie, she's something special, although she's got problems, she's a bit of a naïve idealist.' Giles paused and stubbed out his cigarette. 'We could be complementary, you and I. We could help one another. All I know is, I want a very different life from the one my parents have.'

Giles's parents, as he told Martagon, live in Catford. His father works in John Lewis on Oxford Street selling white goods, as he has done all his adult life. His mother is bookkeeper to a small building firm. His father's elder brother set up a small civil engineering company in Portsmouth, and Giles joined his uncle there on leaving school, qualifying as an engineer on day-release courses.

As soon as he qualified he began to work all hours drumming up new business, starting at the top. Within a very few years the company was five times the size, operating nationwide and expanding, very tentatively, overseas. The head office moved from Portsmouth to Crawley, nearer London. Giles's uncle still chaired the board, but he was ready to retire. Giles, to all intents and purposes, ran Harpers.

'If you're a dreamer,' asked Martagon, 'what's your goal, your ultimate dream?'

'I want Amanda and me to end up in a large comfortable house with a garden and a double garage and an indoor pool in a good part of west London, say Chelsea or Kensington or Notting Hill. And a house in the country for weekends. And children, and dogs. It'll all cost a bomb. An absolute bomb. I want an establishment, and no money worries.'

Martagon was surprised that Giles's best dreams were, ultimately, so conventional. 'I can't envisage anything remotely like that. But then I'm a displaced person, I'm a wanderer.'

'You're a bit younger than me, and you haven't got a family. You'll see. And,' Giles added, 'I'd like to leave something of value – an institute or something, a bit like—'

'Like the Cox Foundation?'

'I suppose so.'

As they waited for the bill, they agreed that you can't be like Arthur Cox without being – well, like Arthur Cox, and that's the problem. They both laughed, and Martagon felt a flicker of guilt at the implicit slight to Arthur.

That first lunch expanded into many, at weekly intervals, in the period leading up to the merger negotiations. It was business, and it was also pleasure. There was a private merger between Giles and Martagon long before the real merger went through. Giles quickly acquired an impressive grasp of the international business. Martagon became fascinated by Giles – by his barrow-boy flashness, his burgundy-red Jaguar – and, even more, by the way Giles ran Harpers.

By the standards of Cox & Co. – Martagon saw this all too clearly after the merger – Giles was ruthless, both with staff and clients. He made cutting corners into a professional virtue. He delegated, and how. He created an internal market within the firm. He felt no obligation to familiarize himself with the detail of any project, and gave hell to anyone who should have known the detail and did not. Martagon was scared, excited and – fatally – flattered. He was mesmerized by Giles, and a little in love with him, as men can be in love with other men without ever wanting to make love to them or even thinking about it.

Martagon's father, who was fond of axioms, used to say that 'God is in the details.' It was in the details that Giles's values and attitudes diverged from Martagon's. Perhaps, Martagon thought now, not God but the devil is in the details. Years later, he said to Marina: 'I think Giles may be the devil.'

She was astonished. 'You've always told me what good qualities he has. How he's a wonderful husband, and loyal to his friends, and so on.'

'That's all true. Maybe he's not the devil. Maybe he's just the devil for me. He tempts me, he brings out a sort of materialism and unscrupulousness in me which I wish wasn't there, but it is and it scares me. He's my bad angel. Arthur Cox used to say that I was his good angel, and that used to be true.'

Arthur Cox took a paternal interest in Martagon when he first joined the firm, though for a while Martagon failed to recognize it as such. Arthur would call him into his private office for 'a word'. He would stand with his hands in his pockets, jingling his small change, looking out of the window with his back to Martagon, and outline a problem. 'I'd welcome your thoughts on this. A fresh eye. The papers are on the desk if you want to take a look.'

Martagon would come up with what he thought was the obvious solution, to be met with silence.

'Well, yes', said Arthur at last. 'That's one possibility. But I wonder if we couldn't do it differently.'

Half an hour would pass, while Martagon did his best to come up with other ideas, and Arthur showed every sign of indecisiveness. In the end Arthur would quite suddenly plump with apparent satisfaction for the first course of action they had discussed, and send Martagon back to his desk. Martagon gradually understood that Arthur, by nature, really did like to turn every possibility over and over. But more importantly, he was quite deliberately training Martagon how to marshal the options, how to separate the essential from the inessential – in short, how to think. About once a week Arthur took Martagon for a drink at the end of the day. Nursing his half-pint, he told long stories about the past heroes of the British engineering profession and their achievements, and about those firms that had overreached themselves, growing so large and grand that they no longer functioned effectively.

By osmosis, Martagon learned. In return he became Arthur's eyes and ears. It was he who spotted the quality of Mirabel Plunket. Arthur was too old-world to give immediate credence to the capabilities of a newly qualified female, but he took Martagon's word for it and put her on the fast track. Martagon was proved right.

'You are my good angel,' Arthur said. Martagon knew that Arthur, as he grew older, relied on him more and more.

Martagon and Giles worked on the merger and planned their Camelot.

Giles was a Chelsea supporter, and always had a season ticket and, mysteriously, access to more. When Chelsea were playing at home, the two went together to Stamford Bridge to watch the match. Mostly, as the months passed, they met at the Harpers' house in Fulham, at Amanda's kitchen table or sitting in the garden. It was Martagon who first used the word 'Camelot' to describe their planned joint venture. He meant it literally.

'The Knights of the Round Table weren't sentimental softies. They were tough, in training, ready to fight their corner,' he said. 'They were armed to the teeth with all the latest dark-ages technology and know-how.'

Giles did not read books, he never had. 'Oh, you're so cultured!' he said mockingly.

But he liked that in Martagon. He really did. Maybe, thought Martagon, that's what he wants from me: my difference. I am coming from somewhere else. 'Sir Lancelot and King Arthur didn't sit around all day drinking spritzers and making daisy-chains,' he said.

King Arthur. King Arthur Cox. How was he going to feel about the new Camelot?

'They did have heavy-duty romances, though,' said Amanda. 'From what I remember.'

'They always ended disastrously,' said Martagon. 'Anyway, this daisy-chain is for Julie.'

'That's nice, she'll like that,' said Giles. 'She really will.'

Planes coming into land at Heathrow, at that hour in the evening, flew over the Harpers' garden at an angle of forty-five degrees every few seconds. Martagon put down his daisy-chain to watch them. Long-haul planes, from the ends of the earth. The sky was clear, and Martagon could pick out their liveries and identify them.

'Weird how they suddenly appear, as if they had just been created. There's that split second between seeing a piece of empty sky and seeing a plane in it. It's too quick, like as if *time* was the wrong category to be catching it in. And think of all those people, in all those planes. Escaping from somewhere, or coming home, or arriving somewhere new and exciting, or new and scary, and all finding – I don't know what . . .'

'Opportunity,' said Giles. 'Actually, what they find is Heathrow.'

'Heathrow is purgatory. Something to be got through before you get to heaven. Or hell.'

'How you do go on, Martagon. Get on with your daisy-chain, it's wilting.'

The day that Martagon met Giles's sister for the first time, Amanda had said, 'Julie's pretty screwed up at the moment.'

She sounded as if she was warning him. She and Martagon were sitting, as so often, in the Harpers' back garden, during that first summer of the merger discussions. Martagon was waiting for Giles, who was late back from the office. Julie, too, was expected.

Martagon had noticed how Giles's voice changed when he talked about his sister. He was fiercely protective of her. Martagon imagined that they still inhabited together their childhood world, in which there was complete mutual trust. Both had reacted against their limited, decent upbringing, leaving home as soon as they could.

'They're the opposite sides of the same coin,' said Amanda. 'Both extremists, both driven – but in different directions.'

Julie, the younger, became left-wing and alternative, rejecting the 'system', dressing herself from charity shops, backpacking to India, volunteering, living on no money. She went on to do Development Studies at the University of East Anglia, when she met Hailu – a clever, handsome Ethiopian seconded for a year from the NGO for which he worked in Addis Ababa.

Martagon had never heard the whole story.

'I might as well tell you, since you're more or less one of the family now.' Succinctly, in her north-country way, Amanda filled him in. 'The next thing was, Julie fell pregnant.'

She and Hailu were utterly wrapped up in one another. Julie didn't make friends easily, and Hailu was her first boyfriend. She didn't dare tell her parents about Hailu and the coming baby. At the end of the academic year they got married, very privately, in Norwich. Julie didn't even confide in Giles. Then she flew back to Addis with Hailu – as she informed her parents in a note posted at Heathrow.

Hailu took the pregnant Julie back to his village to meet his family, and left her there.

'Why did he do that?'

'He thought it was the best thing to do. From what I can gather he's a good young man. Though maybe not up to incorporating a wife into his life in Addis. But he didn't mean to dump her, or not straight away. He told her he'd come and fetch her when he'd found them somewhere to live where they could have the baby. But he didn't come back to the village.'

Meanwhile Julie lived with his mother and sisters in the village – which was hardly a village, just a cluster of round huts, *tokuls*, in the middle of nowhere. It was a very poor area, a 'food-deficit area' in aid-agency language, one and a half days' walk across the bush from the nearest permanent road, thirty miles from the nearest village with a market and shops.

'If you can call them shops,' said Amanda. 'They'd just be rickety single-storey shacks with tin roofs. Julie couldn't write to anyone, and no one could write to her, she didn't have an address even. Julie being Julie, she thought she ought to make a go of it. She still thinks she should have. But she couldn't.'

She had the baby – a boy – there in the *tokul*, and did not recover her health afterwards. She and baby Fasil were never well. Early one morning she put Fasil in a cloth on her back and walked the thirty miles to the big village, where there was some sort of a clinic. The clinic was closed. Hailu's family used to walk all the way home across the bush by night in a group, but she was alone. She didn't have their orientation skills, and she was frightened of hyenas. On impulse, she walked off down the motor-road, not knowing where it led.

She was picked up at dawn by some Dutch aid-workers in a Land Cruiser. In Addis, they helped her to locate the NGO offices where Hailu had worked. He was no longer there, and no one could or would tell her where he was.

The good Dutch people paid for a room for her in the

Ghion Hotel, where she washed Fasil's clothes and had a hot shower. Then, finally, she telephoned Giles.

So Julie came home.

She had underestimated her parents. They were non-judgemental, and immediately besotted with little Fasil. But Julie would not move in with them. She and Fasil were staying with an old university friend in Stoke Newington in north London.

'She's very hard to help,' said Amanda. 'She's having a sort of nervous breakdown on her feet. And I mean on her feet. She's kept up that African thing of walking everywhere, even now when she doesn't have to. She walks miles, all over London, with Fasil in the buggy.'

'Maybe,' said Martagon, increasingly interested, 'it's become a sort of addiction. Or a residual loyalty to that other life. Maybe she's looking for Hailu without knowing that's what she's doing.'

'Maybe.'

A door banged. It was the lattice door that separated the sideway of the house from the back garden.

Coming towards them was a painfully thin young woman with stringy pale hair. She didn't look to Martagon at all like Giles. She was wearing a long denim skirt, a whitish T-shirt, and trainers. A small backpack hung from one shoulder, and she carried a little bottle of Evian water. Martagon stood up.

'Martagon – Julie. Julie – Martagon,' said Amanda, waving a hand, not stirring from her flowered garden lounger.

They shook hands, and Martagon saw that Julie had the same large greenish eyes as her brother.

'Have my chair.'

'No, thank you.'

Julie squatted on the grass. Her voice was thin and

strangulated. She hung her head and her hair fell in strands over her face.

'Where's Fasil?' asked Amanda.

'With my friends. I've been looking for a flat.'

'Did you see anything you liked?'

Amanda's voice had an edge to it. It struck Martagon that she was afraid Julie would have to move in with her and Giles, and that the idea did not please her.

Julie, sensing hostility, raised her head. 'Where's Giles? It's him I really want to see.'

'He'll be here any minute,' said Amanda, and to Martagon, 'Giles is going to help Julie buy a flat.'

'What kind of thing are you looking for?' he asked.

'A basement.'

'A basement? Rather dark and damp, surely,' said Amanda. 'A top flat, where you could see trees and the sky, would be less depressing.'

'I can't bear stairs, and all that scuttling up and down. I'm not an arboreal animal.'

That made Martagon smile. Suppressing the inclination to be facetious about the exigencies of land-use in densely populated areas, he asked her, 'What sort of animal are you, then?'

'A burrowing animal.'

'I hope you find a good burrow, then.'

He laughed, and then saw that laughing was wrong. Julie was crying. Tears dripped down her face and on to her T-shirt.

'I'll get the tissues,' said Amanda wearily, heaving herself off her lounger and traipsing back towards the house. Martagon didn't know whether it would be better for Julie if he followed Amanda into the house, or if he stayed.

'What is it?' he said. 'Please don't cry.'

The silent tears became choking sobs. She was trying to

say something to him. She raised her head and her wet, candid eyes met his. 'All I wanted, all I want, is to be a good person.'

Martagon was on the grass on his knees beside her, his arms around her, rocking her. He could feel her bones through her clothes. 'You are a good person.'

'No, I'm not.'

'You are. I can tell you are. I want to be a good person too.'

'And are you?'

'I don't know. I don't think so.'

Amanda came back with a box of tissues. She raised an eyebrow at Martagon over Julie's bent head. He released Julie and sat on his chair again.

What Julie had said was a trigger for Martagon. 'I want to be a good person' is a childish formulation. There is no sophisticated, grown-up way of expressing it.

Martagon went for a swim. When he was in London, he swam at the Kensington and Chelsea public pool. He hated going to the gym. He hadn't inherited his parents' love for mountain walks. Swimming was what he did. It was his exercise and his drug. For forty minutes or an hour, he swam lengths.

After three or four lengths he relaxed into a rhythm, mind and body functioning slower and smoother. His swimming instructor had told him that skills are perfected by performing the correct movement a thousand times, until a new pathway is carved through the tangled thickets of the brain, and the old bad-habit pathways are overgrown and obliterated. He saw himself slashing through jungles of weed with a curved sickle, which was the one his mother used to attack bramble patches. Then he was racing downhill through a forest on the mountain bike he was given when he went away to school, zigzagging between trees, bouncing off rocks, making for the track of brightness that led into the green valley.

Martagon swam lengths. I want to be a good person. Adults want to be successful, even if being a good person is what they want to succeed at. Even if being a good person is something they try to hold on to while becoming successful – so as not to become a bad person. But Julie wasn't thinking about success in the world's terms, that was for sure. For her, it was about something else.

Martagon came out of the pool and assumed, with his clothes, his normal self.

Martagon wanted the adventure of forming a new company and working with Giles. He felt reasonably confident that the merger would be good for Cox & Co. as well. It was a risk worth taking. It was, as Giles said, an opportunity.

Early on, sitting in Giles's Jaguar with him after a Caprice lunch, Martagon made two stipulations. The first was that if the merger went through, the name 'Cox' must be preserved in the newly constituted firm's name. The second was that Arthur Cox must be titular chairman of the new company for at least a year.

'Of course,' said Giles, throwing up his lighter and catching it. 'Not a problem.'

Martagon, back in the Cox offices in Caxton Street, embarked on a series of discussions with Arthur about the pros and cons. They took the other board members into their confidence. Martagon felt sure they would all come round to his way of thinking, which he did not at this stage make explicit. His only doubts were about Tom Scree, and perhaps Mirabel Plunket – the bright young water-engineer, who now had a seat on the main board.

It was a bit of a problem that Arthur himself, after an

initial flare of interest, moved into his indecisive mode. Martagon should have expected that. He was not too worried, knowing Arthur as he did. He knew he had to give Arthur lots of time, and kept an affectionate watch over him. But then it seemed Arthur lost all confidence in the idea. As the weeks passed his hostility hardened.

'I built this business up from nothing at all. Our people trust me. I'm not about to hand everything over to a bunch of ruffians with no integrity and no respect for anything except short-term profits and the bottom line.'

'We wouldn't be handing over anything. It would be a merger, not a takeover. If it ever happened.'

'Don't you believe it.' Arthur assured Martagon that he knew how Harpers operated. 'They don't think like us. I've known old man Harper for years. He was always a small-time chancer, and that nephew of his is a big-time six-noughts chancer. I wouldn't even trust him in charge of our Cirencester office.'

The Cirencester office was a doss: high gloss, high fees, low-tech, low stress, private clients.

Martagon said, cautiously, that on the whole he was rather impressed by Giles Harper.

'Then you're a fool. He'd be using you. He thinks you have a good reputation and some sense of honour and that it would rub off on him and do him credit with clients.'

Martagon bided his time.

'I'm trusting you,' said Arthur. 'I know I can. I'm trusting you not to lead Cox & Co. down the wrong path. You're one of us. You don't belong with those sorts of people any more than I do.'

Martagon promised that he would advocate nothing which was against the interests of Cox & Co. 'Why should I? I'd be cutting my own throat.'

* * *

After leaving the office that day Martagon went for his swim. Three lengths, four, eight, on and on until he reached the place in his mind where he went. I want to be a good person. Small children are neither good nor bad. They learn how to win approval and how to avoid punishment and how to survive. Martagon's father was a devout Roman Catholic and had talked about saving his soul. That was theological shorthand. For what? Everyone kind of knew what it meant, just as they knew what a lost soul, an unsaved soul, was. Martagon had no religious belief but something in him responded to those phrases.

Martagon swam. I want to be a good person. It's perhaps a question of what you are here for, what you are going to do with your life. You can be 'selfish' and follow your desires and do exactly what you want to do. That's perfectly rational. Why should you waste your one and only life doing what you don't want to do, making choices that go against your hopes and beliefs, against your personal success? That seems completely crazy, or at the very least highly neurotic. Almost, a death-wish. And yet, and yet . . . What about Arthur? I owe him so much.

When he was with Giles, everything seemed possible. But alone in his flat in Earl's Court, Martagon worried not only about Arthur, but about which way Tom Scree was likely to jump. He found it hard to explain to himself his strong dislike for the man, and it bothered him. Scree was a lot older than him – probably in his mid-fifties, thought Martagon. His politics were, proudly, left-wing and unreconstructed Old Labour. That didn't bother Martagon: he envied anyone with such certainties, as he envied people's religious faith. Nor did Martagon resent Scree for being, still, so bloody good-looking – upright and fit, with cropped black-grey hair, tanned skin, blazing dark eyes.

What did irritate Martagon beyond measure was Scree's air of self-righteousness. Scree was a moral imperialist. He always had to be in the right. His face habitually wore an expression of pained nobility, as if he were standing out singlehandedly against all the evil of the world. As perhaps he was. He seemed to have no self-doubt. He seemed sure that he was a thoroughly good person. Again, as perhaps he was. That, for Martagon, was the problem.

Scree was so unpretentious in the way he dressed and presented himself – he never wore a business suit, in an office milieu where a suit was simply an anonymous uniform – that his very unpretentiousness, his rough Tibetan sweaters and scuffed trainers, constituted an act of pretension. Martagon had introduced him to Giles, who asked them both together to Fulham for dinner. Julie Harper had been there too. Scree made Giles – with his flashy clothes and his gold jewellery – seem vulgar. Scree made Martagon feel obscurely in the wrong, always – as perhaps he was, he thought miserably, tossing and turning in his bed.

Scree's private life was an enigma. All Martagon knew was that he had a wife called Ann, who lived in Lincolnshire. Amanda Harper had gleaned over dinner that Ann was some kind of psychotherapist. She never came to London, and no one knew how often or how seldom Scree went home to Lincolnshire. When he was not working overseas, he seemed generally to be in London. But although Martagon had Scree's London co-ordinates – his telephone number, and his mobile number, and his e-mail address – he had no idea where he actually lived.

Scree was a master of the international aid-culture discourse – a matter of mainstreaming gender issues, empowerment, pro-poor growth, sustainability, replicability, capacity-building, good governance – necessary to win funding from government agencies for projects in emerging countries. Martagon agreed with the principles and concepts, but hearing Scree spouting the jargon made him want to throw up.

Western firms, including Cox & Co., working in emerging countries, had to factor into the budget invisible backhanders to middlemen and facilitators. In the campaign against this institutionalized corruption, 'transparency' was the buzzword. 'Transparency in public *and* in private life,' intoned Scree, seemingly the very personification of integrity. Again, Martagon was wildly irritated. He found himself perversely arguing with Scree that practices which seemed to 'us' to be corrupt were in fact an oblique and traditional form of welfare, milking the rich – in this case the rich West – of a few millions to trickle down among functionaries and clerks whose salaries were rarely paid and, in any case, grossly insufficient to feed a family. Scree just looked at him. Scree, the high priest of transparency, was himself the most opaque of men.

At the office things went from bad to worse. Arthur Cox seemed to be losing his grip. Arthur was staying later and later at the office, night after night, surrounded by files and printouts, amassing facts and figures for his case against the merger. He was driving his devoted secretary, Dawn, insane with fatigue.

When he attempted to present his findings, he got lost in a fog. He would shamble in to Martagon with sheaves of papers in his big, shaking hands, and try to locate points and positions on the main grid of his arguments, sinking ever deeper into incoherence.

Martagon was witnessing the terminal decline of Arthur Cox, and it grieved him. Martagon himself could extract and remember the key points and concepts from any mass of data. He could fillet complex documents, and quickly. Who had taught him these skills? Arthur Cox. But Arthur had lost the plot.

'Arthur, we really don't have to bother with most of this,' Martagon said one afternoon, flipping through a stack of files that Arthur had dumped on his desk. 'Look, this one, and this – they belong to the small print. And this one's just brochure-speak. All we need to do ourselves is to have at our fingertips the key figures and the ins and outs of the really crucial issues. I could set them out on two pages of A4 for you if you'd let me. The lawyers and accountants will do the rest for us, if it came to merger negotiations.'

Arthur snatched back the files and plonked his right hand firmly on top of them. He glared at Martagon with his tired, red-rimmed eyes. 'Piss off, Martagon. What do you know about how this firm is run? Nothing except what you have learned from me.'

This was not Arthur's way of relating to anyone, let alone the man whom he called his 'good angel'. Martagon took a deep breath, and a risk. One of the many bonds between himself and the big man was that they had both been brought up reading *Pilgrim's Progress*, and enjoyed quoting it at each other in incongruous settings, like a private code. Martagon said gently, 'You're in the Slough of Despond. You've got to get out of it . . . Think of it another way. Do you remember at the very beginning: "Do you see yonder wicket-gate? Do you see yonder shining light?" That's the way we've got to go, perhaps. Onwards.'

It didn't work.

'If you really think Giles bloody Harper is a shining light, you're more of an idiot than I ever imagined.'

Martagon grimaced. He did not, in truth, think that Giles was a shining light. But he had no shining light in his life to which he could dedicate himself. He did not know that he was looking for one, straining his eyes for it.

Arthur harangued anyone he met in the offices and corridors, falling back on laboriously detailed anecdotes of Cox & Co.'s past triumphs. Martagon, with pain, heard the emptiness of the rhetoric. The message-to-noise ratio, as he put it to Mirabel Plunket, was all wrong.

Mirabel took off her glasses and polished them harder than was necessary on the hem of her shirt. 'It would be more effective, really,' she said, 'if Arthur just threw all the paperwork out of the window into the street and said, "I don't like this merger and I won't have it."'

Martagon had no idea what Mirabel's own position was. They were all still playing their hands close to their chests.

The surprise was, for Martagon, that Tom Scree now seemed not to be altogether hostile to the merger. Maybe Giles had wooed and won him, with what promises Martagon could not even guess. Martagon was beginning to realize that he himself was in Giles's confidence precisely up to the point that Giles decided, and no further.

'Have you been seeing much of Giles's little sister?' Scree asked. 'Funny little thing. Julie. Could come to something, when she's worked through her problems. She needs to be more centred. I said I'd give her a ring.'

'I see her occasionally,' said Martagon. 'Generally at the house.' He felt a fresh stab of irritation, compounded by an unwarranted jealousy, and despised himself for it.

'Amanda Harper,' said Scree, 'now she's really something else.'

Whatever that means, thought Martagon, his dislike for Scree attaining critical mass. 'Amanda's OK,' he said.

Amanda was definitely OK. She kept Giles, whom she deeply loved, on the straight and narrow path just by being herself. Martagon had never met a couple who were so thoroughly married. Tom Scree's marriage was an enigma. Mirabel Plunket was in the process of separating from her husband. The Harpers were solid as rock.

Giles liked to tease Martagon about his private life, and had a running joke about all his girlfriends having names beginning with J.

'Was it Jessica last night, or Jenny, or Judith then? When is our Julie going to get a look in?'

Martagon played along. The truth was, he was often alone in the evenings and at weekends. Not that he ever had any trouble attracting women. He never had to be surprised, or grateful, that a woman wanted him. He was tall and well made, and in repose his aquiline features looked sad. Women are attracted to a melancholy man, the unconscious fantasy of each being that she alone will be able to make him happy. When Martagon smiled his rare, slow, sweet smile, his face was transformed and his dark blue eyes came alight. Martagon's smile was like a surprise present, and it drew people to him, of both sexes. He was very likeable.

Attractive people, and those whom everyone likes, are often a bit aloof, out of self-defence. That was why Amanda found him difficult sometimes. She had taken a photograph of him standing in her garden – squinting at the sun, his dark hair lying on his forehead under one of Giles's wide-brimmed straw hats, his mouth long and hard, handsome – unsmiling. She called it the 'Lone Ranger'.

'It's very like you,' she said. 'You look as if there's nothing you need from anyone. You look good in that hat – Giles shouldn't wear big hats, they make him look like a mushroom, they don't suit him.'

There was no contempt or offence in what she said. Giles was flesh of her flesh, she could have been talking about what looked good, or didn't look good, on herself.

Martagon enjoyed being there with them, in the kitchen, in their warmth, quietly.

He'd liked and wanted and even loved a lot of girls in his thirty-eight years, but he'd never been passionately 'in love'. Or not for long. He feared and distrusted 'in love' as a hysterical frenzy, and hated the brief periods when he was overwhelmed by it.

'It makes me tired just thinking about your life,' said Giles.

'What's your problem?'

It was Martagon's private opinion that Giles did not have a strong sexual drive. He was sensual rather than sexual, and his sensuality was expressed in his material possessions and love of home and what he thought of as the good life. He liked women; he liked to touch them when he was talking. He had a way of draping his arm around the back of a woman's chair at table if he found her attractive. He often behaved in a way that with any other man would have been a preliminary to a private encounter. Martagon was pretty sure no such thought ever entered Giles's head. So he could give himself a long rope.

Amanda was enough for Giles, more than enough. Her parents were both dentists, up in Wakefield. She had good teeth. She had studied social sciences at Leeds, and currently had a job in the human-resources department of a merchant bank. She rarely talked about it.

Amanda was what is called a 'big girl', pleasant-looking, blonde, deeply conventional. Martagon liked her intelligence and her forthright manner. He thought of her as the perfect example of a certain sort of quite good-looking, quite good-tempered, competent Englishwoman. She drove a car well, she cooked well, she was no doubt good at her job. Her tastes were ordinary, while Giles had the tastes of an oil-rich sheikh. His Jaguars, which he changed every year, were always top of the range and always burgundy-red. He had had the small Fulham house decorated with thick, patterned carpets, elaborately draped brocade curtains, chandeliers, everything that people like Tom Scree despised. Martagon disliked the drapes and the chandeliers, but he was moved by the verve and innocence of Giles's taste.

Only the kitchen was pure Amanda, with Shaker-style fittings painted blue, oiled wood work-surfaces, a soft old sofa against one wall, and the big, battered pine table.

Martagon happened to be sitting at that table when Giles came home with an oddly shaped parcel, which he unwrapped to reveal what he said was an *épergne*. That was what the man in the shop in Kensington Church Street had told him it was called. It was a heavy ornamental table-centre in the form of a chariot attached to six rearing horses, in gilded metal. Martagon and Amanda stared at it.

'It's the sort of thing the Duke of Wellington would have had on his dining-table. Very imposing,' said Martagon at last.

'Great,' said Amanda.

'But do you really like it?' Giles looked at her anxiously.

'I don't mind it.'

'You don't mind it? Does that mean you're only pretending to like it?'

'I'm not pretending anything. I don't mind it. I don't mind if it goes on the dining-room table or not. I know that you like it, and that's just fine by me.'

Giles bore the object away into the dining room. For him, Amanda was still all mystery.

'She means what she says, she really doesn't mind,' said Martagon, when Giles came back to the kitchen. 'She's happy for you that you like it.'

Martagon liked the way she and Giles behaved together. He was attracted by their marriage, though not by her. He found no glamour in her, and no mystery. Lin Perry, the high-profile Chinese-American architect whom they were to work with on the new airport, was more sophisticated and more cruel: 'Oh, my dear, she's one of these typical blonde English girls. If they're sexy it's without knowing it, in that overweight, singlet-and-shorts kind of way, waving around their big unembarrassed bottoms.'

Martagon was amused by Lin Perry and enjoyed his company.

'Not singlet-and-shorts,' he said. 'If we're talking English girls, it's vest-and-knickers, though I know that means something different where you come from.'

He wasn't particularly conscious of Amanda's bottom. But he did like the look of her soft boobs under the fawn or blue cashmere sweaters she usually wore. He liked her altogether, in fact, rather more than she liked him.

As summer turned to autumn Martagon saw a lot of Amanda, with Giles, during and after the merger negotiations, since her kitchen table became the unofficial forum for the structuring of Harper Cox, and the nearest thing to a family life that Martagon had ever had. Julie was there too, from time to time.

Neither Giles nor Martagon had done management courses, or business studies.

They had worked with people who had and, like magpies, picked up on nuggets of theory and practice. They both had years of experience behind them already, and were heading up successful companies. With the confidence of their comparative youth, they had few qualms about doubling their capacity. Over numerous bottles of wine, mostly consumed by Martagon, they constructed their own mock-models.

'Look how it all begins,' said Martagon, already drunker – again – than he had meant to be. 'In a business, like in any group. Number-one caveman has power over number-two caveman because he's nastier or stronger, so he makes number-two caveman shift the rocks for him. But number-two caveman creates a dependency in number-one caveman, who gets so soft and lazy he can't shift his own rocks any more. Besides, he'd lose face if he did. So he becomes the manager – get it? – and number-two caveman shifts the rocks. Number-two caveman can suddenly turn round and say, "NO," like any employee can. If number-one caveman loses his grip, or his nerve, and if number-one caveman is hungry enough, there's a revolution.'

'Then what?' Giles asked.

'Boring. It just starts again. Number-two caveman takes on the managerial role and gets number-three caveman to shift the rocks. Someone always has to shift the rocks, and there's always someone else sitting on his butt to see that he does it. He's the manager. But maybe he's not really top caveman. There's another one, with even more clout, who tells the managers where the different rocks are to be shifted to. He's the chief executive. He's the man with the big desk and the sexy secretaries in the movies you saw.'

'You haven't said what happens to a top caveman after the revolution,' said Giles. 'But I'll tell you. He can't shift rocks. No one wants his opinion about where they should be shifted to. He's finished. He's dogmeat.'

A silence.

'Management has four prongs,' announced Giles. 'The first is goals. You've got to have goals. Then, motivation. Then, facilitation. Then, evaluation.'

'That's terrible,' said Martagon. 'I hope you didn't think that up for yourself.'

'No, I read it in a book.'

'In a book?' Martagon affected incredulity.

'Oh, ha ha.'

'Let's talk about goals, then.'

'Power. That's my goal. I told you, before.'

'You just want to make people do what you want them to.'

'That's not what I want,' said Amanda. They had forgotten her. 'That's not power. There might be a revolution, anyway, and then you'd be dogmeat. I'll tell you my idea of power. I want to be free to do, by myself, for myself, anything that I want to do. That's power.'

'What's the relation between power and responsibility?' asked Martagon. 'Is power the same as control?'

'There's lots of ways of controlling people,' said Giles. 'You've no idea of the power of compliance. Women get control over men through sex and domesticity and the niceness of everyday, making men dependent, making them soft, like number-one caveman who can't shift his own rocks. Women are like crack-dealers creating an addict. It gets so he doesn't feel good without regular fixes of what she supplies. Amanda's got me that way . . .'

'Don't be daft,' said Amanda flatly. 'Goodnight, I'm going to bed.' And she went.

'It's true, though,' said Giles. 'It's a terrible thing to fall into the hands of a good woman.'

'I should be so lucky,' said Martagon.

He hadn't yet fallen into the pale, seductive hands of Marina de Cabrières. Women like Marina were much more to Lin Perry's taste than Amanda was, and he knew Marina before Martagon did. 'Marina is to die for,' he said.

TWO

Martagon's first impression of Bonplaisir was unexpected. He stepped into the shade of the gatehouse arch, looking forward to seeing the famous façade for the first time. What met his eye was a row of pristine white lavatory bowls, ranged tidily against the stone wall, gleaming in the sun, beneath the open ground-floor windows. From within the château came the noises of drilling and sawing and, further away, the thrumming of a cement-mixer.

Then she appeared round the corner from the gardens. As she came nearer he realized with a jolt that it was the woman he had seen in the café, even though this time she was wearing a white shirt and jeans, and her red hair was loose, hanging in tendrils round her neck. He could tell from the way she met his eyes that she remembered too.

Martagon smiled at her. She smiled back. They shook hands. She made a gesture towards the lavatory bowls and the din from inside the building, and shrugged. 'An army of occupation,' she said.

His heart was lurching.

It was a relief to turn away and recover his equilibrium walking beside her round the gardens, doing the business he had come to do. He had a feeling of dread. There was no reason for it. Nothing had happened.

But something was going to happen.

He was a single man. His relationship with Jutta, his German girlfriend, had come to an end. So what was he dreading?

There's a lightness in stalking on your own through the world, not caring immeasurably about anyone, open to adventure, in no danger of being betrayed or of becoming a betrayer. Once you step with someone else hand in hand into the dark forest, one of you risks getting lost or abandoned or slaughtered.

Marina carried her height well, walking with her head erect, looking straight ahead. Martagon began to do the same, realizing how most of the time he walked with his neck bent, his eyes on the ground a few feet in front of him. He lifted his chin and walked tall, beside this gorgeous woman who was nearly as tall as he was.

Her voice was deep for a woman's, with a catch in it. There was something tentative, uncertain, about that voice, even though she seemed assured as she talked about the money still due to her from the airport consortium. Martagon took scrupulous notes.

She gave him lunch on the terrace. They sat opposite one another. The chair she sat in was high-backed, carved and gilded, with sphinx heads for armrests and great claw feet. Her pale, long-fingered hands caressed the sphinx heads as she talked. Martagon was riveted. He could not take his eyes off her hands, her face.

The château had fallen silent. The workmen, too, were taking their lunch-break. Looking out beyond the gardens they could see five yellow cranes rising above the trees, and hear the whinings and clatterings from the airport construction site.

'How much do you mind all this?' he asked.

'I mind a great deal and I don't mind at all. I'm taking the important things – memories, and money.' She laughed a wicked, sexy laugh. 'And this,' she added, patting the arms of her great chair. 'It's very old, my mother found it in Alexandria. She always sat here, in this chair. I fought my brother, Jean-Louis, like a tiger for it. I'll have it taken back to my place tonight.'

Marina was no longer living at the château. She had moved into a farmhouse ten kilometres away that belonged to the family property and was not part of the sale.

A cheerful, meaty American girl in shorts who was introduced as 'Billie, my assistant', brought out their picnic lunch and arranged it on the table.

'You know Nancy Mulhouse? Billie's her niece.'

'Ah. No, no, I don't know Nancy Mulhouse, I'm afraid.'

'You don't know Nancy? How can that be? Anyone who spends time in these parts knows Nancy.'

'Well, I've never met her,' Martagon said.

People in Provence – expats – were always asking him if he was going to Nancy's big party, or whether he liked Nancy's makeover of her garden, or whatever. It was beginning to irritate him.

'I know Auntie Nancy's keen to meet you,' said Billie. 'I heard her say so to Lin Perry the other night. You remember, you were sitting with him, Marina.'

Billie disappeared back into the château.

The architect of the airport, Lin Perry, being famous and exotic, was obviously a natural as one of Nancy's regular house-guests.

'How can it be that you don't know Nancy Mulhouse?' Marina could not let it go.

'I don't move in those circles, I suppose. I know she has a house round here somewhere, and I know she's from Texas, but I wouldn't recognize her if I was standing next to her at the supermarket checkout.'

'You'd be most unlikely to meet her at the supermarket checkout. If you did, you'd remember her. But you haven't told me how you like the wine?'

'I know it well, I've been drinking Domaine de Bonplaisir for years. It's always been a nice, big, fruity wine.'

'The fields are being ploughed up. It's finished . . . But this is the very best. Nineteen eighty-nine. It must be drunk now before it goes over the top. I liberated the last dozen cases of it before I moved out of here – my brother would kill me if he knew.'

So they drank the wine – one bottle, and then, slowly, another bottle.

Before he left, he wrote down for her his e-mail address.

'Why "marteau"?' she asked. 'It means "hammer".'

'I know. It sounds like my name, only more aggressive, and suitable for someone working in the construction industry. I've worked mainly in Europe, I didn't want to sound too English. Not that I am, my father was Irish.'

'You look very English. In the best way. If in French you say that someone's *un peu marteau* it means he's a bit crazy.'

'I'm not crazy. I'm balanced, like a good hammer.' Balance, he told her, was important. A question of psychological equilibrium, between work and play, public and private, reason and passion. 'I don't usually talk like this to women I've only just met, on a matter of business.'

He had imagined a visit of about an hour. In the event he stayed until dusk, reason draining out of him through a hole in the bottom of the world. There was only himself and her and the private life.

* * *

In those first days they told each other about their childhoods, as people falling in love do.

'I'm a displaced person,' Martagon said to Marina. 'I don't really belong anywhere.'

He told her about his childhood in Bangladesh, which was East Pakistan then. His father Liam Foley was an accountant with a firm of jute exporters, and they lived in a company house. He told her about his mother Jill, who was pretty and clever with that air of slight silliness which pleases most men. Like all Europeans they had servants, and a car with a driver. He was an only child.

'You were a little prince,' said Marina.

'And you, at Bonplaisir, were a little princess, in an enchanted castle. Dhaka was the armpit of Asia.'

Martagon's nightmares were – still are – about the beggars with eyes missing, in dusty rags, with no hands, banging their stumps against the closed windows of the car. Thud-thud, thud-thud. He was told by his parents to stare straight ahead and take no notice. The driver kept his hand permanently on the horn as they inched their way down unsurfaced streets and alleys crammed with rickshaws and bicycle taxis and people. Martagon suffered from carsickness, and sometimes had to ask for the car to be stopped so that he could get out and be sick on the side of the street. The Bangladeshi men standing around would stare at him, and stare harder at his mother as they fingered their private parts through the thin cotton of their *lunghis*.

He told Marina what an embarrassment his first name had been to him. When he was seven or eight, and they still lived in Dhaka, his mother told him that 'Martagon' was the name of an Alpine lily – a *pink* lily, for God's sake. He was appalled.

'Martagon is a really strong, manly sounding name,' his mother said. She showed him the picture of a martagon lily in the illustrated flower-book she had. 'Look how the petals curl backwards, making it look like a Turkish turban. The other name for it is the "Turk's head lily".'

'Is that why Dad calls me Turk?'

'Yes, that, and because you are a young Turk.'

Martagon was not reconciled to his name by knowing that his mother loved flowers, and that on their honeymoon his parents had walked in the Alps where she had been overwhelmed by the beauty of martagon lilies growing wild along the mountain paths. When he went to school he announced he was called 'Mart', which the other boys assumed was short for Martin.

He went on being Mart until he became a student, when the sonorous oddity of 'Martagon' began to appeal to him. Now everyone he worked with, and people in the profession who knew of him only by hearsay, referred to him simply as Martagon, with no second name. He liked the modernity of this. Surnames, in a world where call-centres and public utilities dealt only in first names, were only for intimates.

'And you?' he asked Marina. 'What was it like, growing up at Bonplaisir? What did you all do all day?'

'Maman drifted from one place to another . . . Breakfast in her bedroom, a tisane in the *petit salon* at ten thirty, lunch at twelve thirty in the dining room, then a little rest on the terrace – the same every day. I always knew where to find her.'

Martagon imagined Marina as a little girl, with a short frock and a mop of red hair, running across the courtyard.

'We didn't have many visitors. Papa said visitors made Maman nervous. She was half Greek, she didn't have many friends. Papa spent most of the day in the library with his ancient Romans, he wrote learned articles about them and paid to have them published.'

'What about the wine business?'

'Papa wasn't a wine-maker, though my grandfather was. Our wine-maker was Pierre, the son of our old *viticulteur*. Papa sent him where the Napa Valley wine people train, at the University of California at Davis. Then he ran our operation. All Papa wanted to do was drink the wine. All the time. When Maman had her morning *tisane*, he opened his first bottle of the day. He drank like a – what is it that you say in English? We say, he drank *comme un polonais*. Like a Polish man.'

'Like a fish. He drank like a fish.'

'Fish don't drink.'

'How come your English is so good?'

'I had an English governess, and when I was first grown-up I went to London for about three years. I had to get away, I quarrelled with my father, with Jean-Louis, with everyone.'

'I must say, with such a background it's amazing that you and your brother grew up to be normal.'

'Jean-Louis is not normal. I am not normal either.'

'All I know is,' said Martagon, unable to detach his gaze from her silky beauty, 'that I've never met anyone like you before.'

Marina told him that when their parents died – in a car-crash, six years ago, her father driving – she and her brother Jean-Louis had had a long and bitter quarrel. The airport consortium approached them about selling the land and the château. She was for it, Jean-Louis was against it – passionately, hysterically. According to French law, the property was inherited by both children equally.

They wrangled for months. Jean-Louis, who had no viable trade or profession, was about to be married to a rich girl from Normandy. He planned to sell off the important paintings in order to have some cash in hand, and to live at Bonplaisir on his wife's money. He didn't want his sister living there too, and he couldn't afford to buy her out.

'I was in his way. He wanted me dead. I think he did try to kill me once. Something with the car . . . when I was driving to Paris.'

In the end Marina won, but at a price. Jean-Louis's grand wedding took place at Bonplaisir just before the sale went through. There was a feast for two hundred guests at tables set out in the garden, and a string orchestra, and dancing. Marina was not invited. She was ostentatiously disinvited. The breach between brother and sister was total.

'Pierre speaks to him sometimes, but I do not.'

'What has become of Pierre, now the wine-making operation has closed down?'

'Oh,' said Marina, smoothing her jeans over her knees, looking down. 'I see him sometimes . . . He's a brute, actually.'

'I may have seen him – before it closed, I used to turn in at the "Dégustation" sign and drive up the track to buy wine at the *cave*.'

'Oh, he's dark, and short . . .'

Martagon could not remember. But something about the way Marina talked about Pierre upset his equilibrium, and he told her so.

Martagon and Marina had been seeing each other or talking on the telephone every day for a fortnight when he had to go back to London for a week of meetings. During that week their relationship took a leap forward without their realizing it. When they met again it was as lovers, even though they were not yet lovers.

Marina wanted to show him round the château before it was changed beyond recognition. 'I still have my keys.'

The teams of workmen always made an early start, and

knocked off for the day, after closing the place up, around four thirty. In the early evening, when an eerie quiet had fallen on the gardens, Marina let Martagon into the château.

They walked slowly, without speaking, through vast, dim, empty rooms. In each room Marina released the catch on the shutters and opened them a crack. Shafts of sunlight revealed particles of plaster-dust floating in the air. Coils of electric cable, bags of cement and paint-pots lay stacked in corners. All the walls and ceilings had been roughly covered with white undercoat, awaiting the redecoration. There was no glint of colour anywhere, and no sounds other than their footfalls and the creaks of doors and shutters.

In a small anteroom beyond the big salon Marina threw both the shutters wide open.

'We'll need all the light from here in order to be able to see in the library. Papa used to work by artificial light, but the electricity is off in there.'

The library was the oldest room, she said. It was all that remained of the medieval fortress round which the château had been built.

'The developers can't get planning permission to put windows in, so the builders haven't touched it. I guess it'll just be a storeroom.'

She led Martagon down five stone steps and unlocked the heavy door of the library.

Inside, the air was musty. Martagon could just make out, by the borrowed light from the doorway, a low ceiling and walls lined on three sides with empty bookshelves. Great slabs of stone formed the floor. The walls and shelves had been painted, once, in a colour that had faded to an indeterminate grey-green. The paint on the shelves was flaking off, and the one blank wall was discoloured with damp patches, and darker rectangles where paintings used to hang. Against this wall was a long dark shape like a boat, or a coffin.

'This room always looked quite normal to me, before we moved everything out,' said Marina. 'I had no idea it was in such a terrible state.'

She moved suddenly to a wooden door, about twelve inches square, set into the wall at shoulder height, and struggled with the latch.

'It's hardly ever been opened,' she said, breathless from her efforts. 'Not since I was a child, I don't suppose.'

Martagon went over to help her. She stood close beside him while he released the latch and worked on the thick little door with the aid of the penknife from his pocket.

The door swung open – not on to the dark little cubby-hole or cupboard that he had been expecting. It was an unglazed opening on to a framed fragment of the world beneath a cobalt sky, with a view over fields and vines, a curve of the river, and the forested hills beyond, gilded by the evening light. A miniature of pure beauty leading to infinity. Martagon took Marina in his arms and kissed her for the first time. It was not enough, for either of them.

'Now, please,' he said.

'Now, here?'

'Yes.'

The long dark thing, in the square of brightness from the little window, was revealed as a couch. She stripped, slipping off her dress and kicking off her black pants. No bra. Pearly skin and a fiery triangle. Neither of them was shy and neither of them was frantic. What they were doing was natural, inevitable.

Yet for Martagon, making love with Marina was not a homecoming. It was more extraordinary than that. Nor was it an escape, as it often had been before, with other women.

'An escape from what?' she asked, when he tried to explain this to her, propped on one elbow on the uncomfortable couch, stroking her face and her hair.

'From thought. From myself. I don't know. I'm not escaping from anything, with you. It's the very opposite. I didn't know this was how it could be.'

Not a homecoming, not an escape – but an astonishing revelation of a new universe of experience. It might take him the rest of his life to explore and know it, and there was nothing more important.

Marina captured his stroking hand and looked up at him, her pupils enlarged. Her voice even huskier than usual, she told him that he was a beautiful man. 'You are beautiful everywhere, but specially here. I have been looking and looking at this part of you all these long days.'

She was caressing his forearm and his thin sunburned wrist, where the dark hairs curled round his watch.

'Of course,' she said, 'that was because it was the only naked part of you that I could see, then . . .'

When finally she moved from the couch he watched as she retrieved the black pants from the floor, shook the dust off them, and put them on.

'Well, we've done it now,' he said, not knowing exactly what he meant.

'Yes,' she said, standing over him, looking straight at him. 'We've done it now.'

'No going back?'

'No.'

So it began. Martagon was calm, and confident, and at peace with himself and with her.

*   *   *

But the following night, in the garden of Marina's farmhouse, he was thinking about her old friend Pierre again. He knew in his bones that Pierre and Marina had been more than friends. Maybe they still were.

'If Pierre ever comes round you again,' he said, 'I may beat him up.'

'What is your problem with Pierre? You are with me and he is not.'

Martagon said to Marina the thing he had thought to himself, when they had first talked about Pierre. 'He upsets my equilibrium.'

'But, Marteau, if there is perfect equilibrium nothing can ever happen.'

The Provençal night had three sounds. At dusk, the frogs began to croak. Then, the nightingales began to sing. Later, when the nightingales packed it in, it was the turn of the owls.

'A system in equilibrium,' said Martagon, 'is only unchanging till it's acted upon by some outside force. But that doesn't go on for ever, either, and then a steady state is resumed.'

'Does it work the same with people?'

'I'm talking about the laws of physics. It's all about what has to be done to maintain balance.'

'I want to talk about people. What might be the outside force that spoils the equilibrium?'

'You tell me, darling.'

'The outside world? Too-high expectations? A third person coming in and causing jealousy?'

'OK,' said Martagon. 'In physics, it's friction that makes it all go wrong. Friction dissipates energy. Like when I change pounds into francs, a bit is creamed off in commission every time.'

They were sitting in the warm dark, swinging in the

cushioned swing-seat, their bare arms and legs and feet touching.

'We're in equilibrium now, you and I,' said Marina. 'At this moment.'

'Not really. We are swinging.'

'In French we say *se balancer* for swinging. Balancing. Balanced.'

'That's just semantic chance.'

'Don't words mean anything, then?'

'Words mean anything you want. Words can lie. The truth is what actually happens. The results of kinetic energy,' and Martagon dug his bare heels hard into the grass, so that they swung higher. Overhead the stars swung too and Martagon felt a bit sick. I've had too much to drink, he thought. The stars went on swinging.

Astronomers call a star 'perturbed' when it loses its equilibrium because of the gravitational pull of something else. Perturbation is interesting because it can lead to the discovery of a new celestial body. Martagon was too tired to put this into words for Marina. He just said, 'Can we go to bed now?'

Martagon and Marina did live in perfect equilibrium for long hours during their early days at the farmhouse. It was a simple house with tiled floors and only the basics when it came to furniture and equipment.

'Minimalist,' said Martagon, when he looked around for the first time. 'Suits me.'

He wanted to protect and care for Marina – a new feeling, for him. She did not seem to need or want much looking after. He did, however, impress on her the need for better security. She left outside doors standing open, and only rarely locked the place up. It was only her fear of unannounced visits from her brother Jean-Louis that reconciled her to Martagon's insistence that she closed and locked the spiked metal gates across the drive at night, when she was alone in the house.

When he asked if there were any other ways into the property, she led him across the garden to a high wall. It was immensely thick, built in the Roman way, she explained, which was still the Provençal way: two 'skins', or separate walls, of large irregular rocks and stones, with the gap between them filled in with rubble and topped with more rocks.

She opened the door in this garden wall and showed him a small dark cavity, empty except for a couple of spades, and beyond it another door set into the further side. This opened on to a track across the fields.

'You should keep both these doors locked all the time,' said Martagon, 'and we'll hang the key on a nail the garden side.'

Thus he perfected and protected their privacy. In the hot afternoons Marina read film scripts in bed while he worked on his laptop calculating loads and stresses, quantities and costs, at a table in the small shuttered room. Marina turned her pages silently. They breathed and moved silently. The stillness was like a trance, because they were together though apart.

On one of those hot, still afternoons Martagon saw that she had fallen asleep. He slipped into the bed beside her. She half woke and wound her legs – those loved legs – around his. Beneath the stillness and silence was agitation, because lying with her in this way made Martagon's heart beat fast. The submerged agitation was quite enough for now. It was good that Marina did not find his liking for stillness and suspension a threat. There was always the certainty that in the end, or quite soon, or in the next second, the storm of longing would prove too strong and they would be overwhelmed, again. Passion was implicit in the stillness and silence.

He said, when she opened her great eyes, 'You are the only person in all my life with whom I can be for hours at a time without getting frazzled.'

'What is frazzled?'

Martagon's French was not up to finding a translation. 'It's everything I'm not right now, so it doesn't matter. But I must get up. I must ring Giles. He thinks I'm neglecting the work.'

'And are you?'

'Not really.'

'Tell me more about Giles.'

'I'll make the call, and then we'll go for a drink and I'll tell you about Giles, and Arthur, and the merger. It was all a long time ago, but I still think about it.'

What had happened was that the board of Cox & Co. had to decide formally whether or not they wished to proceed with merger negotiations. Martagon was in a quandary. He wanted to do the right thing. He was pretty sure that the right thing for the firm, and for himself, was to go ahead with Harpers. But that meant going against Arthur Cox's wishes. He'd been playing Arthur along. He hadn't been candid with him. That was a tactical and moral mistake. A compass error.

The only right thing to do now was to see Arthur before the meeting and confess that he was going to vote in favour of the merger. He dreaded Arthur's disappointment and disillusion. He dreaded Arthur's sadness, and anger, and accusations of ingratitude. But he had to do it.

He put it off and put it off. Finally, the day before the meeting, Martagon went to Arthur's office after lunch, sweating. The tottering stacks of files had all been cleared away. Arthur was stuffing papers into his briefcase, clearly preparing to leave.

'Can you spare me half an hour?' said Martagon.

'Sorry, old man. Family party. The grandson's tenth birthday. Got to be there. Got to get an early train.'

'Arthur, it's really important.'

'I'll give you fifty seconds, then. Good training. As I've often told you, you should be able to articulate anything important within fifty seconds.'

That was rich, coming from Arthur.

'It's about tomorrow's meeting—'

Arthur interrupted, snapping closed the catches of his briefcase, looking round for his overcoat, 'I don't want to hear it. Not another word. You know where I stand, and I know where you stand. Shoulder to shoulder, as we always have been.'

And he was gone, pushing past Martagon in the doorway, patting Martagon's arm as he lumbered past.

Martagon did not try to follow him.

Next morning, as everyone herded into the first-floor boardroom at Caxton Street, Martagon put his head round Arthur's office door. The room looked stark, as if it belonged to no one. 'You all right?' asked Martagon.

'Bit of a cloud . . . bit of a cloud,' said Arthur, his bulky body slumped in the chair. 'I'm just coming.' Then he raised his head and looked at Martagon. 'Look here – I know you've got your way to make, I know you get ideas in your head, but I can rely on you when it comes to the crunch. If it comes to a vote, you won't vote against me, Martagon, will you?'

Martagon opened his mouth to speak. Arthur cut in before he had got out a word, 'Knew I could trust you. When it came to the crunch. I'm just coming. You go on in.'

Lacerated by his longing to save Arthur from humiliation and defeat, Martagon prayed for a miracle.

It was a long meeting. They sat down at nine thirty in the morning, and emerged, exhausted, at half past five. Arthur chaired it badly. He hardly chaired it at all.

Martagon, as managing director, kicked off. He was well prepared, and ran over all the now familiar ground, setting out evenly the pros and cons, without explicitly indicating his own preference. But knowing that the only thing that would bring about the desired miracle – Arthur's change of heart – was his own persuasive eloquence, he suspected that everyone else in the room could guess where his own hopes lay. He spoke for about twenty-five minutes.

After that, everyone around the table had a say, some at considerable length. There were questions, most of which could be answered by reference to some portion of the stack of papers in front of each board member. Mirabel Plunket voiced the anxiety all shared, but which none of the men would have come out with directly, or not yet, for fear of betraying their insecurity. So Martagon spoke again, to reassure the board that the continuing employment of the Cox & Co. staff would be, so far as possible, guaranteed under the terms of any merger. If – and at this stage it was still only if – negotiations went ahead, this would be his own first priority.

Dawn wheeled in a trolley with chocolate biscuits, cups and saucers, a milk-jug, and a big brown teapot. Everyone shifted and relaxed, welcoming the interruption.

'Ah, rosy-fingered Dawn!' Arthur said, essaying a smile.

Dawn, who was Ghanaian, looked up at him sharply from the trolley, mystified, suspecting a racist joke from where she least expected it. She loved Arthur. Martagon caught her in the passage when he went for a pee, and tried to explain that 'rosy-fingered dawn' was poetry about the sunrise, a quotation from Homer – 'like "wine-dark sea",' he said, floundering.

'Oh, right,' said Dawn.

Martagon went back into the boardroom and sat down with a sense of dread. His hands, though he had washed them, were clammy again.

Tom Scree, who so far had slumped in his chair and said nothing, sat up very straight, as if indicating that he had a major contribution to make. As usual, he looked like an old hippie, and as usual, he spoke like an archbishop. He referred to Arthur throughout as 'Sir Arthur', which gave what he said added weight and formality.

It was not until Scree reached his peroration that Martagon really understood what was going on. For the last twenty minutes Scree had been subtly building up a strong case against merger negotiations, and what he was now saying constituted a personal attack on Martagon himself: 'Martagon has told us that Sir Arthur holds traditional values with which the Harpers' ethos may be incompatible. And yet it appears, from what he tells us, that Martagon sees merit in a merger. Martagon, we do not have to be told, has the interests of Cox & Co., and of Sir Arthur, at heart. Martagon has also implied that Sir Arthur's values and attitudes do not, altogether, tally with those of the modern world, to the detriment of the modern world. It is, nevertheless, as he made clear, the world we have to live in and in which Cox & Co. must survive and grow, without – hopefully – abandoning its high standards and business integrity. Martagon's standards and integrity are not, of course, in question. It is, as he has said, up to each one of us to make a decision based on the information which has been placed at our disposal. Some of this is, to my mind, disquieting. Board members may feel we should obtain further and better particulars than those with which we have been supplied, about Harpers' operations and practice and their financial credibility. Board members may feel that we should commission a report from a major and independent firm of accountants. Be that as it may, I should like on behalf of the board to thank Martagon for his admirable presentation of the situation – as he sees it.'

Scree sat back and squared up the papers in front of him, banging the base of the stack decisively on the table. Arthur was looking more chipper.

Fuck you, Scree, thought Martagon. You're banking on the board being swayed by your speech into rejecting the merger. Then you'll make Arthur believe you 'saved' the firm. Then I'll be screwed. And you'll probably get my job.

Arthur grabbed at the idea of buying time by calling in outside accountants – until he realized that by doing so he would be admitting the possibility of negotiations.

'If we proceed, and I profoundly hope we do not, we shall need them for the due diligence. And we'll need to be very thorough about that, with Harpers. Men of straw, you'll find they are. Men of straw . . . But, no, no, on second thoughts, let us rather save the money. Obviously we are not going on with this. Really, we should bring this meeting to an end. There's nothing more to be said, gentlemen.'

'Chairman, I'm not a gentleman,' said Mirabel.

'Ah, Miss Plunket,' said Arthur, thinking to put things right and making them worse, 'I assure you that, in some platonic sense which I cannot quite define, you are, most definitely, a gentleman.'

'I don't think so,' said Mirabel.

The meeting was falling apart. Martagon, with a stony heart, made an effort to pull it together again. 'As Arthur rightly reminds us, this meeting has to be brought to a conclusion – in both senses. I'm sure we would all prefer consensus, without taking a formal vote. But maybe, Chairman, an indicative vote at this stage might be helpful? Nothing binding – just to give us an idea of where we all stand.'

Arthur made a noncommittal gesture with his hand and turned his head to stare out of the window. It was already getting dark outside. 'As you like,' he said.

Martagon pressed on. There was a desultory, embarrassed, inconclusive show of hands both for and against, with some abstentions. Muttered conversations rose and fell around the table. Dawn came back into the room and whispered to Tom Scree that there was an urgent telephone call for him in the outside office.

Scree pushed back his chair. 'I'd better take it. If you'll excuse me a moment, Sir Arthur.'

While Scree was out of the room Martagon said that as there was obviously no consensus forthcoming, the matter would unfortunately have to be put to a formal vote, if the Chairman was in agreement.

Arthur went on looking out of the window. 'If that is the feeling of the meeting,' he said.

They all sat waiting for Tom Scree to come back. Everyone was tired, and looked it.

'We'll go round the table,' said Arthur, with an abrupt show of energy. 'Starting with you, Tom. This time it's "yes" or "no". Nothing else.'

Tom Scree raised a hand. 'Before we start, I have something else to say – if I may, Sir Arthur? . . . I came to this meeting, as perhaps many of us did, convinced that we should not pursue this merger. We have always been flexible at Cox & Co. Flexibility is a strength, and not a weakness. We still retain the qualities of the partnership established by Sir Arthur, and we have always respected each other's opinions, while conceding to Sir Arthur, very properly, the priority among us – he has been, he is, the *primus inter pares*, first among equals. But we have become, perhaps, somewhat ossified in our marketing and in our business practice. We have lost some flexibility. We need new blood.

'It is in the name of our flexibility that I am speaking to you now and asking for your understanding. I spoke earlier out of the conviction with which I came into the meeting. I heard Martagon speaking, as we all did, but I myself lacked the flexibility to admit to myself the cogency of much of what he was saying. So I spoke as I had planned. As I said then, Martagon's standards and integrity are beyond question. In the course of the past few hours, I have changed my views. I now believe that a merger with Harpers would indeed be in the best interests of the firm, the partners, the management and staff, and that we should proceed. As Martagon made very clear in his initial presentation, Sir Arthur's position as chairman of the new entity is, of course, unassailable.'

There was a snort of derision from somewhere down the table at the vacuous hypocrisy of 'unassailable', then a stunned silence.

The lying bastard, thought Martagon. He guessed that the telephone call had been from Giles Harper, who well knew the day and hour of the fateful meeting.

Martagon was right, and Giles's timing had been perfect. Giles told him afterwards, with the air of one who had made a coup, that he had been lunching all the board members of Cox & Co., and ascertained that, after Martagon, Tom Scree was the key player. Then he zoomed in.

Confidential talks with Scree had elicited the information Giles needed. He discovered what Scree wanted.

Scree was tired of working on projects in India and Bangladesh. He wanted to be in the London office, with time and leisure to pursue some of his other interests. Giles never commented or picked him up on this. He had made no deal, his hands were clean.

On the telephone, Giles had said he was calling on a sudden impulse. He just wanted to ask Tom, as a personal favour, whether he might possibly give up his work in the field and base himself at the London office, to work on the restructuring of the enlarged business – if, of course, the merger were to proceed, after discussions which he understood were ongoing. Giles said he knew this would be a sacrifice, but he hoped Tom would consider it seriously, as his expertise would be quite invaluable.

Scree, with matching cunning, replied that he would indeed consider it. It might be difficult. There could be problems. His tacit implication was, it would have to be made worth his while. The two understood one another perfectly.

Then Tom Scree came back into the boardroom, and performed his graceful U-turn.

Thus Martagon got what he wanted, but not in the way that he wanted. He had himself made a good case for the merger, while scrupulously cataloguing the arguments against it. Tom Scree's *volte-face* had done the rest. Martagon collected the rest of the votes. Everyone followed Tom Scree's lead. Yes. Yes. Yes. Yes . . . all round the table. The only person left unpersuaded was Arthur Cox: 'No. No. No. Over my dead body.'

His was a lone voice. For everyone else, it was somehow not a victory. Mirabel inspected her fingernails, a lock of hair concealing her face. Members looked down at their papers, into their teacups, anywhere, but not at Arthur. Arthur stared out of the window. It had begun to rain. Only

Martagon had not yet spoken. His heart was pounding, his armpits were prickling. Arthur turned his head and looked him in the eye. 'And you, Martagon?'

'Yes,' said Martagon. 'Yes. I am in favour of the merger.'

Silence.

Arthur Cox rose awkwardly and leaned his hands on the table in front of him. 'Under these circumstances,' he said, 'I cannot see how I can continue to take the firm forward. I am suspending my chairmanship of Cox & Co. as of this moment, in the confidence that the understanding as to my own future position, already guaranteed by the other side, will be duly honoured.'

He disentangled himself from table and chair, turned, and stumped out of the room. No one spoke. They heard his heavy steps on the stairs, and then the street door opening and closing. Martagon had been sitting with his head in his hands. When the street door banged behind Arthur, he got up, went out to the lavatory, and vomited.

In the post he received a one-line note from Arthur: 'You have behaved dishonourably.'

That is true, Martagon said to himself. I should have come straight out at the beginning and told Arthur what I really thought. It seemed for a while as though he might be jollied into the idea of the merger, and no bones broken. I thought I was doing the best thing. But it wasn't the right thing.

He wanted to talk to Arthur, but Arthur was not there. Nevertheless Martagon found himself getting up from his desk and crossing the landing to Arthur's office. He opened the door, expecting to see an empty room.

Tom Scree and Dawn were in there. Scree was sitting at Arthur's desk, swinging slightly on the tilted chair. Dawn was standing with her back to the window. Two tea-mugs were on the desk. Martagon had the feeling that he was interrupting something. They both looked at him. He saw that Dawn was in a state. She was twisting a crumpled tissue in her hands, and she had clearly been crying.

'Sorry . . . Another time,' said Martagon, meaninglessly, and backed out, closing the door again behind him.

She must be really upset about Arthur, he thought. And Tom Scree can't be all bad after all, if he is the one person she can talk to about it, and he gives her the time. On a human level, he performs better than I do. I should have thought about how Dawn might feel, and had a word with her myself.

In the lengthy and tedious discussions that followed, between Cox & Co.'s bankers, accountants and lawyers, and Harpers' bankers, accountants and lawyers, Giles's promise that Arthur would be the first chairman of the new firm began to look unrealistic. For if Arthur had not been Arthur, as Giles reminded Martagon in the aftermath, Cox & Co. would not have been up for a merger at all, except on their own terms.

Of course, the board of Cox & Co. – including Martagon – thought it was going to be on their own terms. But as the negotiations and due diligence proceeded, it began to look less and less like a merger and more and more like a takeover – by Harpers. The balance sheets told their own story.

In meeting after meeting, Cox & Co.'s position melted away. From the City's viewpoint, the tensile strengths that Arthur had built into the business were seen, bleakly, as points of fracture. The figures that were now being produced seemed to prove Cox & Co. to be terminally ailing. It was embarrassing and humiliating even for those, like Martagon, who were hell-bent on the merger.

Martagon betrayed Arthur a second time. On the final, decisive day of the negotiations, the two sides attended at the Institution of Civil Engineers in Great George Street, each with their phalanxes of accountants and lawyers, occupying separate suites, next door to one another on the lower ground floor. Messages and memos passed to and fro between the professionals they employed – all of whom stood to gain, fee-wise, from spinning things out as long as possible. Meanwhile the principals were sidelined.

Martagon was sitting with Tom Scree, Mirabel Plunket and other Cox people, waiting to sign the final documents when they appeared. It was after six o'clock when the senior man from their solicitors' firm put his head round the door. 'The other side,' he whispered, 'have made another difficulty.'

'I just don't believe it. If it's about the warranties again,' said Martagon, 'tell them to take a running jump. Everything is in order, we've been over and over it all and so have they.'

'It's not the warranties. It's about Sir Arthur Cox. They are reneging on the arrangement. About the chairmanship.'

Martagon had been half expecting this. But he was none the less furious. 'That is outrageous,' he said, vivified by anger. 'That is just not on.' He picked up his mobile and banged in Giles's number: 'I have to speak to you privately. Right now.'

The two met on the steps outside the building, in the cold, inhaling the fumes of gridlocked traffic waiting to get into Parliament Square.

'These are the longest red lights in London,' said Giles.

Martagon was too agitated for small-talk. 'What the fuck are you up to now?'

'I'm sorry, mate. It just can't be done. My people won't wear it. I did everything I could.'

'You gave me an undertaking. You gave me your word.

Your word of honour.' Martagon heard and hated the whine in his voice.

'Informally. I agreed informally. Cox is yesterday's man. He's lost it. Cox is dogmeat. You know it.'

'I can't accept this, Giles.'

'Come on, sharpen up. This is business. Our business, yours and mine. We're on the point of signing. Do you want to scupper the whole merger, our future, over this one issue?'

Martagon took a deep breath of polluted air into his lungs. 'No. No, I don't.'

'Right, then.'

'I shan't forgive you for this.'

'Yes, you will.'

THREE

The disease of management is worse than other diseases, because it is not recognized as a disease at all. Keen management is seen as a sign of entrepreneurial health. It calls out the best in people – initiative, interpersonal skills, flair for bringing order and purpose, and sometimes even grace, to a complex productive activity involving many others.

It also brings out the worst in them. Greed, and arrogance. That's what Martagon feared. That's what he saw happening at Harper Cox, from the beginning.

But could he expect men and women with special talents, placed in authority over others, to be without weaknesses? If so, almost no one would qualify – certainly no one with the drive, ambition and capacity for risk-taking that were essential to the undertaking.

After the merger, he longed to re-establish some simple contact with Arthur Cox. He telephoned him frequently, but he never seemed to be in his London flat. His Lambourn number was ex-directory, and Martagon had never known it. There were a lot of things he didn't know about Arthur.

Then one evening Arthur did pick up the telephone. 'Ah,

it's Mr Vain-Confidence himself,' he said. 'I don't suppose you remember what happens to him.'

'Yes, I do,' said Martagon, shortly.

Mr Vain-Confidence, in *Pilgrim's Progress*, falls into a deep pit.

Arthur told Martagon a long, rambling tale about a takeover bid he had successfully seen off in the late 1970s, before Martagon joined the firm. Martagon had heard it all before. 'We didn't employ shits in those days,' said Arthur, and rang off.

Those words were the last that Martagon ever heard him say.

A couple of days later, on a day of pouring rain, Arthur was shopping for his wife in Wantage, their market town. He was run over on the square by a white van driven by a local man. An ambulance took him to hospital. He was dead on arrival.

The driver was shattered. 'Gutted', as he said at the inquest. He had noticed Sir Arthur Cox, he said, whom he knew well by sight, standing with two carrier-bags beside the statue of King Alfred in the middle of the square. Then, before he knew it, Sir Arthur had lurched forward and was under his wheels. There was nothing he could do. The coroner attached no blame.

Martagon tried to imagine what it had been like for Arthur. The moment when the van first struck him – shock but not panic, time slowed-down; nothing irreversible had happened yet. The van, braking as hard as it could on the wet tarmac, still ploughed on, and Arthur felt himself falling, his hands letting go the bags, his balance lost, and still the van with its crushing weight bore down on him until Arthur was down, his head hitting the road. You can't put the clock back a single second. A black, spilling crack? And then, nothing.

Is that how it was? They said, at the hospital, that he would have felt no pain. But they had to say that. No doctor ever says, after a fatal accident, that the victim must have suffered inconceivable agony in the eternal moment before darkness came.

Martagon spoke at Arthur's cremation service. Most of the staff of what had been Cox & Co. showed up, as did Giles and Amanda, all of them mixing exotically with the Coxes' Berkshire friends. Beforehand, Martagon composed two addresses. There was the one that he actually gave, respectful, regretful, lightened with anecdotes of Arthur's professional triumphs and his endearing personal idiosyncrasies. He did not actually say, 'We shall never see his like again,' or 'They don't make them like that any more': he avoided the most blatant of the available clichés. But that was the general idea.

Afterwards people came up to him and said he had struck exactly the right note. He met, for the first and last time, Arthur's daughter, flanked by a stockbroker husband and a young son. The one who had a family party for his tenth birthday. Now, when it was too late, Martagon felt a tender curiosity about Arthur's emotional hinterland.

The widow, Lady Cox, thanked him effusively for what he had said. Martagon had met her before, and not liked her much – a dyed blonde who had once been pretty. She was wearing heavy makeup and a furry black hat. Afterwards she sent Martagon one of Arthur's ties as a memento, which caused him to suppose that Arthur could not have confided in her the details of his humiliation and betrayal. Lady Cox did not look like a person in whom one could easily confide. The tie seemed brand new, apple-green silk with white polka dots. Martagon had never seen Arthur wearing it. He had probably been given it for Christmas one year, since when it had lain in the back of a drawer. Martagon would much rather have had one of the creased, dim-coloured woollen ties that Arthur habitually wore with his shabby tweed suits at the office.

The second address, which he did not deliver, and never even printed out from his computer, was about how an honourable man was let down by his friends, by his own intransigent personality, and by cut-throat modern business practices. It was an angry piece – doubly and impotently angry, because the tragedy was built in. It was no good saying 'if only'. Arthur Cox was as he was, Giles and Martagon were as they were, and it's an old sad story.

But actions have consequences. We killed something in Arthur, thought Martagon. I am personally culpable, because I was his good angel and he trusted me.

Giles is, in spite of appearances, a sensitive man – dangerously so. His sensitivity to the state of mind of others is part of his arsenal. He was careful and caring in his attitude to Martagon in the first weeks of the new dispensation, conferring with him over every minor decision. He nursed Martagon over this difficult transition, acting as an expansion joint does, absorbing unusual stresses without deforming the structure. Martagon was mollified by Giles's apparent respect for his judgement. Perhaps it was true, what Arthur had said: that Giles wanted him not only for his professional excellence, but as some sort of moral ballast; he respected Martagon's values as Martagon had respected Arthur's.

Giles and Martagon were now joint chief executives of Harper Cox. They retained on the main board an equal number of Cox directors and Harper directors. Some dead wood was pruned – not discarded, mostly, but redeployed. They terminated the leases on Cox & Co.'s Caxton Street premises and Harpers' offices in Crawley as soon as they could, and acquired as their head office three thousand square feet in a factory conversion in Clerkenwell. Novelli's restaurant on Clerkenwell Green, and the St John bar and restaurant in St John's Street became their homes from home. They expanded the regional offices in the UK and overseas. Martagon recruited (as he put it), and Giles poached (as he boasted) bright new talent, male and female, from all over. Harper Cox was hot. They were the new kids on the block.

There was a lot of work in progress from both sides to be seen through, but they started at once to look for new business. Cox & Co., shortly before the merger, had failed to win the coveted contract for a rural-access roads project in Zimbabwe. Alternative arrangements having fallen through, however, the project came up again. Harper Cox were approached directly; they did not have to tender competitively. Their proposal was accepted. Giles announced that he wished to have special responsibility for Africa; he wanted the Zim project for himself. Martagon let him have it. He himself would take Europe.

Martagon had an ulterior motive: he had met a young German woman, Jutta, who worked in a bookshop in Berlin. She was shiningly healthy-looking, with an alluring waist-to-hip ratio, i.e., she was slim and curvy. Martagon responded to her instantly, bought a book he didn't really want, and smiled at her. She agreed to meet him after the bookshop closed.

With a startling rapidity, they became intimate. For three months they had been seeing each other, on her territory, at weekends. Jutta liked set routines. She would not take kindly to his spending months away on the other side of the world and, for the moment, he didn't want to lose her.

'You don't sound all that keen really,' said Amanda. 'Are you in love with her?'

'Well,' said Martagon, 'I'm not in love with anyone else.'

'Are we going to get to meet her?'

'Maybe,' said Martagon, 'but not yet.'

In consultation with Giles, and while Harper Cox was the flavour of the month, Martagon decided to pitch for a few big European projects rather than a lot of smaller ones. The strategy paid off. They tendered for, and got, the main engineering contract for the new theatre just off the Potsdamerplatz in Berlin. The architect was Lin Perry, so it was quite a coup for Harper Cox.

The Lin Perry. The new Camden Public Library, the museum in Barcelona, the star-shaped sports centre in Singapore. Also, the one who was rude about Amanda Harper's big bottom. Lin himself attracts admiring glances and photographers' lenses whenever he makes an appearance – and not just because of his high professional profile.

Martagon had read enough articles on Lin, before he ever met him, to know that he was what feature-writers call a cosmocrat. He is well known in the US quite apart from his architecture because he was, briefly, a basketball star in his student days. His father is a retired American general, his mother a famously lovely Chinese actress. Lin inherited his father's height and heft, and his long, long legs. He also inherited his mother's features and colouring.

The result is startling. Lin looks like the chieftain of a hitherto unknown tribe. You could not guess what his native language might be. He speaks, in fact, in the attractively drawly, ironic tones of the cultivated New Yorker. He is much in demand on both sides of the Atlantic from artistic women with big hair and bank balances, the sort who host dinners for charity.

Lin's London base at this time was a massive loft

near Tower Bridge, which he shared with George, an obstreperous Airedale terrier. George went everywhere with him. George had a peculiarly piercing bark, and he barked a lot. Martagon did not much like George, and George knew it. Lin was seen about with interesting women – a young first-time novelist, a dancer from Covent Garden – but he guarded his private life ruthlessly. Martagon hardly ever saw him alone. He moved around accompanied not only by George but by a variety of personable young male assistants from his office, who carried the bags and knew the detail. Lin is an ideas man, a broad-brush man.

Lin took a liking to Martagon, as people do, but they didn't become intimate. Their most fruitful professional conversations were on the telephone, when Lin seemed to expand and relax. He would ring Martagon at home at odd times – seven in the morning, eleven thirty at night – wanting to settle down to half an hour's chat about the Berlin work. Lin kept Martagon on his toes, and Martagon liked Lin, and it was doing his reputation no harm at all to be working closely with the great Lin Perry. Jutta was still in Berlin, so his professional and private life dovetailed neatly.

So far so good.

Martagon and Giles hired a whiz-kid financial director who had been going through the books with a fine-tooth comb. The plan was to trim down the workforce to a hard core of high-quality engineering staff, and to hire specialist consultants – sociologists, geologists, economists, financial analysts, planners, environmentalists – on short-term contracts for specific projects. They had been putting off appointing a new chairman. Martagon and Giles had been taking turns to chair the main board.

It wasn't sensible to continue like that, and the other board members let it be known that they did not like it. The two of them were busy with heading up their own divisions, with restructuring the company, and with management problems, and there was no objective guiding hand at the helm.

'The only disadvantage in appointing a chairman,' said Giles, 'is that he could get us, or one of us, fired. The board keeps an eye on management, the chairman keeps an eye on the executive.'

'Nevertheless,' said Martagon, 'I'd feel more comfortable if we had a chairman. It's better organizational practice. Do we want just a titular chairman – or someone who will be properly involved in day-to-day decisions? I could take some soundings, and look out for someone suitable from outside, if you think that's a good idea.'

'No,' said Giles. 'No. We should invite Tom Scree to be non-executive chairman.'

Martagon was speechless. He was disgusted.

Giles, who had been conciliatory for so long over minor matters, insisted on having his way over this. He was supported by the rest of the board, who were all for it. Better, they said, the devil we know . . . Giles had presented the case for Scree, with a charming deference, as a tribute to Cox & Co., and a reparation for the dumping of Arthur Cox. Not that he used the word 'dumping'. It would cost the firm less, too: Tom had intimated that he would be happy to move to part-time. To Martagon, Giles said privately that he only wanted Tom in the chair because Tom was too busy to be inconveniently hands-on.

Indeed, Scree was letting it be known that his true interests reached far wider than the affairs of Harper Cox. He was working, unpaid, in what he could without misrepresentation call the voluntary sector – actually an international organization dedicated to conflict resolution worldwide, funded by a multi-millionaire ex-arms dealer and born-again Christian, domiciled in Houston, Texas.

'Who is he? What's his name?' asked Martagon, fascinated.

'You would not have heard of him. He's a very private person. But the organization is called the Grid Group, you'll have heard about that. There was quite a good piece about us in *The Economist* last week.'

Scree and Martagon were having lunch at Novelli's, at Martagon's suggestion. If he was going to have to work with Scree, he had better try to get on better terms with him. They were meant to be discussing the teething troubles of Harper Cox, but did not get very far.

It appeared to Martagon that Scree's work for the Grid Group chiefly involved first-class air-tickets to first-class hotels in agreeable places, for conferences on the world's potential trouble-spots. The proceedings were then edited, and circulated to government departments, newspapers and journals in Europe and the US, and to an impressive mailing-list of the internationally great and good.

'The international community knows all about Bosnia, Burundi, Bangladesh,' said Scree, picking at his halibut. 'But it would take real insight to spot the spores of conflict in, say, Barbados.'

'It certainly would. And even then, you've only got up to the letter B,' said Martagon. 'I must say, it's a breathtakingly immodest programme.' Martagon, who had come along with the best intentions, was finding it hard to overcome his dislike of the man.

'Surely,' said Scree, 'it's better to do something, to try and do something, than to do absolutely nothing, then throw up our hands in horror and amazement when violence explodes somewhere new.'

'But you can hardly intervene before anything has happened.'

'Public opinion and the media can prevent, or at any rate

moderate, events. At the very worst, our government and the governments of other responsible countries will not be unprepared.'

'You mean our governments will know in good time who to make a quick buck selling arms and warheads to, before we step in and piously bomb the same people to smithereens for making use of what we sold them? Can you prove that your group's activities have ever had any influence for good, that is, towards neutralizing conflict before it can break out?'

'You can't prove we *haven't*,' said Scree, looking at Martagon with his bright fanatical eyes. 'What's your problem, Martagon? I can never make my mind up whether you are a cynic, or a complete innocent about how the world works.'

Martagon could not figure Scree out either. Either he was a hypocrite or he wasn't. Either he was Christ among the Pharisees, or he was the chief Pharisee.

'What I was coming to,' said Scree, 'was that the Group's next conference – in Bali, actually—'

'Still not got beyond B, I see,' said Martagon. 'You've a way to go, Tom.'

'This conference, which is a particularly important one, coincides with the date of the next Harper Cox board meeting. So I shall have to ask one of you to take the chair. Of course I'll let you have my comments in writing, for reference, once we have agreed the agenda. Which reminds me, I'd prefer to have Dawn in my office instead of the woman I've got now. Dawn would be useful, she's familiar with the procedure. She knows where to find things, and she is discreet. I know Arthur thought highly of her.'

Dawn, since the merger, had been acting as secretary to Martagon. There was no reason why she should not now be transferred back to the chairman's office. She would probably prefer it. As Scree said, she knew the procedure. Nevertheless, Martagon was irritated. Nor did Scree's absence from a board meeting really matter a damn. Yet he was more than irritated by Scree's casualness. He was infuriated. Chairing the board was Scree's only crucial function now that he worked part-time for the firm.

'Just one other thing,' said Scree, hauling on his greasy, dilapidated leather jacket, while Martagon offered the waiter his company credit card to pay for their lunch. 'I'd like to have Mirabel Plunket co-opted on to the main board. She has somehow got overlooked. She's very good, and we absolutely ought not to have an all-male board.'

'You may be right,' said Martagon, well knowing that Scree was irrefutably right. Martagon knew, too, that he should have thought about Mirabel himself. Scree had, as always, succeeded in wrong-footing him.

Thoroughly confused, Martagon went for a swim. A good person doesn't just keep society's rules in the interests of peace and harmony. You could be virtually inanimate and still do that. A good person is active – pro-active, as Tom Scree would say – in *creating* the society he lives in, standing up against evil and injustice, risking his own well-being, even his life. If he doesn't do that, the bullies will win. The strong will wipe out the weak. Arthur Cox was weak because he was old. That is nature's way – in nations at war, within communities, in animal herds, among plant species. Humanity has taken it upon itself to mitigate this cruel process. Up to a point.

But it *is* all process. We in the fat West have everything, but it won't last. Rise and fall. Growth and rot. The new feeding on the detritus of the old. Martagon heaved himself out of the pool, for once unrefreshed, unrenewed. He dreamed his old dream about the handless stumps – thud-thud, thud-thud on the car windows. Only differently. The windows were shattered, scattering slivers of glass into the dark interior where he cowered and trembled. Sometimes, during this time, Arthur Cox came to Martagon in dreams too. Nothing happened, there was no story, just a strong presence. It was really a dream about a suit, the one that Arthur had worn for years. He saw in close-up the exact texture of the soft tweed. It looked greyish from a distance, but had a small black and white pattern of the sort called 'bird's-eye'. He saw in the dream the way the jacket hung out at the back from Arthur's broad, stooped shoulders, and the baggy, unpressed trousers with turn-ups, and creases behind the knees.

Where was that suit now? Probably Lady Cox had taken it to Oxfam.

It was several months before Martagon admitted to himself that he was unhappy at work. The only thing he was really enjoying was the Berlin theatre project. Lin's design had caught his imagination. Lin had wanted Martagon on the project because he knew about his experience with structural glass: the theatre was topped by an asymmetrical glass dome, to carry a reference to Foster's design for the Reichstag without seeming to parody or mimic it. It was a challenge, both structurally and aesthetically, and Martagon was absorbed by the problems. He enjoyed the contact with Lin and the frequent meetings with Lin's people at his Paris office.

Events were precipitated by two bad quarrels he had with Giles. The first was about Giles's policy of winning contracts by deliberately undercutting the opposition, while knowing that the work could not possibly be done properly for the quoted sum.

'We'll up the costs when we're on the job,' said Giles. 'It won't be hard to find good reasons.'

'I'm sure it won't,' replied Martagon, 'the main reason being that we seriously underestimated in the first place.'

'What's your problem, Martagon?'

The second disagreement was about Giles's management style. He was fostering competition within the firm, so that each division was beginning to raise the ante, bumping up profit projections artificially so as to be allocated a bigger share of the budget. 'Competition is the only incentive. There's the market, and there's the internal market,' said Giles. 'It's the same difference.'

'I don't think so,' said Martagon. 'Competition is turning into faction-fighting. And what happens when the projections aren't met?'

'Then we give them hell and tell them to do better next time. And they will, they don't want to lose their jobs.'

Martagon found himself brooding bitterly about matters that should have been water under the bridge by now. He went over and over Giles's high-handedness over the merger: the dumping of Arthur, the telephone call to Scree during the key meeting. Giles might still not have told him quite everything: he might, during that call, have promised the chairmanship to Scree in order to copper-bottom his support for the merger. Giles's pleasant agreeableness over so many things, at the beginning, might have been just a strategy to jolly Martagon along, knowing that the issue of the chairmanship was going to cause trouble and that he would have to be adamant.

Giles, it seemed to Martagon, did not know the difference between management and manipulation. He was also taking too much money out of the firm for his salary and Martagon's, which made Martagon uneasy.

Martagon despised himself for resenting Giles's style. His broodings were petty, if only because he knew that Giles thought of the two of them as inseparable partners, almost as brothers, Giles was just being Giles, which included an instinctive quasi-sibling rivalry.

'We can manage this business better, for a better return,' Giles said to him, presenting yet another 'opportunity' which Martagon saw as ignoble short-termism. 'That's why we got together, isn't it? You're not properly focused, Martagon. You lack the killer instinct, you're trying to drive with the handbrake on.'

Giles talked a lot about the Harper Cox 'core values'. Martagon gathered that by this he meant maximizing profits for the shareholders – among whom he, Martagon and Tom Scree, in that order, held the majority of shares.

'I thought "core values" were things like honesty and integrity,' Martagon said.

'That goes without saying. Get a life,' said Giles. 'You're such a prig.'

Martagon was nettled. Giles had a point. Martagon began to feel not only resentful but inadequate. He began to be unwell. Nothing major. His gums hurt and bled. He picked up a nasty case of athlete's foot at the pool. He cut himself shaving, and the tiny wound went septic. There seemed to be a lot more hair in his hairbrush than there used to be. He began to think the unthinkable: first, that he was going bald, and second, that he should leave the firm. It was the only right thing to do.

*   *   *

He wrote his letter of resignation to the chairman, Tom Scree. Within two days, the news was all over the office. Scree expressed his great regret, insincerely Martagon thought. Giles, however, came to him white-faced, chain-smoking. Martagon had never seen him so agitated.

'You just can't do this. What has happened to us? What has happened to our Camelot? What's got into you?'

Martagon hardened his heart, saying to himself that it was only Giles's pride and his panic at what Martagon's departure might do to the firm's standing that were causing his distress.

'There's something big coming up which would be just up your street – a new airport in France. The competition for the design is about to be announced, I had it today from someone at Arup who'd heard it on the grapevine. It'll be huge. They say Lin is interested. We should try to be involved. We should pitch for the main engineering contract. You can't let us down like this.'

Martagon shrugged. 'Your business now, not mine.'

'At least let's discuss this, out of the office. Come and talk it all over at home – with Amanda. Like we always do, like the friends we are. We can sort it out.'

'No.' Martagon was exhausted. He had suddenly nothing at all to say to Giles, who after half an hour of cajolement, reproach, bribery – 'What is it that you *want*, Martagon?' – lost his temper.

'Then we'll buy you out. No problem. Clear your fucking desk by Friday.'

Technically, Martagon should not have left immediately. But obviously, under the circumstances, staying on would have been too painful for all concerned. Arrangements were made. Martagon did not go and see Amanda, though he knew she would be bewildered and upset – both for Giles, and the firm, and for the close little unit that the three of them had become. Perhaps it was four of them. He felt the need to explain himself to Julie.

He met her for a drink in Gordon's basement wine-bar in Villiers Street near the Embankment, thinking she might enjoy its subterranean seediness as he did. She turned up with her backpack, looking concerned. She didn't remark on the ambience. The scabby walls and dark, dripping brick vaults seemed just normal to her. Martagon started to tell her about leaving the firm.

'I know about it already,' she said.

'Giles has told you.'

'Yes, but I knew before.'

'Oh?'

'From Tom.'

'How's that?' Martagon was astonished.

'I see him sometimes. He takes me and Fasil out into the country. In his car.'

Martagon had been planning to explain his resignation to Julie in terms of his antipathy to Tom Scree, so as not to speak badly to her about her beloved brother. Now, he saw with distaste, his strategy was inappropriate. Simply for something to say, he asked, 'In his car? What sort of car does Tom have?'

Julie said vaguely, 'I think it's a Viagra.'

He looked at her sharply. There was absolutely no way of knowing whether she was making a joke or not. Perhaps she meant a Vectra, or a Vitara.

Martagon went independent. He took some of his personal files home, and some to the two-room office suite he rented only a few hundred yards from the Harper Cox premises. He didn't have the energy to look further afield, and he had to move fast. He had business cards printed, and headed stationery:

MARTAGON

Structural Engineering and Design
Multi-Disciplinary Consultancy

With a logo designed by himself of a hammer crossed with a long-stemmed martagon lily, making an X-shape.

'You're such a girl, my dear,' said Lin Perry, when he saw the logo.

'No, I'm not,' said Martagon. He knew he was not.

He took the Berlin theatre project with him from Harper Cox with Giles's unwilling consent; it was after all Martagon himself, rather than the firm as a whole, with whom Lin Perry was working. The main task, now, was to determine the multiple and various specifications for the structural glass.

Martagon set out to rebuild his career from scratch. Later, he saw that the painful break with Harper Cox was the best thing that could have happened to him. During the first thin months he did some design work for a firm that built expensive, bespoke, one-off conservatories. In the process he learned, as others in the field were also learning, how best to exploit glass as a 'strong material', and how to create all-glass structures with no supporting steel or wood anywhere. He designed glass beams and glass staircases. He gained confidence. He was working on using hollow tubes as supports, convinced that the load-bearing capacity of glass was still underestimated. He dreamed of designing a bridge – a footbridge – made entirely of glass. The technology was not up to speed for that yet, but in another couple of years it might be. He asked himself continually, 'What if . . . ?' He grappled with problems of heat loss, condensation, ventilation. He wasn't the only one at it – but he was positioning himself among the three or four architects and engineers at the cutting edge of his speciality, though he was too absorbed to realize this straight away.

It took a year before there were more incoming than outgoing calls to his office, but after two of his structures were published in the technical journals the world started to come to him. Soon he was being offered more work than his small office – himself and two assistants – could handle.

He was interviewed by a charming and clever woman for the *Architects' Journal*, and gave a series of lectures on glass technology to post-graduate architects at the RIBA. He was invited to give papers at conferences and to sit on panels. He became a voice on radio programmes about state-of-the-art design. An article on the increasingly close and ambiguous relationship between architecture and engineering in *Architecture Today* featured his work flatteringly, and included a photograph of him. A production company invited him to present a TV series to be called *Best Buildings of Our Century*. He declined. He received – along with an increased flow of junk mail and charity appeals – invitations to previews of prestigious new buildings, and to gallery openings. People to whom he was introduced at these parties and gatherings shook his hand with smiles and nods of recognition when they heard his name.

So Martagon was a success. But if the world had found him, he had not yet found himself, though he loved the work. He still felt adrift. Most weekends he went to Germany to see Jutta, who attached herself organically to his inner self whether he willed it or not – just as living tissue, he thought, creeps forward with mindless determination and cleaves to the ceramic glass of a prosthetic called the Douek middle-ear device. He'd read a paper about it. For he was reading and thinking about nothing but glass, obsessed by its unexpected elasticity and sudden fickle brittleness, and by the way it transmits, reflects and refracts light, sculpting the very air into a form of his choosing.

He experimented privately with working models in a workshop in Bethnal Green with a talented pair of Czech glass-workers, father and son. His clients found it hard to believe in the compressive strength of glass; making models was the best way of convincing them – and himself. ('What if . . .') Old Jan and Young Jan had no conception of impossibility, and no fear of trying out something new and rash for Martagon.

Occasionally, during those five years in private practice, he saw Julie; and she told him about a novel called *Oscar and Lucinda.*

'The woman in it inherits a glassworks and tries to build a glass church. It's her lover's idea. They have this obsession about it. They are both compulsive gamblers.'

'And?'

'I haven't finished the book yet. But I think something shatteringly awful is going to happen.'

'I'd better read it, then.'

'It's very good. It won the Booker Prize. It's not about now, it's set in the late nineteenth century.'

'Glass was in the air, then. Technology creeps along then suddenly takes a leap. Glass is in the air again, right now.'

Julie copied out for him a verse by a seventeenth-century poet, George Herbert:

> A man who looks on glass,
> On it may stay his eye;
> Or if he pleaseth, through it pass,
> And so the heaven espy.

'He wrote another one,' she said, 'about man being made

of "brittle crazy glass" until God anneals the gospel story in him. I don't know what "anneals" means, though I can kind of guess.'

'Anneals. That's a technical term. To do with toughening, and fusing, by heat. I'm using annealed glass now. He must have been really interested in glass.'

'I don't suppose so. Not for its own sake. He was thinking about stained-glass windows in church illustrating Bible stories. He was interested in God. He was a vicar. And dead before he was forty.'

Occasionally, as Martagon left his office in the evening, he saw a burgundy-red Jaguar shimmering round Clerkenwell Green, and quickly looked the other way. He had work, and friends; but sometimes he thought he would not mind too much if he, like the poet George Herbert, died before he was forty. Not so long to wait.

When, in early 1998, Lin Perry remarked in passing that he wished to hell he had him on the airport project, Martagon thought very little about it. He knew Harper Cox had the main contract, and he could not imagine Giles Harper ever wanting to work with him again.

Then Giles rang him up out of the blue, sounding quite normal, as if there had been no break in their communication.

'Look, Martagon, would you consider being a consultant on the Bonplaisir airport project? We're going out to tender now. You know what the contractors are capable of in this area better than anyone. It's all that glass. We're going to need about two dozen different specifications for different sections, and we'll need to get it right. It's a real bugger.'

'I'll come in with you just for the tender process, if that would help. Off the top of my head, I'd say Heaney Mahon would be your best bet. They won't be the cheapest, though. Irish. Part of the Celtic Tiger thing, a whole paw of it, you might say. And they're doing a lot of edgy stuff with glass.'

'That's the sort of thing we need to know. Yes, please come in for the scrutiny of tender. I really want you on board for the implementation too, to see the project through. We're quite far on but we've had some bad setbacks and from where I sit it looks like the whole strategy needs overhauling. We're going to have to work bloody fast now.'

'Giles. Wait a minute. I don't know—'

'You get on much better with Lin than I do, he wants you in on it, and it goes without saying that we do too. Look, I really need you, my old mate.'

They met for a drink. Giles filled Martagon in, at length. Big projects take several years to get off the ground, and Harper Cox had been one of the main players from the beginning.

The inspiration came from the Vaucluse region, as part of a plan to improve on the small airport already in existence at Avignon. The idea was to build a new flagship airport well south of Lyon, with the intention of diverting a profitable tranche of air traffic and tourism from the coastal airports of Nice and Marseille. Lin Perry's design, as Martagon was well aware, had been the winner in an international competition.

There had been opposition from the Marseille mafia, and delays while a commission of civil servants and the relevant ministries in Paris sat on the idea. But the *départements* adjacent to the Vaucluse came on board; a development corporation was set up; the finance came in from private and institutional investors. The budget for the terminal was 150 million francs, the target a throughput of 300,000 to 350,000 passengers a year – as airports go, these days, a small operation, as Giles said. The new 2F terminal at Charles de Gaulle in Paris, for example, had a budget of 2.5 billion francs. The Provence airport, which was to be called Bonplaisir, was more on the scale of Lille's new passenger terminal.

The name Bonplaisir came from the site, acquired with a lot of hassle and at great cost from a brother and sister, local aristos – 'weird people, I gather, at each other's throats' – and was ideal, a flat piece of land with already excellent transport links, and with the Rhône and the autoroute on one side, and the new extension of the TGV railway line on the other. The airport would have its own railway station as part of the complex, though Harper Cox were not involved with that. Plus, the Château de Bonplaisir was thrown in, and would become a five-star hotel.

There had been feasibility studies, and reports from specialist consultants – a sociologist, an ecologist – to provide projections of the probable impact on the area, so that any ill-effects could be factored in and minimized. Harper Cox were contracted just for the terminal, not for the runways or the avionics. But it didn't hurt to do some thinking about the meteorological aspects, because of the impact of the mistral on the terminal building. (Might have to use glass fins for windbracing, Martagon thought as Giles talked.) The main runway, for instance, was running north–south, so that the planes came in and took off with or against, but not across, the mistral.

Giles told Martagon all of this and much more, and in great detail, talking hard for over two hours. He had Lin Perry's original design and some of the plans with him. Martagon kept his cool. He asked a lot of questions. Giles outlined what would be Martagon's particular responsibilities. He mentioned fees – just ballpark figures, he said.

When finally he wound down, he looked at Martagon and said, 'Well?'

'Yes,' said Martagon. 'Yes, I'll do it. I'll come in with you.'

His main work on the Berlin theatre was almost finished. Other projects on the drawing-board could be fitted in.

The following weekend, in Berlin to visit Jutta, he told her that he could not go on with their relationship. Giles's offer had given him the impetus to make the break. Without quite acknowledging the fact, he had been wanting to do it for months, both for his sake and hers – or so he told himself, though that was not how she saw it. The bottom line was that he did not love her. She was a keen bed-partner, and even more keen at planning their future together. He knew that was not what he wanted. It was a painful weekend. He did everything he could to leave her with her self-esteem and dignity intact, and feared that he had not succeeded.

Then, with relief, he flew to Paris and saw Lin Perry. With Lin's right-hand man he pored over the plans in Lin's office near the Sorbonne, and he and Lin took George – older now, and mellower – for a walk in the Jardin du Luxembourg, talking everything over. Then he took the train down to Avignon and hired a car for his first site visit.

The details of his consultancy still had to be finalized with Harper Cox's finance director, but he was not worried about that. He felt as light as air. He saw his way ahead, clear and straightforward. He did not know that the airport project would also bring him Marina. If he had had foreknowledge – which one never has – would he have decided differently?

No.

He returned to the Harper Cox fold and to the Harper family, and began to see more of Julie again. She was not only older, as they all were, but better and happier, having walked away the worst of her unhappiness. She had put on weight – not much, she was still tiny, there was still nothing of her, but she no longer looked like an anorexic or a sickly adolescent from a food-deficit area. She was working for a reputable aid agency in Hackney, as project manager for several sub-Saharan countries.

Martagon at first found it hard to envisage Julie managing anything. Then he began to realize how intelligent she was, and how conscientious. Unlike her brother she read all the time, borrowing books from the public library, and she remembered everything she read. She interested him, and he found himself thinking about her.

He had never before met a woman with Julie's absolute lack of coquetry and flirtatiousness. It was unnerving. He realized that the easy contact he made with most women – even with Amanda, and with women of all ages, plain or pretty – was based on the mutual acknowledgement of agreeable sexual difference. Not so, with Julie.

This was oddly challenging and, after a while, alluring. Julie rarely asserted herself, yet she seemed open and – yes, even available, in the vulnerable, unaware way that a flower is available. She had no self-presentation or 'manner' when she talked to him, so she seemed naked. Talking to Julie is like talking in bed, he thought. She talks in that deadpan desultory way that one normally does only after making love.

All this being so, and since she was not very skilled at making conversation at a supper-table, Martagon concluded that the only real contact a man could have with Julie was likely to be physical.

Not that he had any physical contact with her, beyond social kissing at the end of an evening. He liked her but he did not desire her. If asked, he would have said, in the conventional sexual shorthand, that she was not his type. But once when she was playing with Fasil on the floor Martagon saw that under her usual droopy skirt she was wearing a startlingly white petticoat with a flouncy lace edge. It made him gasp. The white lace was just for herself, and he had to admit he was increasingly curious about that self.

She was reticent, seemingly self-contained. There was an occasion when Tom Scree, at the Harpers' table, had been talking about how unsuited monotheism was to the human psyche, and the lengths to which Christianity had to go in order to sustain such an unnatural idea. The Holy Trinity, for example, making three gods into or out of one. Julie said quietly to Martagon, who was sitting beside her, 'I could believe in the Three in One and One in Three if it wasn't just three. It's such a feeble number. It's either too many or not enough. If it was three hundred, or three thousand . . .'

'What if it was *seventeen*?'

And she had laughed, spontaneously, at that. Julie did not often laugh, so that Martagon felt that she had given him a present. Or that he had given her one.

Julie had found her burrow: a basement with a bit of sooty garden behind. It was in that run-down stretch of Bayswater which consists of long streets of vast peeling stucco houses with pillared porches, all flats and bedsits and rip-off substandard hotels, with no corner shops. The burrow had two bedrooms, one of which she was letting cheaply to a Kosovan refugee woman who had found work in a bakery. She brought bags of unsold croissants and rolls back to Julie and Fasil every evening, and she baby-sat when Julie went out. Julie had made the place cosy in her own way with ethnic rugs and batiks, and pottery mugs and plates, and her books. An elaborate silver Ethiopian cross, which Hailu had given her when they married, hung from its chain on a nail over the gas fire. There were always Fasil's toys around and, of course, Fasil.

He had grown into an enchanting child. Martagon thought about him, too. Julie was transformed into a madonna when she sat with the five-year-old on her knee, reading to him, her light hair falling on his shiny black curls, her pale arms encircling his little brown body. She had stuck a blown-up photograph of herself and Hailu in their student days under the glass top of her coffee-table, and Fasil would stand at the table absorbedly tracing the picture with his finger.

'Daddy,' he would say every time, and Julie would always reply, 'Yes, that's Daddy, with Mummy, before you were born. Daddy's in Ethiopia. That's where he lives. In Ethiopia.'

Fasil would look intently up into her face and mouth the mysterious syllables, silently.

Martagon did not go to the flat very often. He had taken Julie to the cinema once or twice. He always let Giles know when he had seen her, and saw his face light up. Giles's perpetual concern for his sister was his one vulnerable point. Amanda, even now, did not have much time for Julie.

'Poor Julie, she doesn't have a clue,' Amanda said to Martagon. 'And she sponges on Giles.'

'I think he's happy to help her out,' said Martagon.

'Trouble is, he thinks the sun shines out of her arse. I wish she had a boyfriend. It's a pity Tom Scree is married. He's too old, but in every other way he'd be so right for her.'

'I don't think so.'

Not long after that he went back to France, and met Marina de Cabrières, and the world was turned upside down.

FOUR

Back in London after his first weeks in France with Marina, Martagon slept for nine solid hours. On subsequent nights he could hardly sleep at all. He woke every hour, unable to be comfortable in his bed. From four thirty on, he gave up all hope. He ran out of thoughts. Apart from missing Marina, his mind seemed to have nowhere to go.

He gave himself a mental exercise. When he was a child, his mother used to talk about his 'memory bank'. Every treat, every adventure, every mishap or triumph, was an investment in his memory bank. 'It'll pay dividends later,' she would say. 'Nothing is wasted. You'll see.' So now he made a conscious effort to check his investments. It passed the time, until morning came, and after a few nights of it he became addicted. The foreground of his life – even the work, even his preoccupation with Marina – became transparent, in those hours of musing and brooding. He saw straight through them to the background – the past. The pre-dawn hours, in this drifting state, with no particular agenda, passed in a flash or in an eternity; it came to the same thing. It was a state he would not have achieved had Marina been sleeping at his side. Even though he missed her so badly, he knew it was important to be alone for a while. He needed time to regroup.

He was ambushed by memories he had not had before, about the summer trip with his parents to the Tyrol when he was eight, just before he went to boarding-school in England. They were sitting, the three of them, in the garden of a chalet-restaurant where there was a small ornamental windmill.

There was a little wooden man connected to the windmill. The sails of the windmill turned faster or slower depending on how fast or slowly he turned a wheel attached to his arms, which jerked up and down. Martagon pointed out to his father how the windmill's sails came to a stop altogether when the wooden man stopped working the wheel.

'Look again, Turk,' said his father. 'Use your intelligence.'

Martagon looked again. He couldn't think what his father was getting at.

His father gripped him by the shoulders. 'Look now,' he said, in his precise Irish-tinted voice. 'It's not your man who is working the wheel. It is the wind which is working the windmill, and the wheel, and your man. You've got hold of the wrong end of the stick.'

That was the last holiday they had as a complete family. Martagon's father was already ill with the kidney disease that was to kill him, and finding the walks difficult. An old farmer passed them on the mountain track, wobbling along on a white bicycle, carrying a long scythe over his shoulder.

'Are you going far?' he asked in German.

'All the way,' replied Martagon's father. Then, turning to his wife: 'Ah, well, now. Death overtaking me on the road – a phenomenon it would be impossible to invent.'

'Death overtakes us all,' said his wife. They held hands. Martagon, trotting along attached to his mother's other hand, and listening, understood and did not understand.

'Did you see his bike, Dad?'

'I did.'

'It was brand new. A mountain bike. I want one like that.'

'I expect it was his grandson's,' said his father. 'Or, anyway, it will be soon.'

Martagon was at school when his father died.

Early one morning in London, Martagon had a telephone call from Audrey, his mother's cleaning lady. Audrey said Mrs Foley was very poorly. Audrey said a whole lot more, the gist being that she was no longer able to manage. Something would have to be done.

Jill Foley lived out her long, contented widowhood in a 1930s house called White Gates, which had white gates, a crunchy gravel drive, and half an acre of garden. She had not lost her interest in flowers, and her garden – the English garden she had always longed for – became over the years her chief occupation. The house was in a built-up area rich in superstores, light industry, and sports fields. Beyond the suburbs, it was neither quite in London nor quite in the country. It was near the Thames, but not in sight of it. Martagon thought of it as sub-rural nowhere-land. It was everything that he most disliked about what England was becoming. He nearly always lost his way nowadays, when he drove to White Gates, and generally arrived in a bad temper.

As Martagon joined the slow crawl of traffic leaving central London towards the south-west, he noticed that the year was turning. The green of the trees was dull and dusty; some of their leaves were already yellowing. As he drove, he was still thinking about that last Tyrolean holiday, remembering how he had scampered off a mountain track to pee in the pine forest while his parents walked on. His pee made a dark puddle in the squidgy forest floor. For fun, he ran further into the forest, zigzagging between the pines, arms outstretched, being a plane. Looking around, he could no longer see the path, or his parents. There were bad smells of things rotting, and weird noises from the dark pines. He began to run, and tripped on a root, falling on his face on the dank earth. He got up again and ran first in one direction, then in another. The forest looked the same whichever way he turned. He shouted for Mummy, for Daddy, hearing his little-boy voice thin and weak, muffled by the encircling trees. He shouted and shouted, and began to cry. He was *lost*.

Back with his parents on the path, he affected bravado. 'I wasn't really lost, I was only pretending. I'd have found my way back. You were lost, I wasn't. I'd have found you all right if you hadn't come looking for me.'

'It was an ordeal, wasn't it? You were Christian in *Pilgrim's Progress*, or one of the Knights of the Round Table on a quest.' His mother connived, as she would, with his face-saving strategy.

His father was a man for accuracy, for keeping the accounts straight.

'Ah, now, he was only having a pee. It wasn't a quest or an ordeal, or a trial.' Mr Foley's illness made him even more irritably pedantic than usual.

'It was, it was a test of character. I think he was very brave.'

Martagon's mother's appearance was fixed in his imagination and memory at about this time; it tallied with the leather-framed photograph of her which she packed in his suitcase to take to boarding-school that autumn, and which he still had. Crossing Hampton Court Bridge, he saw in his mind's eye her fluffy fair hair, her round blue eyes, and the silver brooch in the shape of a tortoise that was pinned on the lapel of the green coat she had worn for years.

In the past, he had gone to White Gates for Sunday lunch quite often. In the early days of his friendship with the Harpers he had sometimes taken them along with him. His mother liked bustling around providing for the 'young people', and in good weather they ate at a table in her garden. But these days he didn't go to see her nearly as often as he should – and not only because he was working abroad most of the time and, when he was back, dreaded the long time-wasting drive. She greeted his rare but regular telephone calls with 'Well, hello, stranger! I thought you'd forgotten all about me. I've not been too well, you know.' The archness and the reproach irritated him, so that he left it even longer before calling again.

When he did go down to see her, she always seemed pretty well, though increasingly forgetful. She would press him to stay for a meal, for the night – the spare-room bed was always made up for him, just in case. This irritated him too, because it made him feel guilty. He would smilingly refuse to stay for the meal, even if there was a chicken already cooking in the oven. He never, ever, stayed a night. There was something about her yearning eagerness for his company that hardened his heart and made him recoil. If he had had a wife and children, he would be easier with her and less defensive. What he was defending himself against was becoming one half of a little unit, mother and son, all in all to one another, like when he was a young boy. He was ashamed of his lack of generosity but could not help himself. In any case, she never complained. She just let him go.

The white gates stood open. He glanced at the garden,

untidy now with a shapeless, lolling, late-summer luxuriance. If his mother had been well, she would have disciplined the shrubs and herbacious plants, cutting back, shaping, staking, dead-heading. Martagon parked on the drive. He went to the nearest flower-bed and picked an overblown red dahlia. Audrey the cleaning lady, who must have been listening for the sound of his tyres on the gravel, stood at the open front door.

'You didn't need to do that, she's got flowers upstairs already. Your mum's in her bed. Been there ten days now, says her legs won't carry her any further. She's been waiting for you. Father Damian is expected, too.'

Audrey panted upstairs after him. She halted him on the landing outside the bedroom door. 'It can't go on like this, you know. I can't cope. Not the way she is. It's too much, at my age. You're going to have to make arrangements. I'm fond of her all right, but I can't take the responsibility. I'm not family and I've got worries enough of my own.'

'I'll see to everything now, Audrey. I'll come and talk to you in a minute.'

His mother lay in bed, sunken and diminished, her face creased and yellow. Her shoulders were wrapped in the worn old dust-grey pashmina shawl he remembered from childhood. He stuck the red dahlia in a vase of mostly dead Michaelmas daisies on her bedside table, kissed her forehead, and stroked the shawl. 'You're in fashion, Mum. All the girls in London have pashminas now, in all the colours of the rainbow.'

She seemed unaffected by his arrival. He sat down on the chair beside her bed. 'Mum? How are you? The garden's looking pretty good.'

'Paradise is a little disordered right now. All I want is to understand,' she said. 'Men don't want to understand. They want to be understood. No, not quite that, even. They want to be forgiven.'

'Do you really think that?' Martagon, deprived of the expected initial ceremony of exclamations and embraces, struggled to join her in her flight of fancy from a standing start. 'Men do want to understand. They have to. In my job, for instance, I have to understand a whole lot of things, or the buildings and bridges would just fall down.'

'Those are "how" questions, not "why" questions.'

'Mum, how long have you been ill? Why didn't you tell me?'

She said nothing and turned her head aside.

'Look, here I am, asking you a perfectly good "why" question, and you don't answer.'

'Your "why" questions are never the right ones. They never were.'

'Tell me something then, anything.'

She took a deep breath and began to talk fast. 'I was turning out the drawers. Sorting old papers, throwing things away. I came across some letters to your father, dozens of them, from a girl, or a woman, I don't know who she was. Something came apart inside me, like the strands of a string, and I won't ever put it together again. It was – what is the word? Something like "definitive".'

Terminal, thought Martagon, she means terminal. But he did not supply her with the word.

'Oh, Mum, we know what Dad was like, he wasn't that sort of person, it can't have been important, you know he adored you.'

'What shocks me most was that I never guessed, that I couldn't tell. It was probably all my fault.'

'What have you done with the letters?'

'I boiled them.'

'You *what*?'

'I boiled them all up in my preserving pan. With sugar.'

'What did you do that for?'

'To preserve them. I put it all in jars. I've been waiting for you, to give you this,' she said, indicating a plastic Sainsbury's bag lying on the bed beside her hand. 'It's very important.'

What did Martagon expect? More letters, family documents, photographs, perhaps.

He peered into the bag then tipped its contents out on to the patchwork quilt. All there was inside were two chocolate digestive biscuits and dozens of bits of newspaper torn up very small.

'Mum? What's all this?'

He knew her memory had been getting bad. She had always been what people call 'original', which can be a nice way of saying 'eccentric'.

'Can't you see? It's obvious.'

He looked at the scraps of paper and the biscuits.

'You tell me.'

'These are my sins.'

'The biscuits?'

'Don't be silly. All *these* . . .' and she picked up handfuls of the scraps and let them flutter and fall back on to the bed and on to the floor beside the bed. 'My sins.'

Martagon took a deep breath. 'That's an awful lot of sins. I can't really believe you have been so sinful.' He tried a little laugh.

'If you take them away now,' she said, 'I shall be absolved.'

'Easy!' He began to gather up the pieces of paper and to stuff them back into the plastic bag.

'Not in there! Not in there!' She tipped all the bits of paper out again. 'You can't take my soul.' She clasped the plastic bag to her chest.

'I don't want your soul, Mum. I really don't. You hang on to your soul. I can take your sins away in my pocket.' He proceeded to stuff them in handfuls into his jacket pocket, while she watched him carefully. 'They've all gone now, OK?'

'There's some down there – on the floor.'

He picked them up. She lay back, stroking the plastic bag, fatigued.

'What about the biscuits?'

'There was one for your father and one for you.'

'Do you want me to take them away too?'

'You might as well, now. Nothing is for ever.'

He put the two biscuits into his other jacket pocket. She never took her eyes off him. They could hear voices downstairs; Father Damian had arrived. He was parish priest at the nearby church of Our Lady of Dolours, which Martagon's mother pretended was called Our Lady of Dollars, since Father Damian was always collecting for something or other.

'Pass me my brush and comb,' she said.

Martagon sat in the background, on her dressing-table stool, while his mother exercised her remaining powers of enchantment on her old friend the priest.

'What do you think heaven will be like, Father?'

'I fear the worst,' said Father Damian. 'I fear the worst, I really do. Heaven is always described, by those who profess to know, in terms of emotions – peacefulness, happiness, that kind of thing. Not much there to occupy the enquiring mind, I fear.'

'We won't have minds, will we, in heaven?'

Father Damian clicked open his holy box of tricks and extracted a thin white stole of office. He put it round his neck. 'In that case,' he said, 'my requirement will be for a very moderate heaven, since mindless I am nothing, and my emotions tend to be only moderate in their intensity. Are you ready to make your confession, now, Mrs F?'

'I already made a confession of my sins,' she said, 'to my son.'

'Ah,' said Father Damian. 'But I haven't heard them for a month, Mrs F, have I? I've been looking forward to giving you absolution.'

'Oh, all right,' she said, 'I don't mind. You always do hate not to be in on everything.'

'This is not about me,' said Father Damian. 'It's hardly even about you. It is about Him. He absolutely insists.'

As Martagon left the room he heard the two of them wrangling about their respective notions of the God in whom neither of them really believed. Or did they? They are both as mad as hatters, he thought. He sat in the spare bedroom on the bed that was always made up ready for him, and looked out over the neglected garden.

When Father Damian had teetered off down the stairs, Martagon went back into his mother's room. She was looking pleased with herself.

'I really gave him something to think about today,' she said. 'He tries to get his own back because, of course, it used generally to be the other way round. What he really liked was confessing his own sins to me, in the old days. I used to put a tea-cosy on my head and look very severe. We did it in the kitchen.'

'Mother!'

'It was only a game, darling. We were younger then. You mustn't worry.' Suddenly tired, she sank down in her pillows. 'I'll tell you how I knew that I had got old. You must remember it, for when it happens to you. It was when I found myself sitting in a chair in the middle of the morning and doing nothing. Not thinking what I was going to do next, not reading the paper, not mending something, not watching TV or listening to the radio, not thinking even. Just sitting.'

And then, in a frightened whisper: 'Has my life been quite pointless?'

'Of course it hasn't . . .' He catalogued her achievements as well as he could. 'You looked after me, you looked after Dad, you've had lots of friends, you are a lovely person and we all love you, and you made your lovely Paradise garden.'

'I grew a purple foxglove once. Or, rather, it grew itself, among the others at the bottom of the garden. Self-seeded. There it was. Not the ordinary pinky-purple they all are, but a real, dark, velvety, royal blue-purple, with black speckles inside. It was absolutely gorgeous.'

'You never showed me.'

'You were probably away. When the flowers began to go over I tied a ribbon round the stem so I would know which it was. I let the seeds ripen and saved the lot. I thought I would raise lots of purple foxgloves and become famous, they would be called Foley's Foxglove, or *Digitalis purpurea v. Foliensis*. I even wrote to the Royal Horticultural Society about it. But nothing happened. The seeds didn't germinate. Not a single one.'

'Perhaps the colour confused the bees.'

'Perhaps. Or it was just a sterile plant. I was ever so disappointed. There never was another one. So that was that.'

'Perhaps the whole thing was a dream.'

'It's true I've always had a strong visual imagination. I can see people in my head as clearly as if they were really there. Can you do that too?'

'I think so.' He conjured up without difficulty the image of Marina, standing in the farmhouse garden and laughing, her hair blowing, wearing a red and white spotted dress. So far as he knew, Marina didn't have a red and white spotted dress. But the image was very real.

'Mum, did you ever have a red and white spotted dress?'

She started poring over her patchwork quilt as if it were a newspaper, and pointed triumphantly at an octagon of red and white spotted cotton.

'I loved that dress. It was the last year that we were in Dhaka. I had two made from the same paper pattern – wait while I find it – yes, this was the other one.'

A blue and yellow diamond pattern. He didn't remember it.

'And *this* was one of your father's shirts, and *this* was the curtains from your bedroom in the Dhaka house, do you remember?'

He shook his head.

She sighed. 'I'd already passed the civil-service exam when I met your father, you know. But of course he was working abroad so I didn't take it up.'

'I can't quite see you as a civil servant, Mum.'

'Why ever not? I would have been very good. I'd have liked to work in the Ministry for the Environment. I'd have liked to have a proper career, like other people. Other women.'

'One can't do everything, that's the trouble. If you choose A, you have to forgo B. It's the same for everyone.'

'The paths not taken . . . I missed an important turning somewhere, and then it was too late. You can't go back. I have no real friends now either, no one I care about.'

'I'm here, Mum.'

'Jesus Christ was a genius,' she said. 'It's simple. The world works perfectly well so long as people behave honourably towards one another. He understood that.'

'I didn't think that you believed in all that – that you believed in God.'

'I don't. God is the Oba of Benin. God is an alderman.' She sighed.

Martagon thought of Julie talking about the feebleness of the One in Three, but decided not to start in on it.

'The trouble is,' said his mother, 'most people don't.'

'Don't what?'

'Don't behave honourably.'

'You behave honourably. You always have.'

If only that were true, thought Martagon.

His mother took a quick peep into the empty Sainsbury bag and sighed. 'Can you take the pain away with you too?'

'Do you have pain? We can do something about that. What does the doctor say?'

'He says I can go home soon.'

'Where's home? You are at home. This is your home.'

'No.'

'Look at all your things – look, your books, your hairbrush, your jewellery box, your picture of me and Dad, and all your clothes in the wardrobe.'

'No.'

'Where do you want to be?'

'I want to go home.'

As he stood at her bedroom door, saying goodbye, she suddenly asked, in a completely ordinary voice, 'How is your nice friend Giles these days? The one who wears those terrible ties.'

'He's fine. I'm working with him again, you know, but on a freelance basis. Giles is great, but I'm not sure that he is *nice*. Actually, he's a bit of a shit sometimes.'

'Sometimes it's the one you'd least expect who turns out to be the good person, the honourable man. You can't make a morality out of good taste in ties.'

'You may be right.'

'He's got a good wife. I always had a lot of time for Amanda . . . You ought to settle down, have a home of your own. Have you got a nice girlfriend, darling?'

Maybe it was that unaccustomed 'darling' which prompted him to say, simply, 'Yes.'

'That's good. Children.'

'I seem to have left it a bit late, for them.'

'Poor children. Waiting for you at heaven's gate with their little satchels and wellingtons. Waiting and waiting. Like the time I was late picking you up from school at half-term and all the others had already been collected. I never saw such a woeful little face. I still think about that sometimes. Take all that jam I made, as you go. I'll never be able to get through it.'

He was thrown by the way she moved in and out of normality, like a fish flickering between shade and sunlight. He could tell it didn't seem like that to her. She could see equally well in what to him was the murk of dementia. He wanted to please and comfort her, which was maybe why Julie's face swam up into his mind when he answered her question about a girlfriend, not Marina's. It was as if his mother could not only read but direct his thoughts, as she had when he was a small boy.

Downstairs in the kitchen, Martagon listened to Audrey for half an hour. He let her talk herself out.

'You have been very good,' he said. 'Thank you.' Then he spoke on the telephone to his mother's GP, and to Social Services, and to her oncologist at Kingston Hospital. Getting through to speak directly to these people took a very long time and a lot of determination. Audrey made him a pot of tea.

Before he left he went round the kitchen throwing open the doors of all the cupboards. He found what he was looking for. On a top shelf was a row of unlabelled jam-jars filled with some greyish substance, their greaseproof-paper covers secured by elastic bands. He opened one of the jars and inspected briefly the stinking papier-mâché sludge within.

'Marrow jam, is it? That's what she told me,' said Audrey. 'I couldn't say when she made it. I don't fancy it, myself. I'd say it had gone off.'

He took down all the jars and, saying nothing more to Audrey, carried them in his arms outside to the dustbin.

The GP had assured him that his mother had some time left. 'She's a strong woman.' Martagon let himself believe it. It was late afternoon by the time he left. In the car, he thought about what she had said about children. His unengendered children waiting at heaven's gate with their little satchels and wellingtons, not knowing it was too late, trusting him to come for them . . . Is that what she meant? He ate both the chocolate biscuits, a dry communion. They made him cough. He was weighed down with dread and loneliness.

Back in Earl's Court, he circled for a full twenty minutes before finding a free residents'-parking space. Another thing he didn't like about England. Too many people, too many cars, especially in London. He remembered Giles saying, during a gossip about Tom Scree, whom they suspected of calling on married women in their homes for afternoon sex, 'But I could never have affairs! Where would I park my car?'

Martagon's London base has always been this tiny house – an urban cottage – in Child's Place, which is a short, narrow street off the east side of Earl's Court Road, not far from the junction with Cromwell Road. It's the only home of his own he has ever had. He bought it when he first joined Cox & Co., and had never seen any reason to move. He still has the same car from those days too, the second-hand silver-grey Porsche.

His was an easy house to come home to, and an even easier one to leave. By now it looked like the pad of a student who was mysteriously approaching middle age, as was precisely the case. It was not very clean. There were piles of books, plans, printouts and drawings on every surface. Apart from two Piranesi prints in the hall, which had been his father's, there was very little individuality about the furniture or decoration; nothing had been chosen because it was particularly attractive or because it suited the little house. He had furnished it sparsely from second-hand shops and from the cheapest Habitat ranges, out of his first Cox & Co. salary cheques.

He was always travelling for his work, and the house was a perch, a pad, not a real home, though over the years he had made improvements and additions: a microwave in the kitchen, a power-shower in the bathroom, a work-station for his IT equipment, which dominated the minuscule sitting room, and a pair of halogen lamps. Over the fireplace in the sitting room hung a large semi-abstract gouache painting in greens and blues, vaguely reminiscent of a woodland scene. He had bought it out of embarrassment at a friend's show, because he wanted to leave and felt he had been insufficiently appreciative of his friend's work in the few minutes' chat he had with him amid the roar of the party. It had been months before he went back to the gallery to collect his picture. The little red dot indicating 'sold' was still stuck to the bottom of the frame on the left.

Martagon was fond of the painting. It grew on him. He always gave it a friendly glance when he came home. As soon as he got back from France, he had stuck in the right-hand corner of the frame a ten-by-eight colour photograph of Marina, his favourite from a whole reel he had shot in fifteen minutes in the lavender field. In this print she was smiling, protesting, thigh-deep in the lavender in a skimpy white dress, her head turned aside and her hair a halo of disorder. In the left-hand corner he had stuck another, smaller, black-and-white photo of Marina sitting in the grass reading, in the farmhouse garden. Behind her was the terrace and the long, low house. The shutters, which Marina had had painted olive green, came out dark in the picture; and the big fig tree, out of shot, cast its pattern of shadows on the flagstones of the terrace.

The lavender-field picture was too large to stay upright, held in place only by the right-angle of the frame. Martagon found some Blu-Tack in his desk and stuck down the drooping upper left-hand corner of the print. Getting this right seemed absolutely important, much more important than work, or ringing the Harpers, or attending to the tottering pile of mail. When the photo was secured exactly as he wanted it he leaned his elbows on the mantelpiece and studied its every detail. Then he looked at the smaller one, letting what it showed remind him of what it did not: the approach to the house, down a rough track that led through a wood with overhanging branches forming a dark canopy overhead, then out into the sunlight and over a little bridge, with cherry orchards on both sides. From there onwards the house and garden were visible, screened by lines of olive trees on each side of the track, sheltered by steeply sloping vine-fields on three sides.

He ached to be back there. Separating from Marina was like a surgical operation. He felt damaged, in shock, and homesick for a home.

White Gates had never been his home, but he didn't like the idea that it would soon no longer be there in the background of his itinerant life. He had been thinking about the problem of the house all the time as he drove back, so as not to confront too soon the complicated grief about the real issue – his mother – which was waiting to assault him. He would never want to live there. But it was full of stuff – a lifetime's accumulation. What would happen to all that? Perhaps he should buy a bigger place of his own, and furnish it with the family possessions. Leave Child's Place, the child's place, and move along. But by himself? He would not have the heart for it.

Fumbling for his doorkey outside the house in Child's Place, he unloosed from his pocket a flurry of his mother's paper sins, which fluttered away on to the damp pavement, where they stuck. He let them lie. Once in the house, he took off his jacket, upended it over a black rubbish bag, and shook it. The sins fell out of the pockets, some of them into the bag, some on to the kitchen floor. For the rest of the evening, off and on, he retrieved stray sins from where they had drifted – under the sink, out on to the hall carpet, from the soles of his shoes.

He gave himself a large whisky, and another. Then he sat down and e-mailed Marina.

> M: *I love you. Would you ever, could you ever, come and live with me in England?* M.

He sat and waited for an answer. It came, but not until one o'clock in the morning.

> M: *I am just back from having dinner with Lin P. and Nancy M. at La Fontaine in St Martin de la Brasque. I had the courgette flowers and then the lapin, exactly like when I was there with you. I miss you every moment. Lin is very excited about what you are doing with the glass. Nancy says you are her man of mystery because she still*

has not met you. Marteau, I love my country and my life here. I love you too. Would you ever, could you ever, come and live with me in France? M.

Martagon went up to his bed. He curled up, chilled and lonely, under the dank duvet, racked with shuddering dry sobs because his mother was dying.

In the event he had to go abroad again almost at once, to Berlin, where there was a design crisis with one of the subcontracted companies on his theatre project. The Harpers were sympathetic and helpful about his mother. Giles finalized the arrangements that Martagon had set in train, to have Mrs Foley transferred from White Gates to a hospice at Thames Ditton, and Amanda and Julie went with her and saw her settled. Julie told Martagon that she said, on their last visit to her, 'It's such a relief to me. You are his family now.'

'And so we are,' said Julie, without sentiment. 'You know we are.'

Within two weeks at the hospice, Mrs Foley went home. That is, she died.

Martagon heard the news by telephone. Sitting in his overheated hotel room, he became icy cold, and the autumn sunshine outside took on a black glitter. He remained cold until after the funeral.

He was honest with himself. It was not that he was going to miss her unbearably, not that at all. What chilled him, body and soul, was the enormity of death – her death – and the pity of it. Where was she now, the real she? Gone. Gone where? He was appalled when he thought of how he had kept away from her, withholding himself, with a lack of kindness and generosity of which he should have been incapable.

The stock phrase 'the dear departed' did, he discovered, mean something. His mother was dear to him and she had departed. For most of his adult life, she had never gone anywhere at all, and it had been his departures that counted: 'I can't stay, Mum, I have to be at Heathrow in a couple of hours.' Now it was she that had gone, departed, taken her departure. He was the one left behind.

Martagon sold White Gates – it went within a month. He sent most of the contents to auction, and the residue to Oxfam. He gave Audrey five thousand pounds and told her to take any of his mother's clothes and handbags that she wanted, and she sensibly took the lot.

He kept his mother's books. He gave Giles and Amanda six Irish eighteenth-century silver spoons, which had come from his father's family. He gave Julie his mother's tortoise brooch. He took back to Child's Place her wedding ring and her engagement ring, a small sapphire set between two even smaller diamonds, and the family photographs, his mother's old walking-boots, her curved sickle – her 'slasher' as she called it – and the worn old pashmina shawl.

He wished, afterwards, that he had also kept her patchwork quilt, the palimpsest of his childhood. Looking at it might have triggered more memories, of things that he had forgotten about his father and mother. And he began to think about her – about the trajectory of her life, the paths taken and not taken; her longing for Europe and England when she lived in Asia, her pleasure in the long dreamed-of English garden, which she created all on her own. Because his mother had loved England he began, in a spirit of enquiry, to think a bit about England, too.

It occurred to him, when months later he was lying in the

grass in the garden of Marina's farmhouse, on the day of the airport opening: Perhaps, if my mother had not died, I would never have got involved – not *so* involved – with Julie.

FIVE

In London in the late autumn of 1999, following the death of his mother, Martagon was depressed. Ignoring the invitations on his mantelpiece, alone most evenings, he drank to make himself sleep. All he wanted was to be with Marina, in their enclosed and private world. Not as a substitute for his mother – no one could be less like her, or less maternal towards him, than Marina. He had never even seen Marina in the company of children.

He conjured up a picture of her with a baby in her arms and saw her as altogether lovely. But not quite real? Babies and small children cry and make demands. He knew that from Fasil, and had seen Julie's patience, and her tiredness.

But, then, Julie was a single parent. Amanda had let slip that she and Giles were planning to start a family; that was perfectly easy to imagine. Amanda's warm largeness, and her kitchen world, would absorb not one baby but two or three noisy, squabbling, lively, small people quite naturally. Giles might set out to be a disciplinarian, but in practice he'd be indulgent and ineffably proud. Amanda would be a focused mother, her relationship with Giles would change. The children would come first. How would Giles like that?

Martagon's mother always said that having a child transformed a woman's life more utterly than love or marriage. He knew that although his parents loved one another, it was he, Martagon, who had given meaning to her life. He had experienced this knowledge as a burden, when he grew up.

Yet it was knowing he came first with her that gave him his sense of himself and his ability to be alone. Lapped in her approval, he didn't need to prove anything to anyone, or test his attraction or value. That was a weakness, though, in some situations. Not enough drive – the thing Giles was getting at when he complained that Martagon lacked the killer instinct, wasn't firing on all cylinders. Martagon sighed, and dragged his attention back to the plans and calculations on his desk.

He had every reason to go and see Marina often, because of the airport. He and the contractors, Heaney Mahon, were sourcing most of their materials in France, and using French firms both for the manufacture and the installation of his glass. Martagon used an empty bedroom at the farmhouse as his office. Sometimes Billie was there for the day, word-processing Marina's revises and reports on scripts. She was an equable presence. Martagon hardly noticed her. She did not blaze like Marina did.

Now that the weather was growing cooler, they spent more time indoors at the farmhouse, and lit fires in the evenings. They talked and talked. Martagon was curious about other men she had been with. She didn't want to tell him anything, at first.

'*Tous les hommes sont les salauds*.'

'Excuse me – I'm not a *salaud*, a shit if that's what you mean.'

'No, not you, Marteau. But I don't know what to tell you. It always goes wrong . . . It went wrong with Erik.'

'Who's Erik?'

'Erik Smedius. He's Swedish.'

'Film-director? *Blood On the Snow*? I really hated that movie.'

'You are wrong. It's a great movie, Marteau.'

She told him about her affair with Erik. It had started as pure fun. Erik was an idyll-maker, he had taken her on trips to Bali, to St Petersburg, and to his family home in the north of Sweden where they had been quite alone for two weeks, in the spring, with the snow melting and the wild flowers coming out. She had never been so happy. 'I adored him, during those two weeks.'

'So what went wrong?'

Marina shrugged. 'I can't explain. It sounds so stupid. We were on the plane from Stockholm, coming back to Paris, after that heavenly time. He was talking about our future life together. Suddenly I was shaking, in a panic. It was all too much for me. I was terrified. He was so intense, so serious, so happy, he was so much in love, I just could not take it. I began to be horrible to him, on the plane. He didn't understand.'

'I'm not surprised.'

'I had to get away from him, from *it*. I broke it off, just like that. I told him when we got to Paris that I didn't want to see him any more, I wanted to go back to Bonplaisir by myself and he wasn't to ring up or write to me or anything.'

'You ran out. That's what you did.'

'I didn't run.'

'You ran out. My father used to bet on horses, it's a racing term. It means that the racehorse suddenly opts out of the race and veers off-course, towards the rails, and won't be brought back, and there's nothing the jockey can do about it. It sounds to me as if you are – or were – frightened of such extraordinary happiness. Perhaps you are frightened of ordinary happiness too, I mean with a man. Are you?'

'Maybe. I'm not used to it. I couldn't handle it, not with Erik. Perhaps because he was so wonderful. He really was. I'm used to the horribleness of Jean-Louis, and Papa. When he was drunk. I loved Papa very much and he did things to me which were not nice, when I was little.'

'You never told me that before. Poor Marina.'

She shrugged again. 'It's how it was. I am – how shall I say? – comfortable with it.'

'But it sounds to me that you end up punishing men for what you think they are like. Or punishing yourself for – I don't know, I'm getting in a muddle, and it sounds so trite.'

'I know Erik was very sad for a long time. He did not understand. Friends told me. It was after Erik that I started up with Pierre.'

'The wine-maker. You said to me once that he is a brute.'

'He is a brute. But I've known him since I was a child, he is so familiar, he is part of the home world, he didn't make complicated demands, he doesn't love me. He likes sex, and he likes hurting. That's why I say he's a brute.'

'Marina, it's different now. It doesn't have to be like that. You don't have to hurt or be hurt any more. You're safe with me.'

'I think so.'

That night she lay in his arms peacefully. Then turned half away, saying as if to herself, 'Everything is all right now,' and fell deeply asleep. Martagon continued to lie still with his eyes closed, his body touching hers where it chanced to. In the hallucinatory state of half-dream in which reason sleeps and unreason wakes, a vapour-trail wreathed itself loosely round his head and around hers in a figure of eight; and around their bodies, and around their ankles. He breathed with her breathing. Their peace was a lake within which the waters of two rivers cannot be separated.

'We are becoming the same person,' she had said, as they went up to bed. 'Only together are we complete.'

Martagon opened his eyes and saw the full moon shining through the skylight window. He looked at the bright flood of her hair on the pillow. He scrutinized her sleeping face. If her face were made unrecognizable by some terrible accident, would he still know her from her body? He tried to memorize her total appearance, to know her by heart like a poem, from the the pearly skin of her shoulders to her heavy, relaxed legs. She had painted her toenails an underwater shade of blue-green.

'Everything is all right now.' He would make it all right for her, and keep it that way.

Yet the moment was temporary and temporal and something would happen to end it. At the very least, one of them would have to get out of bed. And one of them would have to die before the other. He faced the reality of that. One of us *does* have to die before the other. But if the equilibrium exists at all, it exists, notionally, all the time. It's just that we don't always have access to it. Our separateness in the world, our disagreements and discordances, make reference to it. Disequilibrium can only exist because we know what equilibrium is.

Martagon, back in London, with Marina on his mind all the time that he was not working, found it hard to maintain his equilibrium, and to believe that they were together even when they were apart. There was a signboard he passed just before Dijon whenever he was driving south to Provence. He always looked out for it – *Partage des Eaux*.

He liked knowing he was crossing this line beyond which the rivers and underground streams stop flowing towards the Atlantic and start flowing towards the Mediterranean, towards Marina. Driving north, *Partage des Eaux* spelt separation.

He thought about himself, and her, and the way they were together. He thought about Marina as Marina. What was she doing, at any given moment, away from him?

What kind of person was she really? Surely no one so exquisite could be less than intelligent, honest, kind? Beauty is 'only skin deep' as they say. Beautiful people can be shallow or uninteresting or malevolent. He could not read her mind or her thoughts. She thought and dreamed in French, for a start. They had come together from different places, and he could not retrace the way she had come. The Château de Bonplaisir had formed her, and her world was there, and with the *gratin* of Paris society. If she were not so lovely, would I still love her – for her character, for her mind, which I can never really know?

The questions are meaningless. Marina is a world, and she has a world – several worlds. She is damaged perhaps, but not broken. What is important is that I love her and know I can take care of her. The real beauty is not in the love object but in the loving.

There were so many Marinas. She was a bad long-distance communicator. Martagon would e-mail her, and she would reply within a day or two. He longed always for the sound of her voice. But when they spoke on the telephone it was rarely a success. He only rang when he was missing her badly, and usually put the phone down after the call feeling disappointed, or dissatisfied. Marina had a quick, sharp tongue – he could well imagine her being 'horrible' to Erik. Over the phone, when he could not see her smiling face, she could sound dismissive or impatient just when he needed her to be loving and supportive. Perhaps it was a language difficulty. Her near-perfect English was deceptive, she missed the nuances.

He sent her picture postcards from the different places he went for his work, and the occasional short letter. He was no letter-writer and neither was she. In the days of Jutta, Martagon used to get letters twice a week at least – six or eight pages every time, each covered on both sides with her dense, curly handwriting. Jutta's letters had been about what she was doing, what she was thinking, what she was reading, and how she was feeling. Jutta's letters analysed his infrequent letters to her, and his character and personality, and her own, and their relationship – endlessly, and in depth.

In early days he had been touched and impressed by Jutta's letters. Later, he had come to dread the familiar fat envelopes with German stamps, lurking in wait for him on the doormat in the mornings or when he came home from work. Long before he found the strength to break with her, he was just scanning them, quite unable to plough all the way through. One of the blessings of the end of their relationship had been the cessation of the letters – after, that is, a final spate of accusations, reproaches and pleadings, which had only gradually slackened and stopped.

It's a terrible thing that once you've stopped wanting someone, all you long for is to get out from under and go on with your own life, somewhere else.

For a cool second he saw how it would be if he stopped loving Marina. No more heartache and longing, no more hectic agitation and raw vulnerability, no more inconvenience and endless plans and arrangements, no more anxiety about the future, more time for his work – and his mind emptied of her overwhelming image, set free to meander, like in the past.

The next second, as awareness of the reality of her returned in a hot flood, he knew he did not have that choice. Marina had given him a new self, more alive and vivid. He could never go back to what he had been – temperate, disengaged – even if he tried to. It was about his desire for Marina and sex with Marina but it didn't stop with sex, it started there. The poem Julie had copied out for him was pinned up in his office. He had just been 'a man who looks on glass' before. Now he looked through it and saw, in the brightness beyond, how life should be lived.

His thinking about glass was changing as he changed, and as his knowledge and skill moved forward. He was working on the very edge and looking over it, while remaining just within the constricting terms of the building regulations and EC construction laws. When he first began to specialize, he had made an unquestioning connection between glass and lightness. The ideal he had had of transparency, of glass walls liberating space and removing the barrier between inside and outside, now seemed to him simplistic and even wrong. There had been a hysterical frenzy for transparency, triggered by expanding technologies. But the difference between inside and outside is central to organic life – our bodies, our homes, our perception of safety and danger. That's an anthropological truism. It's basic. Breach the barrier and there is only meaninglessness and disintegration. To appreciate lightness and transparency there must be a countervailing visual weight or darkness. An all-glass structure can be as oppressively opaque as a windowless bunker.

He was moving on in his mind somewhere beyond the mere design of transparent building skins. Or moving back to an old wisdom, perhaps; the traditional techniques to do with the colouring, shading, and decorating of glass had been known to craftsmen four thousand years ago. What interested him most now was an extension of what they knew: high-tech surface technology, coatings, dynamic sun protection, thermotropic layers, air-sealing, shading systems, machine-drawn coloured panels and coloured foils, and the unlimited effects possible by the creative use of lasers and holographic optical elements. What remained a constant was the drama of working with glass – its paradoxical elasticity and brittleness, and the challenge of outwitting gravity and danger. Something possible in theory, and on the drawing-board, must always be tested to destruction. Glass is unpredictable.

Thinking large, and with his mind filled with Marina, Martagon missed something small. Everything had been going very well. Bonplaisir was due to open 'on time and on budget' in February 2000. Running through the specification for the point-fixing systems of the glass curves of the roof one afternoon in early December, he experienced a sharp stab of unease. It didn't look quite right. But it must be right.

He shared his worry with Giles. There were a lot of problems on the airport project. They were all tense. Lin had his anxieties too. Martagon went through this one with Tim Murtagh, the resident engineer at Bonplaisir, and the rest of the team a dozen times. It must be right.

He glanced at his watch. He had a flight to Marseille in a couple of hours. There wasn't time, now, to check his notes and calculations or go through the whole thing again on the computer. Marina was expecting him at the farmhouse. He had to be there, he wanted to be there, he was living only to be back with her. He could always make some local phone calls once he got to the farmhouse. He could run over to Bonplaisir and have a chat with Tim.

I have a right to my personal life, for God's sake. I'm not about to put in peril the only relationship that matters to me. He quashed his unease, packed his bag and left.

Once back with Marina, in paradise, everything dropped away. He stopped worrying about the point-fixing systems. They gave a little dinner party together for the first time.

'It's for Virginie.'

Martagon had never even heard of Virginie.

'She was the housekeeper at Bonplaisir from when I was a child, right up to when we sold it, but she was much more than that. She was a real mother to me, more than my poor mother ever was. It was Virginie who looked after me when I came home after the bad times, whenever I was ill or unhappy, she was always there, she didn't ask questions, she just was there.'

Virginie was ill herself now. She was old. Martagon winkled more out of Marina. She had paid for Virginie to go to a convalescent home after an operation, and she saw her regularly. 'I owe her so much, I can never repay.'

This was yet another Marina, a caring Marina with a sense of obligation and responsibility. Martagon was touched. The dinner was designed as a thank-you to Virginie, and a celebration of her partial recovery.

'She doesn't go out much, and soon she won't be able to. It's like a last treat – well, maybe it won't be her last treat but I'm afraid it may be.'

Billie, her assistant, came too. Yet again, he failed to meet Billie's aunt Nancy Mulhouse; she was in Texas. Marina had also invited Pierre, who was to give Virginie and her ancient husband a lift to the farmhouse in his jeep.

They couldn't find a tablecloth in the farmhouse, so

Marina dragged the linen sheet off the bed – none too clean – and used that instead.

'I'm not sure that it's not a tablecloth really anyway,' she said.

'You are such a slut,' Martagon said to her. 'Such a gorgeous slut.'

He liked the way tall, strong Marina folded the tiny, wizened old woman in her arms and rocked her, when she arrived. He liked Virginie's gaze of uncomplicated love for his Marina. He felt happy and proud at first, sitting at the other end of the flower-decked table as her acknowledged partner, struggling with his French, admiring the old woman's unaffected dignity, joking with Billie, refilling her glass – and, even more often, his own.

It was the presence of swarthy, monosyllabic Pierre that soured the event for him. Pierre did not conceal his intimate familiarity with Marina and with the house. He told her, brusquely, there was too much salt in the *daube*. Late in the evening, when dessert was served and fresh wineglasses were needed, Pierre got up and fetched them from the kitchen without having to ask where they were kept. Holding in his right hand a cluster of glasses by their stems, Pierre leaned over Marina's shoulder to put them on the table. He let his left hand rest heavily on the nape of her neck for a long moment, while looking straight across the table at Martagon with an expression of contempt and defiance. Marina gave no sign of noticing anything at all and went on talking.

Martagon was so enraged that he could hardly breathe.

Pierre didn't return to his place. He lumbered out into the garden, presumably to relieve himself. After a few seconds Martagon followed him, knowing that the others would assume he was doing the same thing.

Outside in the cooler air, his head swam. He had drunk

too much and too quickly. It was dark, but the garden was weakly illuminated by the light from the kitchen windows. Keeping in the shadows, Martagon moved quietly, following Pierre, who took the key from the nail in the massive garden wall and was unlocking the door. Perhaps he was intending to relieve himself in the field outside the garden. Or perhaps he habitually used the cavity in the wall between the two doors as a toilet. That was just the sort of disgusting thing he might do, thought Martagon.

Martagon knew that the second, outer door in the wall was locked, because he had locked it himself and taken the key into the house. As Pierre entered the cavity Martagon dashed forward and slammed the door shut, trapping Pierre in the narrow space. He couldn't lock him in, so he leaned against the door, his feet and legs braced, pitting his whole weight and strength against Pierre's efforts to open the door. He could hear the man swearing. He wasn't going to be able to hold the door closed for long: Pierre was heavier than he was. What the hell was Martagon going to do next? His French wasn't up to expressing his rage against Pierre verbally, and anyway his rage was ebbing. The wine singing in his veins, all he really wanted to do was to slide down with his back against the door and sit on the threshold laughing his head off.

Time to sober up, though. Pierre would start shouting soon, everyone would come running from the house, and then how would Martagon explain himself? The English sense of humour, perhaps: a practical joke. But he'd be a dead man. There were those old spades in the cavity, and Pierre would be murderous when he got out and saw Martagon.

There was a lull in the grunting and shoving from inside the wall. Pierre was thinking, or listening. All of a sudden Martagon moved away from the door and sprinted into the deep shadow under the olive trees. The noise Pierre made tumbling headfirst through the door muffled any other sound. Martagon moved swiftly through the trees away from the wall, so that when he emerged he encountered Pierre at an angle, seemingly coming from somewhere in the vicinity of the drive.

He thought, If Pierre goes for me I'll have to smash his face to smithereens. But Pierre just muttered something incomprehensible and went back into the house. Martagon followed him, laughing inwardly. Nothing had happened. Another path not taken.

It became quite cold after midnight. Marina decided, at that late hour, to light a fire. She threw on to the blaze an armful of lavender from a vase, which made the air fragrant. When the guests had left, Martagon collected up the empties.

'The six of us got through a dozen bottles!'

Marina shrugged. 'It's good wine, my darling,' she said.

'But old Monsieur and Madame hardly took any,' he reminded her.

He started to say something about Pierre, but bit it back. The story of his half-baked exploit would sound foolish, and both he and Marina had drunk enough to say things that shouldn't be said. He must summon the confidence to believe that Pierre was part of the past.

I do have that confidence. But I'm drinking too much these days, Martagon said to himself. I'd better watch it. Marina too. There is altogether too much alcohol in this relationship, even if it is good wine, my darling.

He and Marina remade their bed and slept entwined on the wine-stained tablecloth.

Martagon stayed for five days, and the parting was harder. Marina drove him to Marignane, the airport for Marseille, and for the whole hour they hardly spoke. He sat well away from her, looking out of his window at the landscape of pines, vines and baked earth, which soon for him would be only a memory. Marina generally drove with one hand on the wheel and the other lying between them, on the automatic gear lever. He often touched that hand with his, or twisted his fingers in hers – for a minute, or for five minutes. He often put his hand on her thigh – for a minute, or for five minutes, and her free hand would leap up to cover his.

Today both her hands were on the wheel. He did, without averting his gaze from his window, put his left hand on her thigh. Her bare forearm moved to crush his, but she kept both hands on the wheel. He pulled away his hand.

He glanced at her. Her profile was set, aquiline, the corner of her lovely mouth a little turned down. She passed a bent forefinger under one of her eyes. Were there tears in her eyes? Probably not. Probably just irritation from dust, or the sun.

The grief of leaving her made him angry, ungracious.

Once on the plane back to London, his unease about the fixings flooded back a hundredfold. He suddenly saw exactly what might have happened. His mind had been working on the problem without his knowing it.

He took a taxi to his office, switched on the computer, and concentrated. The bolts were the problem. It was a matter of a nano-measurement, but it mattered. It mattered absolutely. There might still be time. He rang Tim Murtagh at Bonplaisir. No answer. He looked at his watch. It was eight thirty – nine thirty in France. Everyone had gone home.

He passed a sleepless night. First thing in the morning he rang Bonplaisir again, his stomach churning as he waited for Tim to answer.

'We've got it put together – I'm talking about the roof! The big top! – and we've got it up,' said Tim. 'It's taken them four days, working overtime, but it's up. We finished at six thirty last night. Looks great!'

'It'll all have to come down.'

With those few words, all hell broke loose over Martagon's head – from Heaney Mahon, from the lawyers, the client group, Lin's people, Harper Cox's people, Giles himself. It was everyone's worst nightmare come true.

Martagon had to convince them that there was no safe alternative. The great curved panels were compromised not only by having the 'wrong' bolts taken out. Two panels were damaged when Tim's team and the contractors were bringing them down. The whole lot had had to be manufactured all over again, sending the cost of the project spiralling by millions of francs. The 'liquidated damages' – the pre-estimate of likely losses to be suffered in the event of delay – were well overshot. Bending the glass was a major operation, at a temperature of over 600 degrees centigrade. The manufacturers had already moved on to other work, with its own deadlines. Martagon's new panels had to wait their turn.

The opening of Bonplaisir was postponed for five months. There was an ugly symmetry in this. Five months' delay, because of five days Martagon had spent with Marina. If he had given his whole attention to the problem the moment he suspected an error, it could have been corrected before they began to erect the roof. Martagon did not attempt to deny responsibility. The salvaging of honour lay in acknowledging his dishonour.

'How in hell did this happen, Martagon?' said Giles, exhausted by another day of meetings and telephone calls. Giles had the experience to know that in a project of this complexity there were bound to be snarl-ups, and up to now had never implied that he thought Martagon was personally to blame.

'I took my eye off the ball for a moment,' Martagon said curtly. He did not say he had been with Marina. Nor did he tell Marina about the disaster.

Lin Perry did not come down on him like a ton of bricks. When he and Martagon spoke on the telephone, he wanted to talk mostly about George, who had a hernia problem. Lin knew exactly what he was doing. His publicity people got busy with their contacts in the British and French media and sent out press releases. They saw to it that all newspaper reports on the delayed opening made it absolutely clear that it was not due to any architectural design fault, but to engineering problems.

It was Giles who minded most – because of the money, because of Harper Cox's reputation, because he personally had hired Martagon and put his trust in him. He didn't say much more about it, but Martagon felt the disappointment and anger behind his studied normality.

I'll make it up to Giles. I don't know how, but I will. Perhaps in some personal way that would really mean something to him.

There was egotism in this as well as remorse and a proper humility. Martagon didn't like feeling morally inferior to Giles. He stopped going swimming, and put his energies into the work, not wanting to confront his own thoughts. Am I a messer, a wanker?

'What are you doing for the millennium?'

Martagon was sick of the question. If he'd been asked it once in London, he'd been asked a hundred times. Yet here he was asking Marina all the same, over the telephone, 'What are you doing for the millennium? We should be together. But you'd have to come to London, I can't get away again right now, I've got too much to do. We have a bit of a crisis on our hands, I have to see people, do stuff. Will you come?'

She wasn't sure. She thought not. She had a lot of work to get through by the end of the month. And then, Nancy Mulhouse was giving a big party in Provence, and there was another party she had been asked to in Paris. 'You might come to Paris. It would be wonderful if we were in Paris together for the millennium, wouldn't it?'

'It would, my darling, it would be magical, but it's true what I told you. I've got meetings back to back right until the very last moment.'

Marina was stubborn. Martagon was equally stubborn. Why would she never come to London? He could, conceivably, fly out on the evening of 31 December, though he most probably wouldn't get a flight at this late date. Besides which the plane might fall into the sea, he told her, if the electronics went down. He didn't believe that; but it was Marina's turn to fit in with his requirements, just for once. Neither did he fancy sharing her at a party with *le tout Paris*, a horde of society and media types he didn't know. If Marina had a fault, it was that she was wilful. She was also, perhaps, selfish. Her script-editing work was scheduled to suit herself. She could have come over a few days ahead of time, and done her work in his house. She had never even seen where he lived. Didn't that interest her at all?

Amanda rang him at home first thing in the morning: 'Have you seen the papers?'

'No?'

'Tom Scree has got a peerage! Tom is a lord!'

'WHAT?'

'Listen, I've got it here' – there was a rustle of newsprint over the line – 'Thomas Carew Scree, and then it says "For services to development". And there's a picture of him at the top of the page.'

'I don't believe it.'

'Have a word with Giles.'

Giles had had no idea, he said. Tom would have known for some weeks, but certainly he hadn't tipped the wink to anyone at Harper Cox.

'But why Tom?'

'Why not Tom? They have to give these things to someone. Tom gets what he wants. He must have gone all out for it. But he'll be a proper working peer, the government'll get their money's worth.'

'Do you mean he paid for it?'

'Oh no, I don't suppose so. But now I understand why he's been in and out of the DfID office so much. And I saw him having lunch with the minister at the Caprice some time in the autumn. He's been putting himself about, big-time. We saw him on *Newsnight* banging on about this group he heads up . . .'

'The Grid Group. Conflict-resolution stuff. He doesn't head it up, it's some old Texan mogul.'

'Right. Anyway. You'd have thought he did, by the way he was going on. And then do you remember he wrote that arse-licking letter to *The Times* defending some crap planning policy, back in the summer? Very Tom Scree, very New Labour.'

'I never saw that,' said Martagon. 'I was in and out of France all summer.'

'I wouldn't have seen it either,' said Giles, 'you know I never read anything but comics. That's what you think, anyway. But Mirabel Plunket saw it, and she showed me.'

'Well, I'll be buggered.'

'Me too,' said Giles. 'But it's good for the firm, it won't hurt having "Chairman: The Lord Scree" on the Harper Cox letterhead. Or perhaps you don't put "Lord Scree". Perhaps you put "Baron Scree of Leake".'

'Of *where?*'

'Leake. You have to be the lord *of* somewhere, don't you?'

'Is that Leak as in drip, or Leek as in Welsh vegetable?'

'It's where they live in Lincolnshire, in the Fens. Leake with an E. So, yes, drip, basically. We'll have to give a party for him. A small dinner party, Amanda says. We're going up to Amanda's family in Wakefield for the millennium. Julie too. Big get-together. See you after that.'

Martagon knew the decent thing to do would be to ring Tom and congratulate him, but he couldn't bring himself to.

'What are you doing for the millennium?'

Martagon had a last-minute invitation from the wife of an acquaintance in the industry, a property developer for whom he had done some work. Her husband had chartered a launch to go up the Thames from St Katherine's Dock to the Dome, and there were one or two places unfilled. Martagon knew that the woman fancied him. That was the reason he had been asked. He did not find her in the least attractive, but he was glad of the invitation, and accepted.

So there he sat, squashed at a convivial table under cover on the upper deck with a bottle of champagne and a plate of lobster in front of him, and around him pleasant people, many of them professional friends or good acquaintances. His hostess was fully and shriekingly occupied with her husband's guests and clients, so there was no danger from that quarter. He had his mobile phone with him so that he could ring Marina, as they had arranged, at midnight. He didn't have much to say to anyone, but it was better than wandering the streets on his own, or sitting in front of the television in Child's Place. Better to get pissed in company than by yourself. Idly, he watched people excitedly milling about, moving up and down the gangway that led to the lower deck where the bar was.

And then he saw them.

The stairway was momentarily deserted except for this couple slowly coming up. It was like watching a film in slow motion. A very tall, glamorous, eye-catching couple. When they reached the top, they paused. Heads turned.

The man was exotic, with slanting cheekbones and eyes and an impressive physique. He was wearing an extraordinary ankle-length overcoat made of some shaggy, whitish animal-hair. The woman also wore a long coat, of quilted mulberry-dark satin with an edging of glistening black fur down to the ground. One long white hand was on the stair-rail, the other held her coat together at the throat, half hidden by fur. Her flaming hair was piled on top of her head, with curling tendrils escaping to frame a lovely face.

'Heavens!' breathed the plump Irishwoman next to Martagon, with whom he had been chatting amiably about people they both knew in Dublin. The man opposite her, a stranger to Martagon, swivelled round to see what everyone was looking at, and turned back to the table.

'Lin Perry and Marina de Cabrières,' he said, with fat satisfaction. 'Well, well. The A-list. We're obviously at the right party.'

'Wow!' said the plump woman. 'Do you know them?'

'I know that's Perry because I know what he looks like from photographs. And I met *her* once, at a party in the South of France. At Nancy Mulhouse's, do you know her?'

'No, no, I don't . . .' said the woman. 'But isn't *she* just gorgeous?'

'I didn't know she was going out with Lin Perry. There was some talk when I was down there that she was carrying on with a local man who makes wine. A very local man, by which I mean a bit of rough. She's quite a number. Apparently she's come into a lot of money. Sold the family silver or something.'

'They make a lovely couple, though, don't they?'

Martagon, who seemed to himself to have turned to stone, heard his voice say, 'They aren't a couple. She's not going out with Lin Perry.'

They looked at him with interest. Just at that moment the scene changed and there was a general rush towards the open section of the deck. Chairs were pushed back, tables half overturned, voices raised, as everyone scrambled for a good position. It was five to twelve, the boat was approaching the Dome, a magic mushroom throbbing with changing coloured lights; it was nearly time for the fireworks. Lin and Marina were swallowed from sight in the throng. Martagon remained at the table motionless, paralysed. He felt as if he had been hit on the head.

Either he believed in Marina and in her love for him, or he did not. He had moved light years away from his old, rational self. All belief, all trust, is irrational. Martagon made an act of faith.

At two minutes to midnight, alone where he sat, he retrieved his phone from his jacket pocket. He called up Marina's number and pressed the 'Yes' button. She answered at once: 'Where are you?'

'Where are *you*?'

'Darling Marteau, you won't believe this, but I'm in London! On a boat on the river! I was in Paris, and Lin had these two tickets for Eurostar, and we came over this evening.'

'Why didn't you call and tell me?'

'I wanted to give you a surprise, I wanted to make you suddenly happy! I had to come on this boat with Lin as he had been so kind as to bring me over, and when you rang like you said you would I was going to give you this surprise, it was a plan. Are you surprised? Are you pleased? Where are you, where shall I come and find you?'

'Where exactly are you on this boat?'

'Right at the front of it . . .'

And then their phones went down, since absolutely everyone all over the time-zone was ringing up someone else, because it was midnight and cannons were firing and hooters hooting and bells ringing and lasers shooting green arcs and fireworks blossoming in the sky and falling in bright showers over the gleaming dark Thames and on the crowds on the banks and on the small boat where Martagon fought his way through the crowd to Marina's side and they were together for the millennium.

'Hi, Martagon,' said Lin Perry. 'You want to come on into the Dome with us?'

'Hi,' said Martagon. 'No,' he said firmly. 'No. I think Marina and I will take a rain-check on the Dome.'

And, after a second's stand-off, that was that. Marina was smiling at him. She linked her arm in his. Martagon took a deep breath and relaxed. They were together. That was all that mattered.

Martagon could not get used to having Marina staying with him in Child's Place. This house was where he had longed for her, missed her, telephoned her, thought about her so consistently that it seemed impossible she could actually be there. It was defined by her absence.

Being in bed together was different in London. They heard the roar of the traffic on Earl's Court Road, watched the wavering pattern of naked branches against the street-lamp. Marina felt cold all the time, and Martagon had to get out all the blankets and coverings that he possessed.

'I've been suffering from jealousy,' he told her. 'I'm jealous of every boyfriend you ever had. And I'm jealous of the people you see in France when I'm not there. I'm still jealous of Pierre.'

'You're so funny. You don't have to worry about Pierre. He and I understand each other.'

'That's what I'm afraid of. And now I'm jealous of Lin too.'

'You idiot! Lin is gay. Well, a bit gay.'

'I've never heard anyone say that about him.'

'Even when he loves a woman he is perhaps being a bit gay.'

'Does he love you?'

'Of course. He loves the way I look, he loves us both to dress up and go out. Like on the boat.'

'Narcissism *à deux*.'

'Perhaps. And perhaps you could say the same of us, you and me. It's not a crime.'

'Why do you love me, Marina? Why do you want me? You could have anyone.'

'Because I do. Because of the way we are. I want to be with you. The person you love is the person you want to be with. There doesn't have to be a reason.'

'But can I trust you, my darling? Don't laugh any more, it's serious. For me.'

'I am serious now. Are you always faithful to me? The only reason, Marteau, that a woman will be unfaithful to the man she loves is to protect herself, to escape from his spell, his total monopoly of her passion and her thinking, to give herself back to herself. For a short while.'

'And then?'

'And then, having done that deed, she can inhabit her relationship with the one she loves more rationally.'

'Love is not rational. But I don't think it's irrational of me to love you. It is an absolute. The one absolute of my life.'

He did not ask her whether she had in fact 'done that deed'. He did not believe she had. Jealousy is pitiful, ludicrous, unattractive. He would have nothing more to do with it. He had pinned his future on the romantic principle and he would see it through.

The Harpers' little dinner for Lord Scree was not a success. It would have been satisfactory to combine a celebration of his peerage with a public announcement of the imminent opening of the new airport. Now that was off. There was a shadow over the occasion.

'A bit of a cloud . . . A bit of a cloud,' as Arthur Cox used to say.

The big surprise was that Tom's wife Ann came up from Lincolnshire for the dinner. She turned out to be a dark-haired, handsome, bespectacled person of high seriousness, wearing a full floral skirt and a beige jersey strewn with a pattern of pearl beads. Her lack of social grace endeared her to Martagon.

'I never know what to wear in London,' she confided to him. 'It's the skirt problem. A total nightmare. I always wear trousers, you see. I feel like a female impersonator when I get all dressed up, I feel as if I were in drag.'

'You look very nice,' said Martagon, 'though you could have worn trousers if you'd wanted. Look, Marina is, and so is Julie.'

'Tom said he thought a skirt.' Ann Scree was anxious. So was Martagon, anxious the whole time, in case Marina should be bored.

Well, of course she was bored. The only question was, how was she going to handle it? Over drinks before the meal, in the sitting room, she sat talking to Giles. She was in sleek black Armani, and she had had her hair done for the occasion, curled and ringleted into a burning bush that stood out from her head. Whore's hair, thought Martagon, when she came down the stairs at his house, ready to go.

'Marina, what are you *like*!'

'What am I like?'

'Pure heaven,' said Martagon.

In the Harpers' sitting room, she looked confident, exotic and female. Sitting beyond Giles with no one to talk to – Amanda and Scree's wife had gone into the kitchen – Martagon studied Scree with an intensity of dislike that had almost the fervour of love.

He observed, as he bit his nails and nursed his wineglass, Scree's social technique. Scree talked in a low voice, leaning well back in his chair. This compelled the women to whom he was talking – in this case Julie Harper and Mirabel Plunket – to lean sharply forward, their elbows on their knees, simply in order to hear what he was saying, and thereby, involuntarily, giving an impression of extreme and girlish eagerness. Scree was obviously getting off on the combined and exclusive attention of the two women, looking from one face to the other as he explained the full implications of the reform of the House of Lords with special reference to his own role as he saw it.

Mirabel responded by wriggling about on her seat, crossing and uncrossing her legs continuously, and fiddling with the buttons of her cream silk blouse. She kept putting up her hair in a knot then unwinding it again, shaking it loose as she posed some question, then winding it up again.

Julie sat still, as serious as a nun, the wide neck of her black sweater showing her thin throat and part of her shoulders, inviting speculation.

Scree's eyes raked them both, missing nothing – and flickering more and more frequently away and beyond them, to the sofa where Marina sat with Giles.

Amanda had set the table in their ornate but minuscule dining room, with Giles's *épergne* in the middle. Squashed round the table were Giles and Amanda (one at each end), with Tom Scree on Amanda's right and Martagon on her left. Ann Scree – Lady Scree – was on Giles's right. Marina was placed on Giles's left. Mirabel Plunket and Julie made up the party. Tom Scree dominated the conversation, his accent more pukka and public-school than usual – because he'd just been made a lord? Because his wife was there?

He's always been a name-dropper, Martagon was thinking, and the House of Lords is giving him a wonderful new raft of names to drop . . . Scree, sitting opposite him, was telling a long and intrinsically boring anecdote only in order to drop a particularly impressive name at the end of it. Or that's what Martagon presumed, having heard the anecdote before. When Scree got to the punchline, he fumbled it, he could not remember the name. 'Oh, God,' he said, clicking his fingers, rocking in his chair, 'this is terrible, you know exactly who I mean . . .'

Martagon, in contempt and pity, swallowed what was in his mouth, tersely supplied the missing name, and immediately refilled his mouth with steak-and-kidney pie.

'Yes, yes, that's right!' said Scree, managing to make Martagon complicit in the whole dreary business, and Martagon the actual name-dropper.

Amanda floundered somewhat, not contributing much to the flow of talk, darting in and out of the kitchen.

Julie, between Martagon and Lady Scree, seemed paralysed. She never was much of a talker at parties. Martagon noticed that she rarely took her great grave eyes off Scree's face.

Marina was in the middle of telling Giles about a film, now long forgotten, that she had starred in as a child. Martagon hadn't heard about this before and was interested; so was everyone else, so that now Marina held the table. She was being funny and entertaining, repeating her lines and her actions from the film. She made everyone at the table laugh and look at her and admire her. She may well be bored, thought Martagon, but there's absolutely no way that she can be boring.

Whereas Ann Scree . . . but Ann Scree was patently nice, and admired her horrible husband.

Martagon was already drunker than he would have wished to be.

'What kind of therapist are you?' he asked Ann, across the silent Julie. 'Structural? Mechanical? Electrical? Or just Civil?'

'What kind of engineer are you?' she replied. 'Jungian? Freudian? Cognitive? Behaviourist? Or just Alternative?'

Really Ann Scree wasn't too bad at all.

When everyone was leaving, dragging on their coats in the narrow hallway, Martagon had to nudge Marina – who was being over-tenderly embraced by Tom Scree, whom she had met that evening for the first time – towards the kitchen, in order to thank Amanda, who was loading the dishwasher. Marina, too, was a little drunk, and caressed him briefly, shamelessly, in the dark hall.

'Do you think I should also tell our charming hostess,' she said, in her sexy stage-whisper, 'that no one over the age of twenty-two should be *allowed* to wear an Alice band?'

Giles, helping Ann Scree with her coat, was a foot away. Martagon closed his eyes for a second and prayed that he had not overheard.

As he walked through London with Marina at his side, Martagon looked at the men who looked at her. He wanted to see what strangers saw. He observed in action what he knew from his own experience – that a man's reaction to a pretty woman is involuntary and automatic. Some were drawn to her face, the automatic first glance returning again, and again, as if the men's heads were twitched by a wire. Most stared only at her body, at her tits and belly, as if faces were an optional extra. A woman with a good body is desirable even if she has a face like a dog. Some men fixed Marina with a dull, torpid gaze while chewing or scratching themselves, like cattle watching a train go by. Like the street-corner men in Bangladesh who eyed his mother, when he was a child.

Now that nearly everyone in his circle knew, or at least suspected, that he and Marina were together, Martagon wanted to talk about her. After she went back to France, he wanted to say her name out loud, to hear her beauty praised.

He started with Julie, whose uncomplicated manner towards him never changed. She was also the one person he thought had not put two and two together.

'What did you think about Marina? Did you like her?' he asked her casually, on the bus, after a concert he had taken her to at the Barbican. They had heard Mahler's first symphony. Julie had found it uncomfortable. Too wilfully disordered, she said. Almost embarrassing. Whereas for Martagon the music was miraculous, evoking the disturbance and fulfilment of passion better than words ever could. Not that he said that to Julie.

Julie was silent for a moment before she answered his question about Marina.

'She's very – well, *theatrical*, don't you think? But I don't know how nice she is really. You can't tell.'

Julie did not seem to want to say any more, and Martagon didn't press her.

'That was a great evening, thank you very much. What did you make of Marina?' he asked Amanda, in her kitchen, a week after the party.

Amanda, who was topping and tailing beans for supper, gave him a long look. 'Well . . . Of course, she's incredibly glamorous. That amazing hair, and that suit . . . Is she rich? She looks rich.'

'Yes I suppose she is, very rich now, because of selling the land and the château. Not that that's the point one way or another.'

'Well, it must make a difference. It makes her not like other people. Not that she ever could have been, with her looks and that background.'

'No, she's not like other people. You liked her, though?'

'I honestly don't know, I was so busy getting the dinner and everything, I didn't talk to her properly, we didn't really connect.'

'We must set up something else so that you can get to know her. She's really wonderful, she's great fun too.'

'You're a dark horse, Martagon. Who would have thought it? Is it the real thing this time?'

'It's the real thing.'

Then Giles came in and they changed the subject. When Martagon left, Amanda gave him a hug, which was unusual for her, and said, 'Just remember, there are no free lunches.'

'Yes, there are, if you are prepared to pay for them.'

'Oh, Martagon. Take care of yourself, though.'

To Giles, in the pub, Martagon said: 'Marina really enjoyed that evening. She asked me to say thank you. She really liked you and Amanda, and she loved what you've done with the house.'

Why on earth did he say that? Just in case Giles suspected she hadn't liked the house, and just in case he had overheard what she said in the hallway . . .

Giles raised an eyebrow. 'A bit flamboyant, for my taste.'

That, from Giles of all people!

'She's a lovely woman, though, mate. Classy. Loads of personality. Quite a handful, I should think. I've heard she's pretty unstable, like the brother. You and her aren't really an item, are you?'

'Well . . .'

'You're a lucky man. Make the most of it. That sort doesn't stay around long. But keep your eye on the ball . . .'

'It's all right, Giles, for God's sake, everything's under control now.'

Martagon had no desire at all to talk to Tom Scree – Lord Scree – about Marina. But Scree, meeting him in the reception area at Harper Cox a couple of days later, drew him aside. 'Fine woman, Marina.'

'Yes, she's beautiful, isn't she?'

Scree paused, eyeing Martagon speculatively. Then, 'What I call a phallic woman. Older than she looks, I'd say. Wouldn't mind seeing her with her kit off, though.'

Martagon's first instinct was to thump him. His right fist, clenched, rose up all by itself. Then he pushed past Scree, out through the glass doors and into the street, breathing heavily, his armpits pricking with sweat. Tom

Scree. What a shit. Worse even than I imagined. What a filthy little ferret.

All in all, Martagon rather wished he hadn't indulged himself by talking about Marina to his friends. He went for a swim.

What did Scree mean, a 'phallic woman'? Psychobabble picked up from his wife, probably. Maybe it just means a potent, effective woman. Marina is certainly that. There's a lot of the male in her, even though she's so seductively female. There's a lot of the female in me, for that matter. We balance each other. We reinvent each other. She's not exactly what people mean when they say 'feminine'. Female is what she is. Male is what I am, what she makes me.

Lovers inhabit a citadel of erotic imagination, in which they are brilliant, potent, beautiful – young. It's not quite how they are perceived. As soon as they left the citadel and engaged with the 'real world', Marina became what Julie called theatrical, and he himself flailed about, seeking approval, risking betrayal.

Swimming lengths, Martagon wondered whether their world of love was inauthentic, illusory. Yet surely it was as 'real' as anything else? I used to think that happiness was just a by-product. Now I think it's an attitude, or an orientation. When I feel like a loser, when I suspect the god has left me, I can climb back into the citadel and be safe and whole. There may be inflation, yes, hyperbole, yes. But the passion of love is still authentic. It's the only unarguable authenticity there is.

SIX

Martagon had other European projects to attend to as well as the airport. He couldn't bear to part with Marina even for a day unless he had to, so in March he took her with him on a site visit to the theatre in Berlin, now near completion and solemnly named the Neues Erasmustheater. She seemed excited by the idea: 'I want to see what it is that you do, Marteau.'

They drove across the heart of Euroland from Bonplaisir in her new black Alfa Romeo – Lyon, Strasbourg, Frankfurt, Berlin, 1,500 kilometres. They took three days. It was their first little holiday together. He wanted to give her what her beauty and his love demanded, and booked a suite at the Adlon beside the Brandenburg Gate.

He took her to the office of Lin Perry's people first. Lin himself wasn't there, but Martagon showed her their models and Harper Cox's plans. She was amazed, as outsiders always are, by how small the auditorium was in comparison with the spaces needed for storing sets, for offices, workshops, rehearsal rooms, dressing rooms, staff canteen, public spaces, bars, restaurant, walkways, staircases, lights and flies . . . Martagon felt bound to explain that although Harper Cox were the consulting engineers on the site, he himself was only one of many outside consultants.

'Harper Cox are responsible for the foundations and structure. Then there are acoustics engineers, and the M and E people – that's the mechanical and electrical engineers, for the lifts and stage lights and so on.'

'And you are here for Harper Cox and Lin, because of the glass. You make yourself not important. You are not romantic, Marteau.'

'I'm romantic about you, Marina. If you don't understand that, you don't understand anything.'

'But about your work.'

'About my work, too.'

It always did give Martagon a terrific buzz to see a big building under construction. That's what had kept him in the business, he told her – the continuity of the co-operative thorny process leading from concept to realization, and the creation of a new thing in the world that would last longer than anyone who had worked on it.

'It's just a job and a living, to some people in the industry. You say I'm not romantic about it, but I am. Working on something like this theatre, or the airport, is as near as I can get to what it must have been like working on one of the great medieval cathedrals. I get quite consumed by it, as a test of best practice and honour.'

'It's a bit unfair that Lin gets all the publicity.'

'Top architects like Lin Perry are the stars of the construction industry. They're the only ones with glamour as far as the general public is concerned, you're right. They are artists – Lin calls his Paris office his studio, for God's sake, he talks about "authoring" a building. You have to remember that like all artists they live on the edge, too.'

'He must make lots of money, surely, from something like this.'

'Big projects like this theatre or the airport involve a massive financial turnover – but a turnover is what it is. Lin has to hire more people in his office, and so his profit is not nearly as big as you would imagine. By the time of the opening celebrations, he will already have had in nearly all the money due from the clients, months ago. So unless there's another big project on the table, or unless the office has a steady line of minor bread-and-butter clients, the famous architect Lin Perry may have precisely zilch in the bank at the very moment when he is being most fêted and flattered.'

'And the engineers?'

'We live on the edge in the same way. We co-author, if you like, with the architect. We're essential. We just get on with it, our basic job is to turn the architect's vision into a structure that will stand up. Tomorrow you'll see Lin's design for the airport, just five sheets of paper, which got him through the first phase of the international competition. His drawings are impressionistic beyond belief, even though Harper Cox was already involved at that stage. The detailed working drawings were submitted at a big presentation to the jury in the second phase.'

'So you guys make it stand up. But without Lin's vision there would be nothing to make stand up.'

'Correct. And working with architects on their visions is the fun bit. There's an old joke in the industry, in England, about the difference between horrifying and terrifying: a building put up by an engineer without an architect is horrifying, and a building put up by an architect without an engineer is terrifying. But it's not really like that any more. Particularly with specialities like my structural glass. A few architects' offices actually include engineers nowadays, and vice versa. There shouldn't really be rivalry, though there still sometimes is. It's like in *Oklahoma!*, "The farmer and the cowman should be friends . . ."'

Later they sang all the songs from *Oklahoma!* that they could remember, as they showered together in the hotel.

Lin Perry flew in from Paris that evening and came for a drink with them at the Adlon, striding through the foyer looking like a barbarian chief in the long shaggy white coat he had worn on the millennium night. Behind him came a South East Asian youth holding back a panting George on a lead.

Lin greeted Martagon and Marina fondly – 'My dears' – in his beguiling New York intellectual's accent. He introduced 'Deng, one of my assistants'. He immediately sent Deng off to take George for a walk. George had a microchip in him now, Lin said proudly, a 'pet's passport', so could travel in Europe with him.

Lin then settled down to chat exclusively with Marina, bringing her loving messages from people in Paris whom Martagon had never heard of, and gossip about friends in Provence – Nancy Mulhouse, and French people with names that were the names of places. Martagon could only suppose that was because they were all *vicomtes* and *ducs* of somewhere or other. Every now and then Lin lapsed into rapid French – his French was perfect – then returned to English with an apologetic gesture towards Martagon.

Martagon struggled not to feel redundant. He and Lin had a meeting fixed for the next day, so there was no reason for them to be discussing the theatre's problems there and then. Martagon could see that it would be graceless, and excluding of Marina, if they were to talk shop now. He wished, though, that she did not look so sleekly happy talking to Lin. Being so much alone with her, this was a social Marina he had rarely seen.

The real Marina is mine, he told himself, remembering the night.

The other two had their diaries out now. 'Oh, we can go, can't we, Marteau?' asked Marina, turning to him at last. 'April the third? Nancy's giving a big party for Lin's birthday. It will be wonderful.'

'Yes, you too, Martagon, of course!' said Lin, quickly. All too clearly there had been no 'of course' about it.

In any case Martagon didn't even have to look at his diary. The third and fourth of April had been earmarked for weeks as the dates for a major get-together at Harper Cox in London for everyone working on the airport project. He had already begun to prepare the progress report he would have to present. There was no way that he could be absent.

Marina looked devastated. That cheered him up a bit. She then looked cross, which cast him down again.

'You go, anyway,' he said to her.

'Yes, yes, I'll go.'

Lin, rising to leave, confirmed with him that their meeting in the morning was to be at nine. On hearing that Martagon was going to be taking Marina on to the site after their meeting, he offered to show them round himself. Martagon longed to say, 'Don't bother,' but thanked him effusively instead.

So Martagon was not in a good mood when he and Marina went on out to dinner at a restaurant recommended to them by Lin. Neither was she. She could not accept that his London meetings were so important that he could not be in France for Nancy Mulhouse's party.

'I thought you and I were together. For always. Are you always going to be somewhere else?'

'Of course not.' Obviously he would always rather be with her than not. At the same time he was disappointed and angry that she now seemed to have so little concern or respect for his work, and it showed in his voice. 'I'm not going to Bangkok, for God's sake, only to London, and missing one party isn't a tragedy.'

'Yes, it is, because it is an indication of how it's always going to be.'

'I do far less long-haul travelling now. But you know that's how I've always lived, getting on planes and disembarking in strange new places with a job to do and people to organize and manage, and living in extreme ways – either working in pestilentially primitive conditions, or staying in five-star hotels. And, yes, always looking forward to being somewhere else.'

'And when you get to somewhere else, are you then happy?'

'Not always. Not particularly. I get terrible jet-lag. And I get lonely in the hotels in the evenings sometimes. I think I'm probably happiest of all when I'm on the train to Heathrow, or settling into my window-seat on the plane with the stewardess handing me a drink. Travelling first-class, in every sense.'

'That can't be an end in itself. So what, in every sense, is your destination?'

'There has to be a central task, around which all the excitement and pleasure and power are spun. The central task is the work itself. I think I'm a bit uncomfortable with the idea of a destination.'

'Then surely you are not on a real journey, a real path,' said Marina. 'You are just wandering about. Always wanting to be on the move, restless, planning your next trip. It's a neurosis.'

'I'm happy with the idea of being a wanderer. Or I have been.'

'But it's not good to be merely a tourist in your own life. Always moving along.'

'Marina, I think you're talking about yourself, not me. Take a grip. I have the central task, I told you, the work, it's the steel core.'

'The central task could be different. Work is work. The people who know how to live do as little of it as possible, it seems to me.'

'Then they don't really love their work, they only half love it.'

'Is it only half a love, your great love for me?'

'You are the most important thing that has ever happened to me. You have given me a reason for living, you have made the world beautiful to me. Without you, I would merely exist. I have discovered with you what love is. I have made you the centre and purpose of my life. It is for always. You are my shining light. You know that, Marina.'

Marina smiled, seemingly satisfied. She was looking astonishingly lovely and luminous that evening. He saw how the other diners in the restaurant, both men and women, kept looking at her, as he himself had the first time he saw her in the café in Aix. She put her hand across the table on his, and said what she sometimes said in the private darkness of night, 'We are becoming the same person. Only together are we complete.'

Then she put it to him.

She had a proposition, she said. Why did he not give up his London base and come and live with her, all the time? That was what they wanted, to be together. She was rich now. She had enough money for both of them.

They would let the farmhouse, and buy a pretty old house in a wonderful location, and renovate it and build on. He had all the expertise to direct the operations, to be the *maître d'oeuvres*. They would have everything exactly as they wanted, with a bedroom on the ground floor opening on to a private lawn hedged in with rosemary, like he'd told her he dreamed of. They would have an orchard and an olive grove and lovely gardens. They would create the perfect life. He could go on working on prestigious projects that really interested him. He could design and build his own studio, his own private space.

'It sounds just too good, like a dream come true,' he said, dazzled.

'Why too good? Why should not dreams come true?'

And the central task? Martagon gazed at Marina, thinking about it.

The central task will be to use the freedom and experience that we have, to build our world. Accepting some necessary curtailment of freedom and new experience, in order to preserve what we are creating.

There's so much poetry, he thought, so many novels, so many theories, about the ways that things go wrong between men and women. The lyrics of songs dwell on loss of love, regrets, heartbreak. Gossip is always about infidelities and separations.

The trouble is that grief and longing inspire the best poems, the best novels, the most heart-stopping songs, the most gripping gossip. There's precious little analysis or art or even talk about goodness, happiness and fulfilment, apart from the fairy-story ending: 'They lived happily ever after.' And that should be the beginning of the story, not the end.

He and Marina, two equal adults, can write that unwritten story by living it. By bearing witness. It is a privileged central task worth devoting the rest of life to.

'You're right,' he said. 'Why should not dreams come true? We will be doing something exciting and new. It'll take courage and determination because it won't always be easy, darling.'

'I know horrible things must happen, it's the same for

everyone. But we will be together and that will be – what was it you called it? – the steel core.' Marina stretched her arm across the table and put her hand over his once more. 'Marteau, I should like to have your child. Your children. Our children. And soon. I don't have much time.'

That, from Marina, was a rare kind of admission. She had always refused to tell him how old she was. Martagon took a deep intake of breath. His unengendered children, who wait at heaven's gate . . .

'Is that true, about having children? I can't really believe it. We'll think about it, darling.'

'I think about it already, all the time.'

And so, from then on, did Martagon.

In the morning, Lin and Martagon and Marina put on yellow hard hats, neon jackets and steel-toed boots to go on the site. Marina looked bizarrely elegant, and Martagon laughed at her. He had a whole raft of detail to be checked and inspected, but Marina was seeing the whole. He kept an eye on her. A construction site is noisy and scary if you aren't used to it.

Watching her, he experienced anew through her eyes the astonishing, timeless sight of hundreds of skilled men (and a few women) working intently and fast – riveting, welding, sawing, hammering, measuring, drilling, fitting, consulting with each other, shouting to each other across vertiginous spaces from planks across scaffolding and temporary stairways, moving up and down the structures like busy monkeys. It struck Martagon that Julie Harper, 'not an arboreal animal', would have hated it. Marina was loving it.

Lin left them for a moment while they climbed to the very top and stood on a high platform under Martagon's glass dome, looking down into the well of the auditorium.

Everywhere there were crates, copper piping, joints, ducts, coils of cable, pieces of timber, panels, steel joists, girders, beams, valves, cisterns, dangling ropes, swinging lamps, piles of tools, and everything covered in fine dust. Marina, absorbed in the scene, leaned perilously over a scaffolding bar. Martagon had a nightmare vision of her falling from the great height. He pulled her back roughly.

She was not pleased. 'Don't treat me like a child.'

'Then please, darling, be more careful. There's always the danger of falling, or of having something heavy fall on you, in spite of all the health and safety regulations. In the past, dozens of men would have had fatal accidents on a site like this one.'

Lin reappeared and they clambered down a level, down ramps and round dark corners, emerging into dazzling sunlight on an exterior platform, to see an overwhelming panorama of the new Berlin rising above the old. Construction work everywhere, the skyline broken by towering cranes and gantries and, more or less opposite them, Norman Foster's Reichstag building. Martagon pointed out to Marina the refurbished Stasi buildings and the great arches of fat pink and blue tubes straddling the streets, supplying and extracting water from deep excavations. He turned to Lin for help in identifying a spectacular new building, which had seemingly sprung up since his last visit. Lin was waiting well behind them.

He shook his head, tight-lipped. 'I can't come any closer,' he said. 'I'm phobic about heights.'

This was so surprising that Martagon warmed to him again. But Marina wasn't happy either. She turned away from the panorama that so elated Martagon. 'It spells money. It spells power. It spells Germany. You have to remember where I'm coming from. I am French, I am Greek, my Greek grandfather was killed by the Germans in Crete.'

'Do you think the German people didn't suffer too? Think of the bombing of Dresden. Think of what happened to Berlin itself, for that matter.'

'The Germans brought it upon themselves.'

'There's always been the other Germany, the Germany of music and philosophy and liberal thought. The war and its horrors are all in the past, darling. Germany's done penance. We have to move along.'

'Move along to where? I am thinking, I have sold the house and the land that my ancestors cared for, and which was left in my care, for money, and for other people to make even more money. I shouldn't have done it.'

This was not the happy Marina of their life alone together, nor the socialite Marina of the evening before. This was yet another, self-doubting, insecure Marina.

While they went round the theatre her proposition had always been in his mind. The dream come true. It would have to be his dream just as much as hers. No one can inhabit someone else's dream without resentment. How would he survive as a person, without making his work the central task? He imagined the perfect house that they would make, and then saw it filled with chattering French people who were not his real friends, and international expats including bloody Nancy Mulhouse – who was growing monstrous in his imagination – and himself, drinking too much, and growing fat, and struggling with the language, with depression growing in him daily like a cancer. The seriously rich cut themselves off from the lives of ordinary people, they are made characterless by leisure, they are magnificent lepers, unable to be really at ease except with one another.

But rich people can also do good, and use the wealth to make the world a better place. He knew examples of that too. Surely he could settle, find repose, make a home, have a family, become a good person. Their thoughts of last night had been the right ones.

'My reasons for selling really were unworthy,' she said, when they reached ground level. 'Basically, it was just my desire to spite Jean-Louis and my fear of death.' Two yards away a pneumatic drill was massacring an inoffensive stretch of pavement.

'Fear of *death*? What on earth are you talking about?' he shouted.

'Fear of *debt*!' she yelled back, and they laughed, and the bad moment passed.

She waited while Martagon went into the Harper Cox Portakabin to have a brief discussion about claddings, and to countersign contractors' bills. There was a last-minute problem about the mastic in which an interior glass wall was seated. It wasn't gelling properly. Martagon wrote out a variation order for a new specification, knowing it would add something to the costs. He ran through the schedule again and sorted out the sequence of remaining operations – the critical path – and had a word with the overall site engineer, a calm German. All the time he kept an eye on Marina through the window of the cabin: she was sitting on a bollard, her shoulders hunched. He suspected she was still disturbed. Or perhaps she was just cold. She had the most expressive body. He could read her body as he could not read her mind. Martagon was so attuned to her that he felt her unease as his own.

When he had finished, they walked a while. He showed her the vast curved façade of the Sony building, and the new British Embassy, and the Daimler-Chrysler Building with its glass core shielded by louvred terracotta. She was interested but she was not a walker, and she soon flagged. So then they went and sat together for a long time in the Café Einstein on Unter den Linden and got a bit pissed on champagne, and she was her radiant self again.

She held up a full glass against the light and gazed into it, close up.

'What the hell?' she said. 'Do you like that expression? I learned it from Lin. What the hell? All I know is that here is a whole world of liquid gold with lots of clear little bubbles rising from the bottom to the top, on and on. Where are they all coming from? There's nothing and nowhere for them to *be* coming from. And why do they all fly up, on and on, and not round and round like a snowstorm?'

'For someone from a wine-making family, you are ill-informed.'

'So tell me.'

'You don't really want to know, my love.'

Martagon was expected back in London. He had a dinner invitation from Giles and Amanda, which he had accepted, and an appointment with a bread-and-butter private client in the country, in Dorset, for whom he had designed a glass-covered swimming-pool in co-operation with a local architect who was refurbishing the property.

He was not, however, ready to leave Marina. There was too much unresolved. He e-mailed Giles apologetically, jettisoning the dinner date, and sent another e-mail to the Dorset client saying he had unexpectedly been summoned to a project in Prague and would contact him the moment he was back in England. The Prague story was a complete lie, but by the time he clicked on 'Send' he almost believed it. He said to Marina, 'I have three or four more clear days. Home now? Or shall we go somewhere else?'

'We'll do it your way this time', she said, stroking him. 'We'll go "somewhere else".'

'Without a destination?'

'Yes.' Still stroking.

'Marina, I love you so much.'
'Yes.'

Two days later, on a clear day in the Dolomites, they saw a golden eagle soaring against the dramatic craggy peaks, and stopped the car to wonder at it.

'They can live for a hundred years,' said Martagon,

'I don't think so.'

'That's what my mother told me. She loved these mountains. Maybe she was wrong about the eagle. But looking at that great creature, I could believe anything anyone told me about it.'

And then, after a pause: 'It's exactly six months ago that my mother died.'

He thought, for the eagle the idea of 'six months ago' has no meaning, even if it is hundred years old. Every minute of the hundred years has equal value and actuality. It lives in the eternal moment. It doesn't know past and future. Some people see the past as the only determining reality – the Jews and the Irish because of their history; and psychoanalysts and their clients. The present for them is a shadow of the past.

I bet Giles never thinks about the past. He lives in the present, and projects his plans and dreams into the future. Lin, too. I think Lin's a bit of a fantasist, and his greatest fantasy is himself.

Marina, for me, makes sense of past, present and future all at once. Maybe that's why, when we are closest, we seem to be in the eternal moment. Like the golden eagle.

'You are my golden eagle,' he said to her.

'Your mother,' she said, 'are you missing her?'

'I'm not sure. It's as if I'm only just getting to know her, I think I have only begun to understand her since she died.'

He tried to explain to her how in his mother's lifetime he had never related to her in an adult way. He had remained a resentful boy, withholding himself from her loving clutch, struggling for independence – because, before Marina, he had never had another focus for his emotions. 'So if I appreciate her more now, it's because of you. Everything is because of you.'

The next day the weather changed. They found themselves at midday in low cloud and driving rain, the Alfa sprayed with water and mud from the wheels of juggernaut trucks. Visibility was appalling. Martagon was driving.

'What does *Notweg* mean in German?' asked Marina. 'I keep seeing these turns off to the right every so often saying *Notweg*. Why so many turns to the same place?'

'It's not a place. A *Notweg* is an emergency escape route. If our brakes failed, say, on one of these steep mountain roads, I could veer off into a *Notweg* and avoid disaster. It's a very sensible safety measure. A *Notweg* could save your life, and other people's lives . . . Do you know what we are coming to now?'

'We could be anywhere, in this filthy weather. But we must be going over the Brenner Pass. I saw the signs.'

'Yes. The Brenner Pass. It always seems to me extraordinary. The junction of Europe. Italy and Switzerland behind us now. Austria and Germany ahead, with Austria stretching away into all of Eastern Europe. And to the north and west, France, Belgium and the Netherlands.'

'And Britain?'

'Oh, Britain – Britain is, well, Britain is that disconnected space-station somewhere far away to the north-west.'

As he talked to Marina and the juggernauts thundered past, crisscrossing Europe from corner to corner, Martagon for the first time saw Britain, and especially England, for what he thought it was.

England, so self-important. Yet England has absolutely nothing at all to do with this landmass of interlinked peoples and cultures, with its informal frontiers, its languages smudged and merging along national borders. Why should they bother about England, or even think about England, unless in connection with rock groups, or royal scandals, or Manchester United, or BSE, or – for the very old and those interested in history – the two world wars? The only useful bit of the off-shore space-station is the City of London, into which the world beams its money-shuffling transactions.

'But everyone in Europe has to speak English,' Marina objected. 'English is the language of commerce, science, the Internet.'

'That's because of the US, not because of us. Why should Europe give a toss whether Britain belongs properly to the EU, whether we join the monetary union or not? All our blustering and posturing in Brussels looks just pathetic, from here. The Europeans must witness it with bored amusement. We think we are important, we think we matter to this continent. Well, we don't. If it matters to the Brits to join the euro, if that's the consensus, then fine, but we should be modest and businesslike about it and present ourselves acceptably. We used to be respected for justice and what was called fair play. Morally, now, England just spells football hooligans.'

'It's not pretty to talk about your own country like this. I could never speak about France with so little respect. Though if it means you will live in France, then of course I'm glad you feel this way.'

'Well, what do *you* think? About England, I mean.'

'What I think is that geo-politics is not your field, Marteau. There must be more to it all than what you say. When I go to dinner-parties in Paris and sit next to ministers or people of the *corps diplomatique*, they never talk about England like you do.'

'How do they talk about England?'

'They are interested, intrigued – maybe they think they do not quite understand.'

'And what about you? You still haven't said.'

'The two dearest and most honourable men I have ever known have been Englishmen.'

'Two?'

'One is you, of course, I'll tell you about the other sometime. It was a long time ago, when I was young and living in London. I don't want to live in London, but I like going to London, like that millennium time. All French people love going to London. Everything is there, on what you call your off-shore space-station. And English people are tolerant, much more than French people. Lin told me that if he were a black American, he would much rather live in London than in Paris or anywhere in the US. In London, no one disapproves of you if you are different or deviant. Or if they do, they don't show it.'

Martagon suppressed an impulse to cross-question her about the other Englishman. It was never any good pressing Marina to tell him something when she didn't want to. He'd find out another time. He suppressed, too, his irritation at her constant references to Lin. When did Marina have these conversations with Lin? *Chez* Nancy Mulhouse presumably. Forget it. He thought about English tolerance.

'Tolerance isn't the right word. Tolerance implies that there is something which must be tolerated, and a prejudice which has been consciously overcome. It's not quite that, in England. It's more that nobody really cares what other people are like, or what they do. English people don't give a damn, unless there's some threat. English tolerance is more like indifference.'

'The effect is the same. An acceptance. It's even better, because there are no noble overtones. No self-congratulation. Another thing, Marteau – I think perhaps you really do not know your own country very well.'

'That's true. Perhaps I should do something about it.'

'You were in Asia when you were a little boy, and when you did go to England you were shut up in a boarding-school. Now you are grown-up, you are always somewhere else.'

'Not any more. I am going to be with you.'

'Well, that's somewhere else too. Not England, again. We will have to plan for this, Marteau. You will have to prepare – sell your little house, I don't know what else . . .'

'I can do all that.'

'Are you sure?

'I am sure.'

'Sure like a contract?'

'Sure like a contract. We have a contract between us.'

'No running off into a *Notweg*?'

'I'll take it step by step,' said Martagon, 'and stick to the critical path. I'm not going to screw up my chances of life with you. No, darling, no *Notweg* at all.'

His first day back in London, he checked his messages on his home phone and found one from Lin Perry's office asking him to call.

He was put through to Lin straight away. Lin was not ignoring him now. Lin had an exciting proposition to put to him about Aviaplus.

Aviaplus is a consortium of architects and consulting engineers based in Copenhagen, which specializes in the design and building of airports from inception to completion. They provide a multi-disciplinary package, from design to site-management, including avionics, construction, finishes, landscaping, noise-management, everything.

Lin didn't have to explain much about Aviaplus to Martagon. He had been tracking their success, having noted with professional and personal interest that this idea of multi-disciplinary practices, providing a neat one-stop-shopping solution for clients, was the way the industry seemed to be moving. It suited his own ideas and his own way of working very well.

Aviaplus, Lin said, were expanding, and had approached him – through his friend in the firm, one of the partners – with a view to his joining them for work on special projects. 'It's something that would be right for me, and now I'm coming to the point,' said Lin. 'I think it would be right for you too. Sven says they want me to bring a small team of my own people with me, and I'm hoping you might be interested. I like working with you, we make a good team.'

Martagon's first reaction was one of pleasure, and relief that his dereliction of duty over the Bonplaisir specification had not discredited him with Lin. It struck him that perhaps Lin didn't know all the details. Giles was loyal, a good professional and a good friend, and not a blame-thrower. Thank God for Giles.

'Well, thank you very much for thinking of me. It's certainly an attractive idea.'

'It needn't be full-time if you didn't want, but it would be regular work and a good base-line of regular income. You'd be able to take or leave other projects that come up for you with some sense of security. It would mean basing ourselves in Copenhagen for a while, but that wouldn't hurt. We'd probably open our own studio there.'

'The thing is, Lin, that unfortunately I don't think I can do that.'

'Obviously you can't say yes straight off. You'll want to think about it.'

'I can't even think about it. I have another contract.'

'Oh, yes? May I ask . . . ?'

'It's under wraps at the moment, I'm sorry to be so difficult.'

'Give it some thought anyway, and come back to me. It's so obviously a terrific opportunity, it could be a turning-point for both of us. With the experience I'll get there, I might think of a launching a "package" practice of my own in a few years, and then the sky's the limit. Literally, since we are talking airports. I'm convinced that the multi-hub mega-monsters like Chicago, getting bigger and bigger, will soon be a thing of the past. Dinosaurs . . . Are you listening to me, Martagon?'

'Course I am. I'm thinking. You may be right, but what about these bigger and bigger planes? Like the Airbus triple-decker superjumbo?'

'The Concorde story all over again. It's an eleven-billion-dollar gamble, and it won't even get off the ground if the Pacific Rim goes into recession. They won't get the traffic. Boeing are going the other way, into smaller planes, smaller than the 747. The mega-airports are already becoming unmanageable. Everyone's rebelling against airport hassle. It'll be back to small is beautiful. I just know it.'

'Well, me too,' said Martagon. 'For a start, the security is rubbish at the moment. The hassle can only get worse. Or something really bad will happen, sooner or later.'

'What do you mean exactly?'

'How would I know? It's just a feeling I have.'

'All the more reason for you coming on board. We'll be security mavens, if that's what turns you on. Look, Bonplaisir's been a good experience. We could be on the cutting edge of the new concept, the new twenty-first-century generation of airports.'

'Lin, I can't come in with you on this. I'd like nothing

better than to work with you again. I've really got a lot out of it. But I'm . . . I'm committed elsewhere. Long-term.'

'Nothing's all that long-term, Martagon. Can't be. Not in our business. But if you aren't convinced, we can hedge our bets. We do Aviaplus-plus. We get involved with the mega-stuff as well, while it lasts. There's a big development study coming up on Hong Kong International, they'll be inviting consultants to tender later in the summer. Contract to be awarded in the autumn. Might be something for you and me there, working together. And then there's all the new possibilities for off-shore airports. That may be the way to go, for any location that's not landlocked, not only for East Asia.'

'Are you thinking of Kansai International? Renzo Piano and Ove Arup. Stunning. But it's sinking into the sea, apparently, now. BA have pulled out, haven't they?'

'Kansai was too big, too early for the technology, and they went for some cheap solutions. It'll get put right in the end. I was really thinking about Yokosuka, south of Tokyo. A new floating airport built on massive steel platforms, they're testing them now.'

Martagon was engaging with Lin against his will. He could not help being interested. He would love spending time in the Far East again. He would love the challenge of creating floating glass palaces, heavy as hell but apparently weightless, poised between air and water. He could see his dream of a glass bridge becoming a reality. The problems and the solutions. His mind raced.

He took a grip.

'I'll have to take a rain-check, Lin. Count me in for small projects, Europe-based. But I'm not in the market for the long haul.'

'You undersell yourself. Chances like Aviaplus don't come along often, not yet. It may be a once-in-a-lifetime opportunity, for us. Everything's in flux in the profession right now, it's a marvellous time to be working. We're at our peak, you and me, you're the leader in your field now, Martagon. The good time doesn't last. There's new people coming up all the time. You have to catch the tide. But I guess you must know what you are doing, my dear.'

'Thank you again, Lin. I shan't forget it.'

'There is a tide in the affairs of men . . .'

How does that go on? Martagon, in his house, turned to his bookshelves and looked it up in the dictionary of quotations.

> *There is a tide in the affairs of men,*
> *Which, taken at the flood, leads on to fortune;*
> *Omitted, all the voyage of their life*
> *Is bound in shallows and in miseries.*

Shallows and miseries. Bloody Shakespeare. Martagon shivered.

He had committed himself to catching a different tide, towards a different shore. The primacy of private life. He had passed the first test. He had kept faith with the transforming love on which he was staking everything. He had kept faith with Marina.

SEVEN

If England, seen from the Brenner Pass, was not Europe, then what was it? One sunny Saturday in early May, Martagon drove down to Dorset for a last site visit at the house where he was doing the covered swimming-pool. His clients were successful, sociable types with a clutch of student-aged children. Gregory worked in advertising, Jane was a partner in a TV production company. Clump House, on the seaward side of Beaminster in Dorset, was for their holidays and weekends. The rest of the time they lived in London. Martagon got on well with them; they had been ideal clients, receptive to his design ideas and willing to afford the best materials and finishes. He felt they were probably decent, worthwhile people, making the best of their lives.

Driving west through Wiltshire and into the relaxing emptiness of Dorset, he felt an unfamiliar relief at being out of London.

I am in England now. London is not England. London is an international trading-post. The romance of commerce. There is everything and everyone from everywhere in congested London, and at the same time there is nothing and no one. Or not for me.

Off the A303 now, winding down lanes into stone-built villages intersected by streams, and up again on to ridges, framed by the arcs of the downs. Martagon responded to the architectural minimalism of the landscape and its three clean colours – the pale green of the bare hills, the light blue of the intermittently glimpsed ocean, and the creamy stone of the farms and cottages.

If England has a native architectural genius it is – or was – for small-scale domestic building. And for gardens.

There wasn't much for Martagon to do in his professional capacity at Clump House – just signing-off the contractor's work, checking the settings of the pump, and the air-seals and fixings of the glass, and general 'snagging'. Jane did not much like the pool's door furniture, Gregory was not absolutely happy with the blue-green of the exterior woodwork. Neither problem was really his responsibility, but he discussed alternatives at length and proposed suppliers with better ranges.

Afterwards they sat in the garden with drinks. He had been asked to stay to lunch. It was a good garden, with white tulips in tubs where they sat, primroses clotted under the boundary hedges, and bluebells in the shade of chestnut trees at the far end of the lawn. The planting around the house was relaxed and opulent, the colours delicate. There was a pond, with flag-irises and lily-pads. The spring-flowering shrubs were not showy, but they bore comparison for beauty with the lotus and orchids he knew from the Far East, the jacarandas of Africa, even the lavender of Provence.

My mother would have loved this garden. What would Marina make of it all? If everything goes according to plan, she will probably never even see it.

Martagon felt a pang. Now that the job was over, he himself might not see these people or this place any more, either.

Solitary himself, he had a weakness for happy families. He sometimes met couples in England whom he would like to have as friends. And, quite often, he never saw them again. It was as if every couple already had their long-established, close, familiar circle, and although they were interested in meeting strangers, there was really no need, or no room, in their lives for extra people. It was not an active or a hostile exclusion; it was as if it just did not enter their heads to enlarge the group.

Because of the circumstances of his life, Martagon had no close group of his own apart from the Harpers and the people he worked with. He had friends, but he still had no tribe of his own. When on occasion he followed up a new acquaintanceship with a telephone call and the suggestion of another meeting, he never felt rebuffed. But he had sometimes sensed not only pleasure but surprise, and an anxiety, in the voice on the line. There were plenty of exceptions, of course, especially in London. Women on their own were generally all too pleased to hear from him.

They had lunch outside – the first time this year that it had been warm enough, said Jane. Feeling contented and expansive, Martagon surprised himself by saying into a moment of quiet, 'I love England.'

He didn't know what response he expected. Pleased smiles perhaps, placid agreement. Instead there was a silence, as if he had said something a bit shocking. Then Gregory spoke. 'Well, one doesn't often hear *that* said.'

'Why not? The Scots love Scotland, the Welsh love Wales, the Irish love Ireland, and have no trouble saying so.' He remembered his conversations with Marina: 'The French certainly love France, and say so. Likewise Americans, Italians, everyone. It's natural to love your country, isn't it? You love this place, that's quite obvious.'

'This place, yes,' said Gregory. 'We do. There is not

much beauty around in this country. Not in the towns, not in the daily behaviour, not in the laddish beeriness. There's no beauty now even in English football. This is our safe haven, our world which we have made. Do you have somewhere special like that?'

'I suppose I do . . . An old farmhouse among lavender fields and vineyards in France, in Provence.'

'There you are! *Not* England.'

They began to talk at him rather than to him, in fluent marital counterpoint. They knew he had been born abroad, had worked abroad, was always on the move. He was like all expats, with a sentimental dream of an England that had long gone even if it ever existed. Patriotism and nationalism were in any case petty and dangerous. They led to the social exclusion of minorities. They led to fascism. They led to war. So much was wrong in this country – the class system, the gulf between rich and poor, corruption in the police, racism, homelessness, greed, materialism, underfunded schools and universities, failing health service, disastrous public transport, congested roads, hopeless rail system, insensitive planning, agribusiness, the arms trade, the tabloid press, political spin, the drug culture, teenage pregnancies, family breakdown, dumbing-down of the BBC, craven sycophancy towards Europe – or else towards the US (they argued between themselves over that one).

Martagon was not altogether surprised. He had heard most of this before, with different emphases depending on whether the speakers leaned to the left or to the right. He couldn't guess which way Gregory and Jane voted, since their dissatisfactions seemed to cover the whole political waterfront. He thought they probably belonged to what Marina called *la gauche caviar* – they were 'champagne socialists'. The difference this time was that he had never said, 'I love England,' before, because he had never before felt that he did.

And why did he now? Because he was planning to make his permanent home elsewhere, and knew he was burning his boats, and needed to honour the country he was abandoning? Because his mother had loved England, and since her death he was seeing with her eyes as well as his own?

He let them have their say. The parting shots were the same as the first: as a habitual expat, he had no right to make judgements about England. To hear him say, 'I love England,' was – well, it was just a bit embarrassing, Jane said.

Her condescension nettled Martagon.

'Embarrassing! Embarrassment is a third-class emotion. It's so *English*, for God's sake.'

'There you are. We *are* English.'

'If I had been a real foreigner, would you have been saying all these things to me?'

They smiled and shrugged.

'Nearly every point you made would be valid for any country in the developed world. Not all of them for all countries, but many of them. In lots of countries the gaps between rich and poor, and institutional corruption, are far worse than here.'

They shrugged this off too. 'That's their business.'

'Maybe this is what's wrong with England,' said Martagon. 'The begrudging English can't love their own country. Yet you love each other, and your children, and your friends, knowing that no one is perfect. A believer doesn't stop loving God because of a few bad priests. And what if I had slagged England off for all the reasons you have just given me, instead of saying, "I love England"? Wouldn't you have leaped to England's defence for the same reason, that I don't live here all the time and so know nothing about it?'

At that they laughed, the subject was changed, another bottle was opened. Martagon was shaken nevertheless. He had not realized the extent to which he could be perceived as an outsider. Nor did he like the idea of the English as an insular people riddled with self-dislike, alienated within their insularity, like rats – no, mice – squabbling in a cage.

Perhaps the trouble is that we English – for I *am* English, he thought – have always found our meaning-structure by administering other nations. The empire has long gone, and the British Isles are separating out.

England has only herself to administer, and looks inward, and doesn't like or even recognize what she sees. Gregory and Jane, and people like them, are part of the problem. They don't involve themselves in practical politics. They are outside the political process unless they are given a place in the House of Lords like Tom Scree; they despise most politicians, and create their 'safe havens', as at Clump House, from where they give tongue about England's inadequacies.

Yet to make a garden grow is a fine thing in itself. It takes work. England needs weeding, fertilizing, pruning, cultivating. England needs to be cared for, and taught to care for herself again. Mother England. The garden of England. If only.

On his way back to London, Martagon stopped at a country pub. He sat at a table by himself. There was a jolly group of people at the bar, among them a prosperous-looking man in late middle age. He raised his glass of beer and said heartily, 'Now that's as good a pint as you'll see in a day's march!'

Back on the road, Martagon could not stop thinking

about that man. He was so stagey, such a stereotype, like an actor playing a retired English military man in a bad movie. 'A day's march', indeed. What crap. Yet the man was not being phoney or false. He was being himself. You couldn't have got a 5p piece between him and the role he was playing. What would have happened if he had asked that man whether he loved England? He would have stared, and perhaps said gruffly, 'What's that meant to mean?' He did love England, but he wouldn't be able to say so simply, he would have had to crack some joke about disastrous cricket scores against the West Indies. He would have been 'embarrassed'.

Martagon wished he had put his theory to the test. He very nearly turned the car round to drive back to the pub. Instead he played the scene over again in his imagination, saying once more to the military-seeming man, 'Do you love England?'

This time the imagined conversation came out differently.

'What's that meant to mean? You collecting for something?'

'No. It's just a question, I want to know whether you love England.'

'Course I do. Goes without saying.'

That's the point about the English. What they really care about goes without saying, so they don't say it.

Martagon was confused by his foray into middle England. It reminded him of a conversation with Giles Harper, long ago, at one of their lunches before the merger when they were first getting to know one another. Giles was describing his sister Julie, whom Martagon hadn't yet met then, as one of the 'frail ones' who occurred in nearly every family nowadays. More than there used to be? Martagon asked. Was not the incidence of frail ones more or less constant, only we all talk about it more freely and are more concerned? Giles was certain that there were more frail ones than in the past.

Martagon didn't know enough about families to make a judgement. But if Giles was right, perhaps it was because there were no more certainties. The social structures are too fragile, the boundaries too translucent for true security. Everyone lives in glass houses. There is too much unsorted information beamed in from outside – information overload. Some people never find a culture they can thrive in, or they latch on to a shallow, temporary one in which they can't put down roots. The strong ones, like Giles, are OK. They graze, they grow fat on the mixed diet. Giles, accounting for the 'frail ones', had said vaguely, 'It's because of the globalization of absolutely everything.'

'But globalization is a relief to displaced persons, to people who don't belong anywhere, like me, perhaps like Julie. We can belong everywhere, instead.'

'Julie does belong somewhere,' said Giles sharply. 'She belongs with her family, she belongs with us.' Goes without saying, he might have added.

Martagon said aloud in the car the verse Julie had given him:

'A man who looks on glass
On it may stay his eye;
Or if he pleases, through it pass
And so the heavens espy.'

Perhaps the view of heaven is inward, not outward. I must ask Julie what she thinks it really means.

I recognize something of myself in Giles's description of the frail ones, even though I am a healthy and successful man. I have no hinterland. I'm a figure in a landscape that stretches as far as the eye can see, with a network of paths taken or not taken, and no signposts. When Arthur Cox used to quote, '*Do you see yonder wicket gate? Do you see yonder shining light?*', he was trying to teach me to take the long view in business at the expense of short-term profit-taking. It means more than that to me, now. Marina is my shining light, my destination. I used to be like the English tennis players, no BMT, no Big Match Temperament. Giles saw that. Perhaps I still am? No, I'm not.

On the car radio he listened to a report about FIFA and the upcoming vote on the venue of World Cup 2006. England seemed to think she had a divine right to host the competition. But England was behaving appallingly – reneging on a gentleman's agreement to support Germany for 2006 in return for Germany supporting England's bid for Euro '96. What's more, the commentator recalled, the FA had reneged a couple of years ago on a signed agreement to support Johansson as FIFA president, because they thought Sepp Blatter would be more favourable towards England. Actually, Blatter was supporting Africa for 2006, so it was all pointless anyway. Beckenbauer, the veteran German player, was going around saying that once he had trusted 'the word of an Englishman'.

Perfidious Albion. Something had gone wrong. Dishonour, arrogance and gracelessness from start to finish. The good people are still there, though, in England. Getting on with it in thankless, badly paid, essential jobs. Looking after their families and communities. Pursuing their private passions. Cultivating their gardens.

Martagon was happy to get back to the cosmopolitanism of central London. He found two messages waiting for him at home. One was from Giles, asking him if he had been in touch with Julie in the last few days. Giles sounded anxious. The other was from Marina, asking him to call her. She sounded anxious too.

Martagon had a busy schedule. When he understood just how distraught Marina was, he flew to Marseille just for the day. Only another month, he thought, with flickers of excitement and anxiety, and I shall be flying into Bonplaisir.

Marina met him with the Alfa Romeo at Marignane, and they drove into the city, to the old port area, and found a place to have lunch. He parked the car some distance away, and they sat together without getting out. He was waiting for her to tell him what the trouble was, but she wouldn't tell him straight away.

'*Tous les hommes sont les salauds*.' That's all she would say.

Martagon hated it when she talked like that. He looked away from her out of the car window. A mechanical excavator was lifting silt from the port in its dinosaur jaw. 'You don't think I'm a shit. You know I am not. And there was the other Englishman. You said he wasn't a shit either. Who was he by the way?'

'Is it the moment to talk about that? I have so much on my mind today.'

'Yes, it is the moment.' Suddenly, he did need to know.

'It was when I was in London, when I ran away from everything at home. We were both so young. Just a girl and a boy, really.'

She told him the story. Her young Englishman was a friend of her brother first, they had met on a skiing holiday. Jean-Louis had given her his London telephone number. His family lived in the country, and he was as lonely in London as she was. He was training to be a vet. 'I liked that about him. I've always loved animals.'

'I didn't know that – which reminds me, I've been meaning to ask you for ages, but I keep forgetting. Why are there dog-bowls on the kitchen floor at the farmhouse? You don't have a dog, unless it's a secret dog.'

'What an odd question. Why should you be interested in that?'

'I'm interested in everything about you.'

'The dog-bowls are for George. Lin leaves him with me sometimes when he has work to do and meetings and so on at the new airport.'

'Horrible dog.'

'No, no, he's a very nice dog . . . Shall I go on telling you?'

'About the vet. So what was he like?'

'He was simple and sweet, not smart, and not experienced, and he wasn't a city person, he liked walking. Neither of us had much money, we would get a train out of London at the weekends and go for walks, and he would tell me the English names for trees and flowers. He thought I was like he was. I mean, he had no idea how complicated life was. My life, anyway. But I did love him because – well, for every reason, and I tried to be what he wanted me to be. He'd never had a real girlfriend before.'

'He must have adored you.'

'Yes. That's why it got so awful, in the end.'

They had slept together, in the flat in South Kensington that Marina shared with another French girl. Then he asked her to marry him. He was that sort of young man – conventional, singleminded, not very imaginative perhaps. He had their life all planned out. They would wait till he qualified, and then he'd get a practice in the country, and they would start a family.

'And I said yes. I was so touched by his wanting it, by him wanting me. No one had ever asked me to marry them before. But inside, I felt sick. I squashed the feeling down.'

'Was it the thing I said to you before, that you perhaps couldn't cope with the idea of being happy, the way ordinary people are happy?'

She didn't know the answer to that.

The crisis came when he arranged for them to go down and visit his family for the weekend. They lived in Shropshire. (Marina found it hard to pronounce 'Shropshire' and had to spell it out before Martagon got it.) They were going to tell his parents they were engaged.

'We were on the train, going away for that weekend. I was wearing a blue dress he specially liked. And after about half an hour I began feel ill. I had to say something or do something. I was desperate. He didn't notice, he was reading the paper. I was in the corner seat, I just sat staring out of the window.'

The train stopped at a station and people got in and got out. Just as the guard was blowing the whistle for the train to start, Marina jumped up, opened the train door and was out on the platform as the train began to move away.

'I didn't decide to do it, in my mind. I hadn't decided anything. I just did it. Like when you suddenly get out of the bath, without having actually decided to, do you know what I mean? Only it wasn't like getting out of the bath. The train was already moving, I fell over and hurt my knees, and my bag spilled open and everything in it rolled all over the platform. By the time I had picked myself up, the train was gone. So I didn't see . . . I didn't see Jonathan's face. That was his name, Jonathan. He was so good.'

'Poor bloke.'

'I never saw him again, ever.'

Martagon's mouth fell open. Outside the car, the excavator halted its grinding movement abruptly, mud and stones spilling from between its teeth. The operator jumped down from the cab of the machine and walked away. Lunchtime.

'But, darling, what you did was cruel and it solved nothing. The way through is the only way out, you have to go into a problem to get out the other side.'

'Don't you be horrible to me too.'

'What do you mean, "too"?'

'I had to be cruel. To make him see. Also I was in such a state, you've no idea. Like I said, I didn't decide anything, it happened.'

'You say you loved him, and you let him love you, but then you hurt him. Like with Erik.'

Marina had gone straight back to France that same day, back to Bonplaisir and the comforting arms of Virginie. She made Jean-Louis call Jonathan to say it was all over. 'Jean-Louis betrayed me, though. He said horrible things about me to Jonathan. He said I had been seeing other men all the time anyway.'

'And had you?'

'Oh, sometimes. I was very young, Marteau, and away on my own for the first time. It was all an awful misunderstanding.'

'I suppose I can see how it happened, just about. When was all this?'

It was in the mid-1980s, when Martagon himself had been working with Arthur Cox. 'I might have met you then in London too.' His heart turned over at the thought that he had missed knowing Marina sooner. 'You must have been all girly and new. Do you know what's become of Jonathan?'

'I expect he's found a nice sensible English girl and settled down.'

'Let's hope so. Three children and a Volvo.'

'And a nice dog!'

Martagon found the story disturbing. Marina didn't seem to see the pattern in her behaviour. She had no insight. In essentials, the story of Erik and the story of Jonathan were one and the same. However, she was older now, and more mature. Patterns can be broken. Forewarned, he would damn well see to it that history did not repeat itself a third time.

The mistral was blowing strongly. In the walk from the car to the restaurant, Marina's hair was whipped into knots and tangles. When she attempted to overcome the disorder her comb broke in two. 'I hate this wind,' she said. 'I hate it, I hate it.'

Her present distress was about her brother Jean-Louis. Over a bouillabaisse, which she hardly touched, she told Martagon that he was now challenging her right to the farmhouse and to the objects she had taken from the château. He was reneging on their previous agreements. In particular, he was asserting his right to the big chair. The Alexandrian chair, the chair she sat in. The chair with the sphinx arms. His long, handwritten letters, with paragraphs crazily highlighted in yellow, cited ancient laws of inheritance, which made no sense to her. He had rung her up, drunk, at two o'clock in the morning, threatening her life. That's why she had told Martagon.

He couldn't bring himself to take it as seriously as she did. She seemed to him more agitated than frightened, and almost as if she was enjoying the drama. He tried to suggest as much, not unkindly.

'No, Marteau, please, it's not a game. It is serious. I am really terrified, I daren't go to sleep, every little noise makes me think it is Jean-Louis coming to do something to me.'

'Then he's crazy,' said Martagon. 'You are crazy too. Have you seen your lawyer? Have you been to the police?'

Marina dismissed the idea with a violent gesture, nearly

knocking over her wineglass. Martagon caught it as it tipped.

'Don't be ridiculous. There are things about France you don't understand. There's absolutely no question of involving the police. It would make a public scandal. This is between Jean-Louis and me. It is a private matter, a family matter. What shall I do?'

'You could let him have the chair, if that would quieten him down. Then we could fight for the farmhouse as a separate issue.'

'He will never have the chair. How can you even think that? I want you to help me think how I can shut Jean-Louis up for ever. How I can hurt him very much. Either he will kill me in the end, or I will kill him. Really.'

Martagon took both her hands in his across the table. 'Look at me, Marina, and listen. If you go on like this, you are the same as him. As bad as him. It is *folie à deux* again. You must not let this idiotic thing with your brother ruin your life. Our life.'

She looked at him from under her lashes, sideways, infinitely seductive.

'Pierre would kill Jean-Louis for me, I know. If I asked him to.'

'Well, I would not. Don't even think about it.'

'You are so English . . .'

Martagon, exasperated, slapped down a 200-franc note on his sideplate, gripped Marina by the wrist, and half dragged her out of the restaurant and into the wind. He walked her along the rue des Catalans, the bay on their left, as briskly as he could get her to go, for twenty minutes, refusing to engage in any more talk about Jean-Louis. Then he turned and walked her all the way back to her car, and they sat inside it, free of the tearing wind, in a capsule.

Martagon put his arms round the beloved woman beside

him. 'Darling love,' he said, 'I'll always look after you. I'll always help you. I'll never abandon you or abuse you. You mustn't be crazy. Or not too crazy. You can be a bit crazy, it's part of what you are. But not so it separates me from you.'

She clung to him, stroking his wrist, pulling at the hairs round his watch. 'I want to be with you all the time. I am always all right when I am with you.'

'You shouldn't be alone in the house right now. Can you go and stay with Nancy or someone? Or have Nancy's niece – what's her name? The nice girl who works for you. Billie. Ask Billie to come and stay with you.'

'I'll do that. It's a good idea. Billie is a sensible girl, I can really talk to Billie. But when will you come?'

He knew what she meant. 'Soon. By the end of this year, when I have tied up my loose ends. We will get married next spring, perhaps, when your cherry-trees are in bloom. Do you think?'

She looked at him, transfigured, unspeakably beautiful. 'Will we really be married?'

On the plane back to London, he wondered why it irritated him so much when Marina said, 'You're so English.' A lot of decent, straightforward people are English. Like Arthur Cox. Like Jonathan.

Martagon thought about Marina's 'pattern', and reminded himself that lots of young people screw up their love-lives in painful and dramatic ways. It had all been too soon for Marina, with Jonathan, she just wasn't ready. As for Erik . . . But who was Martagon to criticize her, anyway? He himself was not always decent and straightforward. He'd let Arthur down, for a start. He banished the memory. That was quite different, of course.

*   *   *

Back home that evening, he found another message from Giles on his answering-machine. Giles was still anxious about Julie. She was still not answering the telephone. Apparently Hailu, Fasil's father, was in London. Something bad might have happened. Did Martagon by any chance have a key to Julie's flat?

No, I don't, thought Martagon. And then – yes, I think I do. There had been that evening after the Mahler concert when he had taken her home, had a coffee with her, and left his briefcase in her flat. He rang her office in the morning to ask if he could go in to pick it up, and she had told him about the neighbour with the spare key . . . But where the hell was it now?

It was in a saucer in the kitchen along with two AA batteries, a radiator key, some German coins, and a red badge saying 'What's Love Got To Do With It?', which had been slipped to him at some party by the developer's wife who had invited him to the millennium bash.

He rang Julie's bell, and waited. No response. He let himself into the flat. No one in the living room. He went through to the bedroom, like a burglar.

Julie was on the bed, curled up, a box of tissues beside her.

'It's only me,' he said, and went to sit on the chair by the bed. Julie had been crying. A lot. Her face was very pale.

'Where's Fasil?'

'With Hailu. With his father.'

'Is that the trouble?'

She shook her head.

Martagon went into the kitchen to make them both some instant coffee. It took a while to get Julie to tell him what was going on. Hailu had appeared from nowhere, that is from Ethiopia, and had been 'really nice'. Hailu was a businessman now, with an import-export business in Addis. He was really lovely with Fasil. Hailu was staying with a cousin who lived off the Harrow Road. He had taken Fasil back there with him for a few days because Julie was upset and in trouble. Fasil was having a great time, Fasil was thrilled to see his daddy.

'Hailu's not trying to take Fasil away from me or anything. He's a really good person.'

'So what's the trouble?'

At this Julie began to cry again. Martagon waited.

'It's Tom . . .'

'Tom Scree?'

In fragments, between sobs and gulps of coffee, the story came out. Julie's story.

Julie had been going out with Tom Scree, that is, sleeping with him, for six months. Tom Scree was a wonderful lover and a wonderful person, she thought. Of course he was very busy, and important, but he came round whenever he could, nearly every day. He told her his marriage was dead, and she shouldn't worry about it. He made her feel special, he told her they would be together for ever. She had been happy for the first time in her life, or at least since she had first been with Hailu in Norwich. There had been no one else in between.

'So what happened?' Anger was rising and spreading in Martagon like a forest fire. Plus a certain satisfaction. He'd been right about Tom Scree all along.

What happened, basically, was that Tom got the peerage. Lord Scree of Leake was now under media scrutiny. There must be no sleaze to uncover.

'You aren't sleaze,' said Martagon.

'Anyway,' said Julie.

Lord Scree was moving on. What's more, his wife Ann had let him know that she was interested in taking her proper place as Lady Scree. If there were going to be parties at 10 Downing Street and tickets for the new Royal Opera House and invitations to the Royal Academy annual dinner, she was going to be there. She was putting Lincolnshire on the back burner and they were looking at houses in Notting Hill.

'But he told you the marriage was dead.'

'He told me lots of things. She is still his wife. He's a bit afraid of her, I think.'

Julie did some more crying. Martagon made some more coffee and elicited the rest of the story.

Lord and Lady Scree were going to be a high-profile couple, in London. There was no way that Tom's life with Julie could continue. He told her that nothing was for ever, that no one could take away what they had had together, but that it was over.

'And there's something else, as well . . .'

The something else took longer to get out of Julie.

'There were other people too. Women, I mean. Girls. Lots of them. Including in the firm.'

Martagon racked his brains.

'Mirabel Plunket?'

Julie shrugged her shoulders. 'He says that was just a one-night stand and that he regretted it. She became fixated – that's what he said – and he just wasn't interested.'

'Poor Mirabel.'

'There's worse. OK, I'll tell you. It's so awful. I think he only told me all this horrible stuff so that I'd know that I had no special claim on him, that I wasn't the only one. It's what hurts more than anything. You know Dawn? The nice black girl?'

'Of course I do. His secretary, who was Arthur Cox's secretary.'

Tom Scree, as he told Julie when he was breaking with

her, had been Dawn's lover too. A long-time lover. He had a child with her, a little girl. All the time he was seeing Julie, he had also been seeing Dawn and the child, whose name was Karen. Dawn had been dumped now, too. But he was going to pay Dawn money for Karen's education.

'And to keep her mouth shut, I wouldn't wonder.'

'No, he said he didn't want to avoid his responsibilities.'

'Well, he would, wouldn't he? He's such a hypocrite. How old is Karen?'

'I don't know. But younger than Fasil.'

Martagon was silent. He was remembering the day of the fateful merger meeting at Cox & Co., when he had opened the door of Arthur's office and found Scree and Dawn together in there, and Dawn obviously distressed – because of Arthur, he had thought then. She must have just discovered she was pregnant. Presumably she had taken maternity leave, later, when Martagon had already parted with Harper Cox.

'What hurts most – what hurts most – is that he was so loving about Fasil, he used to talk about how mixed-race children were not disadvantaged, how the genetic mix gave them greater potential physically and mentally and in every way, how they were the future. And all the time he must have been thinking about Karen, not just Fasil . . . I just don't know what to do. Will you help me? I haven't told anyone about it. I haven't seen anyone.'

'Of course I will help you. If I can.'

'Tom talked about you sometimes. I don't think he likes you very much.'

'That's fine by me. I don't like him very much either.'

'He said you were involved with someone.'

'We won't talk about me now. We've got to think about you, we've got to get you right. And you must ring Giles. He's really worried.'

'I will. In the morning.'

'Promise?'

'Promise.'

'Shall I come round tomorrow evening and see if you are OK?'

'Yes.'

He kissed her on the forehead and left.

It had been an extraordinary day. He thought of the two women, so different from one another, both needing his support. He had always known Julie as a 'frail one', but had he ever seen Marina in such a state before?

Yes, once. Late last summer. The day they went for a picnic in the Luberon hills. It was his idea. She was against it: 'It will be too hot, and there will be insects. Much nicer here on the terrace, in the shade.'

'We can find shade up there. I absolutely love picnics.'

There were two bicycles in the shed, locked in an angular embrace against a wall hung with sporting guns. Marina's father had used the farmhouse as a hunting lodge, in the palmy days. They considered the bicycles, and decided against. They would take her Alfa.

So they collected up bread and pâté and peaches and cherries, and a tomato salad.

Martagon made the tomato salad. He always did, it was his speciality. He took it seriously. Slice ripe tomatoes quite thinly. Arrange them nicely, the slices overlapping. Sprinkle garlic, chopped not crushed, over the tomatoes, also a couple of *ciboules* – spring onions. A sprinkling of chopped parsley doesn't hurt. Make a dressing with olive oil, white wine vinegar (not too much), one twist of salt, several twists of coarse black pepper, and a pinch of sugar. No mustard: it makes the dressing thick and opaque. You want the tomatoes to *glisten*. Spoon the dressing carefully and evenly over the herbs and tomatoes. Tear up a handful of basil leaves and scatter them on top. Do not turn or stir the salad. That not only spoils the neat arrangement, it makes the slices of tomato fall apart.

Martagon laid out his perfect tomato salad on an oval dish. Marina immediately tipped the whole thing into the plastic box, ruining the arrangement. Never mind.

They put the box with the other things into her blue string bag and added some paper napkins. Also knives. Two glasses. A big bottle of Evian and a bottle of rosé wine. Marina swept up a kelim rug from the floor of the room she called the *séjour* – the living room – and stuffed it into the boot of the car for them to sit on. Martagon was childishly happy.

They drove up the winding bumpy track, left the car, and walked. Martagon, behind Marina on a narrow track, looked with loving admiration at her long straight back, her neat waist, her classy butt, her dear chunky legs swinging along, creamy-white and smooth. Marina, because of her colouring, took care never to get sun-tanned, but she looked like a freewheeling fragment of the sun itself. She was wearing red shorts and a shocking-pink tank-top, her flaming hair licking her shoulders. Martagon felt hot just looking at her.

They chose to make their camp in a spot where sheep, looking like boulders, lay motionless under a clump of trees. It was the hottest hour of a hot day. They spread out the rug in the shade and ate their picnic. Marina had been right: there were ants, and flies, and beetles. The peaches were ripe. The juice spilled down their chins. They drank all the wine.

'If I were to make love to you now, do you think the sheep would be scandalized?'

In the event the sheep, as with one mind, steadfastly

looked the other way. Contented and sticky, Marina and Martagon went to sleep, separated because of the heat, at opposite ends of the kelim rug.

Martagon was deeply asleep when he heard the screaming. He surfaced and sat up. Marina was at a distance from him, out in the sun, hopping from one leg to another, twisting and turning, slapping at her face and neck and thighs, screaming and shrieking. She was covered with flies – clots and constellations of flies, piling on top of one another, moving and shifting and rising idly into the black swirling cloud around her and then returning to her bare skin. Seeing Martagon, she stood stock-still for an instant, the flies settling in masses on her exposed parts as on a cow or a corpse.

Martagon grabbed the rug and ran to Marina. He slapped off the flies and wrapped her up from head to foot in the rug. She stood there, shuddering, uttering single shrieks, as if she would never stop. Somehow he got her, and the blue string bag with the remains of the picnic and her red shorts stuffed into it, down the track and back to the car. She sat inert as he drove, still shivering.

'I am so cold,' was all she said.

Back at the farmhouse she still could not get warm. Martagon made her take a hot shower. He set it going and adjusted the water temperature. He found and put into her hand a fresh piece of the lavender soap she particularly liked. She closed the cabinet door. He lay on the bed listening to the sound of the water as ten, fifteen, twenty minutes passed and she was still in the shower. In the end he opened the shower door, turned off the water, wrapped a big towel round her and dried her as if she were a child. For the rest of the day she lay in bed like a zombie, every now and then uttering shrill single shrieks. Martagon was alarmed. He wondered whether he should call a doctor. Marina became so agitated when he suggested it that he gave up the idea.

'I'll be all right tomorrow,' she said. And she was. Martagon, though, sleeping alone in another room, had a horrible night, and dreamed the stumps dream. Thud-thud, thud-thud on the car windows. He awoke sweating, his heart beating fast.

The thing about my maenad Marina, thought Martagon in London, swimming lengths before work the next morning, reliving the horror of that picnic, is that she is easily alarmed, and her alarm is very extreme. It's just the same with this Jean-Louis business. He switched lanes, to get out of the way of a woman in goggles and a rubber cap doing an impressive racing crawl. I'll always be there to look after Marina. Someone in Provence, in the days when he had heard of Marina but not yet met her, had mentioned in a throwaway manner that she was 'difficult'. Well, who wants an 'easy' person? It would not be interesting. Giles had suggested she might be 'unstable'. So what? I love her for her beauty and vividness. Not even that: I love Marina simply because she is Marina. It's like what I worked out before. One does not fall in love with a woman because she is a good person, though I think Marina is good. One does not fall in love with a woman for her common sense, any more than for her saintliness. Love is something that happens to you and then it becomes something you *do*. It's the act and fact of loving which is the point and the saving grace. The 'worthiness' of the beloved is not even an issue. If it were, how could Marina choose me rather than a better person?

It's because I am I, because she is she, and together we are complete.

* * *

During that day Martagon concentrated on checking the specifications for the glass floor of the arrivals hall at Bonplaisir. This was the feature he was most excited about, and one of the hardest to get absolutely right. It had been done before, but not by him, and not in the way he was doing it. The idea had come to him soon after he joined the project, when he was leaning over a bridge in Regent's Park, watching the play of the evening sun on the water. The sun went behind a cloud and took all the silvery glitter with it. Martagon now saw through the surface – he saw darkly waving weeds, and the darting movements of small fish.

He went to the Glasstec Fair in Düsseldorf to look at high-tech production methods for what he wanted to do, and satisfied himself that it was possible. He explained his idea to Lin Perry, and to Giles, and they were all for it. The glass floor must of course be non-slip and opaque, and therefore sand-blasted – or, better, laser-etched. He was using hefty sheets of annealed compound glass with an acoustic layer to absorb sound, all mounted on glass supports calculated to a far higher load than they would ever be required to bear. But he would also – and this was his big idea – have a series of larger and smaller 'pools' of clear, light green glass, beneath which the ducts, pipes and cables of the different services would be visible, painted in coded colours – like a coral reef, like sea-serpents, like the Sargasso Sea, said Martagon, his enthusiasm getting the better of him.

It put an extra burden on the engineers and fitters responsible for the services, since the under-floor area had to be scrupulously cleaned up; plus, work usually well hidden had now a design function, and was subject to aesthetic criteria, which did not always tally with the easiest way of accommodating the material. But they entered into the spirit of the thing and came up with some bright ideas of their own. Artificial fish, perhaps; or artificial sea-weed; or a mermaid? Or scales and fins painted on the pipes and cables?

I don't think so, said Martagon. He wanted a reference to underwater, not a Disneyland imitation of underwater. He did not want the functionalism of what was glimpsed in the 'pools' to be disguised. The final effect was random. A Coke can was left where it fell, likewise an empty pack of Marlboro Lights. Martagon knew that the workmen were secreting small fetish objects of their own among the painted pipes and cables just before the floor was laid, like dogs burying bones. There were rumours of condoms, but Martagon, discreetly checking, hadn't seen any. He himself, surreptitiously, hid a small photograph of Marina between an emerald green pipe and a blue one.

The glass supports of the flooring had been tested to destruction. Martagon boasted that it would bear a convoy of trucks. Nevertheless, he sat at his computer going through the calculations again and again.

In the late evening Martagon went back to Julie's flat, because he had said he would. She was in bed, but not quite so desperately miserable. Fasil was back, and asleep in his room. Julie had had a bath and washed her hair. It fell pale and smooth round her wan face. She tried to smile at him.

He thought of what Marina always said. 'Do you think all men are shits?' he asked Julie.

Julie said:

> 'Believe it, men have ever been the same,
> And all the Golden Age is but a dream.'

'You have a motto for every occasion,' Martagon said. 'You're like a Christmas cracker.'

'It's Congreve,' said Julie. 'His last poem.'

'What's it meant to mean?'

'It means that even if you are a shit, you're not any more of a shit than men always were. But I don't think you are one,' she said.

She was naked under the covers. Who put out a hand first? Their hands were dry and warm, gentle. Their touches were light but they carried the burning weight of knowing what passion was – transferred, transposed to another person. Perhaps it was the ache of that familiarity, and that difference, which made Julie gasp and Martagon suddenly pull back the duvet, and made Julie lock her arms round his neck and put her face up to his. After that, it was too late to remember anything, and there was only Julie and Martagon.

EIGHT

I can stop this whenever I want. It is just for now. Marina is seven hundred miles away.

Excuse me, so what difference does that make? What is the precise distance that makes betrayal OK? Seven hundred miles? Seventy miles? Seven miles?

The point is that this cannot hurt Marina. There is no way that she will ever know. The thing with Julie has absolutely no bearing on Marina and me, or on our future, or on the way we are. I am committed to Marina.

I can stop this whenever I want. It is just for now.

For three weeks, Martagon went to Julie's flat every evening. He discovered, among other things, that she was writing stories in her free time.

'You really have come a long way,' he said, looking at the small pile of typescript on her table.

'What do you mean?'

'I mean you are in the driving seat. It's like you aren't wearing L-plates on yourself any more.'

'I guess I've passed my test,' Julie replied drily.

'What are you writing about?'

'That one there's about a marriage.'

'Can I read it?'

'Certainly not. It's not finished.'

'Tell me about it, then.'

'What do you think about marriage, Martagon?'

'I think a marriage, a good marriage, would be like the sea with the tide always going out or coming in, except when it's on the turn and the waves are still – but only for a moment, because nothing ever stays the same.' He was thinking about himself and Marina, and how it might be, for them. An act of faith at a time of faithlessness.

Julie raised her eyebrows at him, mocking. 'Oh, my, Martagon. But you're dead right that nothing stays the same. My story is going to be called "The Worst Scenario". I don't think I would ever marry someone I loved.'

'You're so cynical.'

'You're so romantic.'

'I didn't used to be. I am now. I must be getting old. So tell me about the worst scenario.'

Julie told Martagon the outline of her story as they lay in her bed, after they had made love. Martagon held a strand of her hair between his fingers and thumb, rubbing it and rubbing it as Fasil did with the old piece of patterned cotton he used as a security blanket.

'This man and this woman got married and were very happy together. Then he took a job that paid a great deal of money and took him away from home for fifty per cent of the time. She thought that was rather a lot. He did too. But he wanted the job, and the money, and he was used to travelling all the time for his work. She didn't want to stop him doing what he wanted, though she didn't care one way or the other about the money.'

'Why didn't she go with him? My father worked abroad, but my parents were never separated.'

'She could have, if he was posted to one country for

six months or a year. But this is more like a long series of different trips, staying in hotels, moving around all the time. She could go and join him for holidays when he was in an interesting place. But to trail round with him all the time would be the life of a dog. Live like an airhead and you become an airhead. Anyway, she's got a career at home she doesn't want to give up. I haven't got all that thought out yet.'

'You're right that it's not in the culture for spouses to go on all the business trips, however devoted the couple.' Martagon was remembering a night in the New Otani in Tokyo, back in the Cox & Co. days, when he had glimpsed from the lobby one of his colleagues disappearing into the lift with a Japanese hooker. He knew the colleague's wife and had visited them at home in Chelmsford. They were patently a contented couple. He had been surprised at the time – still was, when he thought about it.

'Go on,' he said to Julie.

'Well, they started out on the new life with mutual goodwill. They could handle this. And so they did, after a fashion. When he was away she worked, and saw her friends, and went out like a single person. So, when he was away, did he. It was all rather stimulating, really.'

'And they were delighted to see one another when he came home,' said Martagon, wanting it to be true.

'Sure. But he was always tired, and had his mail, and messages, and the office to attend to. Sometimes she had things arranged, which could well have included him, but he had so much to do, and they were her friends rather than his, so perhaps, he said, he'd give it a miss . . . As time passed they hardly communicated during his periods away, except about dates and times of his returns. He didn't really feel the need now for daily calls or e-mails; and she wouldn't have felt good if she'd faced up to how much she missed him. It was more positive to get on with her life. Sometimes, at his suggestion, when he was at home they would give a dinner party, mostly for old mates of his. They were both good people. It's just that what happens, happens.'

'So what did happen?'

'I'll read you this bit. Remember it's only a summary, though, not the real thing yet.' She picked up her typescript and read:

> 'Really nothing happened – except that they never used the word "love" to each other, apart from putting "lots of love" at the end of faxes and e-mails. The way they were together when they were first going out was all in the past – not that either of them thought about it very much, he hardly at all. The house, and his wife, always seemed in good order when he did come home, and his travelling life just seemed normal. "My wife and I are very good friends," he would say to women in bars in the evenings in all the countries he travelled to. At home, she was saying on the phone, "Yes, he's away as usual, I'll come on my own, if that's all right?"
>
> 'Then he had to retire, because of his age, and he was at home all the time. It was a bit awkward to start with. They slept in separate rooms, because their sleeping patterns were so different. It was just for a while, they said. But he never moved back into what was now her bedroom. They were still good friends, and they never had rows. On a good day, he thought, This was really all I wanted, all along, and tried to believe it. On a good day, she thought, There is still time . . . and tried to believe it.'

Julie put down the typescript.

'So what happens next?' asked Martagon.

'Nothing happens,' said Julie. 'Maybe they've had children, maybe they haven't, I haven't decided yet. They grow older. One of them dies, and then later the other one dies. That's it.'

'Is it a tragedy?'

'I don't know. That's what I have to work out. I'm calling it "The Worst Scenario" like I told you, but perhaps it should really be "The Best Scenario", or "An Everyday Story".'

'I bet you were thinking of Tom and his marriage when you started writing it.'

'Kind of. He read my first go at an outline.'

Martagon was stung. 'OK, so what did he say?'

'He laughed. He said I'd missed out one important thing. He wouldn't say what, he said I had to find out for myself. I asked him again what it was, yesterday.'

'Yesterday?'

'Oh, we still talk. He worries about me.'

Martagon, outraged, sat bolt upright in the bed. 'For God's sake, Julie. That man wants to have his cake and eat it. You shouldn't have anything to do with him any more. He's just messing you about. You should tell him to bugger off.'

'He's away anyway now for a bit, for meetings with his Grid Group people. Apparently Orford Mulhouse has taken a huge villa for them all, in Biarritz.'

'Orford Mulhouse?'

'That's the Texan who finances the Grid Group. I met him with Tom, I must say he's extremely nice, for a rich person. Very modest, very quiet. Someone you can really talk to.'

'What did you talk to him about?'

'I told him about what I did, and he said he'd like to have me in the Group, working for them, they were going to be looking for an administrator for the London office. It'd be in Queen Anne's Gate, Martagon, right beside St James's Park – a bit of a change from Hackney! But I don't suppose anything will come of it.'

'Mulhouse. There's a rich American woman called Nancy Mulhouse who lives most of the time in Provence.'

'Yeah, that's his wife. He told me about her and her French house, when I was telling him about my family, about Giles, and about Harper Cox doing the new airport for Provence. She's in Biarritz with them now. Why, do you know her?'

'No, no, I've never met her . . . Small world, though. It would be difficult for you, I'd think, working for the Grid Group, now that it's all over with Tom.'

'I don't think so. I'm perfectly all right talking to him now, it doesn't upset me, not since you . . . not since we . . .'

He looked down at Julie's face on the pillow. She was sweet, not wanting to say the words, not knowing what words to say. Martagon lapsed back into a comfortable position in the bed and took her hand in his. 'And when you spoke to him yesterday, did he say what it was that you had left out of the story?'

'Passion.'

'Passion . . . I suppose he meant, what did they do about sex.'

'He said you can't suppress passion, it always has to spurt out somewhere.'

'He's the expert,' said Martagon.

'He said the husband would have had adventures with Thai bar-girls and affairs with his secretaries.'

'Like *he* has.' Like most men, thought Martagon, remembering the scene at the New Otani.

'I said to Tom, "It never says in the story that he did

not. I just don't choose to spell it out." And I said to him, "Why just the husband anyway? The wife might have have had affairs too." And Tom said, "Opportunity."'

'Opportunity. Your brother's favourite word.'

'Not in that sense.'

'I think you're being defeatist,' said Martagon. 'You're writing that story to prove that there's no point in committing yourself to anyone, let alone marrying.'

'Listen who's talking.'

'I'd get married, now,' said Martagon, 'if I couldn't bear not to, if I was so taken up with someone, if she'd got under my skin so far that life without her wouldn't be worth living and I wanted to be with her all the time.'

It was on the tip of his tongue to tell her something about Marina. Perhaps not everything, but something.

'But she wouldn't be with you all the time, would she? You'd always be rushing off to the airport, like in my story. Giles and Amanda manage, though.'

'Solid as rock. Your sister-in-law isn't perfect—'

'She's a real cow sometimes.'

'Right. But she provides what Giles needs. She knows what's right and what's wrong. He's not always sure, he'd be all over the place without her. Besides, Giles is basically a settler. Home matters to him. Everyone's either a settler or an explorer.'

'I'm a settler and an explorer. I am at home wherever I happen to be with Fasil. At the moment it's this flat, though that could change.'

'You're a nomad, taking your tents around with you,' said Martagon, looking round at the colourful confusion, and the folkweave curtains shutting out the night. 'Sweet!' he added mockingly – though he did find her shoestring home-making sweet.

'And you're an explorer, I suppose.'

'Certainly. Though recently I've diagnosed in myself symptoms of becoming a settler.'

'How very *un*settling for you! By the way, did you know that Amanda's going to have a baby? She's only just found out for sure.'

'No! That's wonderful. I must give them a call.'

'You might see if they'd like us to go round for supper on Sunday, after we've been out with Fasil, like you said we would, if it's a nice day.'

'Good idea,' said Martagon. One of the family.

I can stop this whenever I want. It is just for now.

A person who is trying to do good feels elated when, occasionally, he does something not good. Something secret, something for *me*. It puts things in proportion. Marina had said something to that effect, hadn't she?

In any case my being with Julie is not being bad. It is helping her to get over the débâcle with Tom. She seems happy with me. Good things can be the result of bad things, such as deceit.

He took Julie to see the film *Magnolia*. He told her she looked a bit like Melora Walters.

'Uh-huh,' said Julie. 'She was a loser. And you're the nice cop, right? Wanting to do good?'

What happens, happens. Frogs falling out of the sky, like in *Magnolia*, or whatever. Martagon has put his house in Child's Place on the market. Waiting for the estate agents to come and value it, he stood at his bedroom window looking out into the sunlit street. On the other side, a little way down, there was a yellow crane in the roadway, and a removals van. A grand piano hung from a top-floor window-frame, half in half out, secured by thick yellow strapping. The great hook of the crane, after two failed attempts, latched on to the strapping. As the crane's neck turned, the piano lurched as if it were going to crash down – and then floated lightly free of the window-space, in a wide arc, over the trees, over the parked cars, swinging slowly round and round, down and down, until it landed gently on the sloping backboard of the van. Once unhooked, it reassumed the dead weight proper to a piano, as the removals men struggled to get it up the ramp into the van.

Two young men were walking up the street. They were a pair, with short haircuts, identical dark blue suits, neat white shirts, and ties. They stood out among the T-shirts and baggy khakis of Earl's Court denizens like extra-terrestrial aliens. They could only be estate agents. Or Jehovah's Witnesses. As Martagon opened his front door to them he half expected to be asked if he were saved.

'It's not had anything much done to it in recent years, has it?' asked number-one agent, who was taller and had a louder voice, after Martagon had shown them round. 'When would you say it had last been redecorated?'

'Oh – in the early eighties, I should think. I haven't had time to do much to it. I put in the power-shower.'

'The whole house needs work.' Number one caressed his mobile phone. Stop that wanking, said Martagon. In his head.

'We haven't seen a kitchen like this for a long time, have we?' said agent number two. 'Pure seventies. Amazing.'

Martagon felt like a worm. He looked at his kitchen. It seemed just like any other kitchen to him. He didn't know what they were talking about.

'It's a nice area. There's a lot of demand. But, like I say, the house needs work. I suppose you wouldn't think of decorating throughout and putting in a new kitchen before we market it?'

'No, I don't think so . . . What could you ask for it the way it is?'

The agents looked grave and paced about from the living room back to the kitchen, with number two agent in his superior's wake, imitating his demeanour.

Number-one agent sighed – then named a sum that seemed to Martagon, who had not been following the escalation of the London property market, to be astronomical. 'That's fine by me,' he said.

He had taken a great step towards his new life, and felt nothing at all. Weightless. When they had gone he picked up his sports bag and left the house straight away. He went for a swim.

What was it about Julie? Martagon was hooked by her physical frailty, her youth, her smallness, her unmarked defenceless self. She never asked him anything about his personal life, about other women, other attachments. She made it so easy.

I love Julie. I've known her a long time, and she is lovable. I'm not *in* love with her like I am with Marina. She doesn't inhabit my imagination. I don't have to think about her all the time. She does not dazzle me or make me shake, like Marina does. She is not a beautiful woman like Marina. She is not beautiful at all, but she is – what? She is flawless. She is a mother, for God's sake, but she still seems as new and fresh as Fasil. She smells of biscuits. So does Fasil. They both smell of biscuits. Her silky pale hair when she has washed it, falling like water. I might feel the same tenderness for her if she was a boy, or my sister. But, no, I wouldn't. When I saw her naked I wanted to consume her and be consumed by her and made pure. As if she were some healing drug. It's about her awkward grace, her thin round arms, her little tits standing out from her ribs, the shallow curves of her, and all of a piece, and her not knowing, not understanding, what she is – flawless.

I can stop this whenever I want. It is just for now.

A bad person lets other people behave responsibly, while he exploits their honesty and reaps the benefits. Like Tom Scree. Am I like Tom Scree? I haven't damaged Julie or Marina, because neither will ever, ever know about the other. If I were to 'confess' to both or either, it might make me feel better but would only make them miserable, and screw everything up.

But if actions have consequences so do inactions. There are silent lies. There are sins of omission as well as sins of commission. What are sins? What someone decides they are. A bagful of torn scraps of newspaper. Why did I avoid thinking at all about my father's unfaithfulness? Did I know I was capable of behaving like him? Get real – all men are capable of unfaithfulness. Lots of men don't even think of unfaithfulness *as* unfaithfulness, but as something that just might happen when you are away from your partner. Virtue is its own reward. What is virtue? What is the reward of virtue? You tell *me*. There must be more to being a good person than just being a well-socialized man who keeps the rules. It's not an absolute, anyway. It depends on your particular society's values and attitudes. Any intelligent person must accept some and reject others. I have a perfect right to do what I want to do. It's my life, no one's in danger of being damaged but me, and it's no one's business but my own.

Nevertheless, Martagon knew that he would have to say something about his plans to Julie.

Sunday was a fine day with a high wind. Martagon, in the old Porsche, picked up Julie and Fasil in the morning and they drove out of London. Into England. Julie sat beside him with the map on her knees, and Fasil was in the back. They drove through the Cotswolds as far as Tewkesbury, where they had lunch in the garden of a pub on the river: swans, pleasure boats, great overhanging trees tossed by the wind.

Afterwards they drove off again into the midsummer countryside, looking for somewhere to rest and where Fasil could run around and play. Driving slower now, in the lanes, looking for somewhere to stop. On the outskirts of a village in the lee of Bredon Hill, Julie spotted a 'For Sale' sign at the opening of a track. 'That looks interesting,' she said.

They walked up the track and found a ramshackle cottage. His London estate agents would say it definitely needed work. They peered in at the windows. It was completely empty apart from a teacup upturned on its saucer on the draining-board in the kitchen. They walked round to the back.

The garden was narrow and sloped down steeply to a shallow trickle of a stream. There were no flower-beds. It was all just grass, thick and soft and dark, uncut for a month, half shaded by the trees and shrubs that enclosed it on both sides and sheltered it, today, from the wind. Fasil ran straight to the stream and squatted beside it, picking up small stones and twigs to throw in. Martagon and Julie lay down on the grass, in a sunny patch, Julie using her little backpack as a pillow. All they could hear was the wind in the trees.

It was peaceful.

Fasil ran back up the slope and threw himself down between them. 'I saw a duck,' he said. 'Why can't we live here?'

'It doesn't belong to us,' said Martagon.

'It's for sale. You said. You could buy it.'

'I wish,' said Martagon.

'You could, you *could*,' said Fasil. 'Then we could live here. Mum and me. And you. We *could*.'

He jumped on Martagon, punching him in the chest. Martagon, laughing, sat up and pushed the little boy off. Fasil turned to his mother, and hurled himself face down across her body, kicking her legs. 'Tell him. Tell him we've got to live here.'

Julie put her arms round her son. 'Go and do some more playing,' she said, rocking him. 'We'll have to be going back quite soon.'

It crossed Martagon's mind that the money from the sale of Child's Place would buy this cottage and put it in order and leave some to spare. Not that that was an option.

Fasil was back by the stream.

Julie said, a little awkwardly: 'I've been meaning to tell you something. I've been talking a lot to Hailu. He wants us to get together again. He wants me and Fasil to go back to Addis with him.'

'Is that what you want?'

They were lying back in the grass again, not looking at one another.

'I don't know. Sometimes I think yes. Mostly because he's Fasil's father. A child needs a father. But I don't know if I could hack living in Addis now. I like my work, I might get that better job with the Grid Group, I've got good friends, I like being near Giles and Amanda, and my parents. Fasil's settled in his school. Also, there's you, now.'

'There's something I've been meaning to tell you, too. It might make a difference. I'm probably going to shift my base to France – quite soon.'

'I don't see why that should make a difference. You're always off abroad somewhere already, as it is, and you'd always be in London part of the time, presumably.'

'It sounds a bit like your marriage story.'

'Except we aren't thinking about getting married.'

'No.'

'And that does make all the difference. We'd both have our own separate lives, and then we'd have our times together as well. I'll have to be concentrating on Fasil a lot for the next few years anyway. We'll both do what we have to do, and when we are together it will be holiday. We'll just let things evolve, see what happens. If that's what you want. I'll always be there for you, Martagon.'

He said, 'I'll always be there for you, too.' Because it was true. In one way or another.

'Is that a deal?'

'It's a deal.'

Martagon scratched his nose where a long grass-stem was tickling it. It had not entered his head before that he could have his cake and eat it. The thought was uncomfortably interesting. Long-term, it would not work. The short-term advantages might save everyone a lot of pain. Things would work themselves out. The only thing you can be sure of is that nothing stays the same. Things would evolve, like Julie said.

He decided to say no more, to let it lie. He propped himself up on an elbow, leaned over, and kissed Julie on her forehead.

As they were getting into the car, Fasil announced he had to pee. Get on with it then, they said. Just in time, Martagon seized him by the shoulders and wheeled him round. 'Never piss into the wind,' he said. 'That's a lesson in life. Maybe that's the only useful thing I'll ever teach you, Fasil.'

'I don't think so,' said Julie. 'At least, I hope not.'

Martagon and Julie fetched up outside Giles and Amanda's

door in Fulham at about nine o'clock that evening. Giles, a bottle of champagne in his hand, took one look at their wind-burned, sun-burned, smiling faces, and said, 'Aha! You two . . . Come in. It seems we have a lot to celebrate.'

In the kitchen with Amanda, they drank to the coming baby. They drank to Amanda. They drank to Giles. Giles said, 'Speaking as a paterfamilias and a man of substance, I want to propose a fraternal toast to – Julie and Martagon!'

Julie blushed and giggled. Martagon, red lights flashing in his head, mimed moronic amazement. What was going on round here? He knew exactly. While Amanda and Julie were finishing the preparations for supper and laying the table, Giles refilled his own glass and Martagon's, and drew Martagon out of the french windows into the dusky garden.

The wind had dropped. They talked of this and that, of Chelsea's prospects, and of the schedule for the grand opening of Bonplaisir, which was imminent. Giles was at his most expansive and vital. Martagon felt his seductiveness, as in the early days of their friendship.

Giles is an angel. Giles may be the devil. Or the devil for me. In this mood, Giles can make me do anything. Like over the merger.

'You know something?' said Giles. 'I've never cheated on Amanda. In all this time. Guess that surprises you, doesn't it?'

'Not really,' said Martagon. 'Not that I've ever really thought about it.'

Giles put an arm round Martagon's shoulders. 'Julie hasn't said much, but she's said something. Amanda and me, we don't want her to go back to Ethiopia. Hailu's a really nice guy, but she needs her family . . . I just wanted you to know, my old mate, that if you and she really became an item, it would be good news so far as I am concerned. Very good news indeed. I know it's nothing to do with me.'

Martagon said nothing. He was glad of the darkness.

Giles hadn't finished. 'I've been thinking, too. I know we had our difficulties, but it was early days for us all and you didn't really give it a chance. Why not come back into the firm? We've both come a long way since then.'

'Things have changed, for me,' said Martagon.

'That's the whole point. You've had your adventures – professional and, if you don't mind me saying, personal – and you'd be coming back in a really strong position. A homecoming, back to your family. We've always been like family, you and us, haven't we?'

'We have.' Giles knew how to touch his most tender spot. He was moved, unable to speak.

'And now – well, now even more so. I won't say any more.'

'No, Giles, not now.'

Martagon did not take Julie home. He left before her, saying he had work to do. When he got home to Child's Place he was unnaturally exhausted. The emotional moment had passed with the effects of the champagne. He was coldly clear-eyed.

It all looked rather different to him now. Giles had seen an opportunity. Giles was offering Martagon a package.

Giles cared deeply about his sister and her happiness. If that meant Martagon, then he would help her to secure him. He cared, too, for Martagon, so long as Martagon did not go off at a tangent. He knew Martagon was a class act and top of the range, professionally. He was ambitious for Harper Cox.

Put all this together, conceal the price-tags, gift-wrap the package, and present it. That's what Giles had done.

Forget the romance of commerce. What about the commerce of romance?

The following Tuesday, 12 June, the newly opened Millennium Footbridge over the Thames between St Paul's and Bankside swayed so violently under the weight of sightseeing pedestrians that it had to be closed. Martagon, fascinated, rang a friend at Ove Arup, the engineers of the bridge, to get the inside story. He didn't get much: ranks were closing. Nothing significant, he was told. We're on the case, we'll probably be doing something with dampers, shock-absorbers. I could do with some shock-absorbers for myself, thought Martagon.

Some days later, Martagon's mobile rang while he was standing on the platform at Earl's Court tube station waiting for an eastbound train.

The call was from Marina. They had spoken the evening before; they had talked about the wobbly bridge, she had told him about the state of play with Jean-Louis, who was persecuting her with telephone calls. He still wanted their mother's chair.

'I've never understood,' Martagon had said, 'quite what's so special about that chair, for you two. It seems out of all proportion.'

'It would take too long to explain, I'll tell you another time.' Billie was with her, just back from seeing her aunt in Biarritz. Marina and Billie were about to have their supper: sea-bass and spinach. Everything had been normal.

The sound quality this morning wasn't so good, the station was noisy, and he had to strain to hear her through the crackle.

'Martagon, now I know. You are a shit.'

She did not seem to be in one of her states. She spoke in a low, expressionless voice.

'No, I'm not. You know I am not. What's up?'

'You have a girlfriend in London. You are a shit. I thought you were different, but you're not.'

Martagon was silent, numb. A train came screaming into the platform and stopped. The different things he might say to her went round and round in his head. He sweated. He was ready to fight for his life, but he needed to buy time.

'I can't hear you properly, my darling. Can I ring you back?'

'What is the point? Is it true or isn't it?'

A voice on the station public-address system: 'There are no Circle Line trains this morning due to a shortage of drivers. Repeat: there are no Circle Line trains.'

'Martagon. Tell me. Is it true?'

Three long seconds passed, quivering with his unspoken 'No' and his unspoken 'Yes'. Whichever way he went, there would be no getting back.

'Yes,' he said.

He heard her intake of breath.

'But I can explain everything. Look, I'll come over. Stay at home, stay at the farmhouse, I'll be with you by afternoon.'

His phone had crashed. He wasn't sure she had heard. He pressed the green button two or three times. No good. He crossed over to the other platform and got on to the next Piccadilly Line train to Heathrow. Fight or flight. He was going to fly, in order to fight.

How could Marina possibly have found out? With adrenaline flooding his brain, he thought hard, his future seeming to depend on finding the answer. What could Marina know? How much could she know? In the train he took out his phone again. He had forgotten to charge it. The signal was weak, but it worked. He cancelled his two appointments in London then called Julie at her office.

Speaking normally – he hoped – he told her he had to make a flying site visit to Bonplaisir. He'd be back in a couple of days.

'Will you be back before we all go over again for the opening?'

'Yes, yes.' And then: 'Julie, just for interest – have you by any chance told Tom about us, in one of those telephone conversations?'

'I don't know, I don't remember . . .'

'You must remember something like that.'

'Well, yes, I did say something, but nothing very private or personal, just so that he wouldn't worry that I was too lonely or anything. I hope you don't mind. I'm sorry if you think I shouldn't have.'

'It doesn't matter now.'

'Martagon – please don't go to France today! Please!'

This was not like Julie.

'But I have to. It's work. Just a couple of days. Speak to you later.'

Martagon leaned back in his seat. He was not thinking about Julie. She had no significance for him at that moment.

Only you, Marina, only you. Only you.

He could guess what had happened. The exact sequence. Tom Scree told Orford Mulhouse, who had taken such a benevolent interest in Julie, that she had a new boyfriend, and who it was.

Why did Scree do that? Easy. Malice and guilt.

Then Orford Mulhouse told his wife Nancy. Or perhaps Scree told them both together, over drinks on a terrace in bloody Biarritz, knowing that Nancy Mulhouse would pass it on to her niece Billie – who, last night at supper, told Marina. Acting sincerely out of concern for her, no doubt. Such kindly people. Scree, Nancy and

Billie had already known that he was involved with Marina.
He could murder the lot of them.

His passport was where he always kept it, in the zipped compartment inside his briefcase. He boarded the next available flight to Paris, where he changed planes. At Marseille he hired a car – a red Ford Ka – and slowly, his mind a blank, took the familiar route to Cabrières d'Aigues and, beyond it, to the farmhouse. Up the track, through the wood, over the bridge, past the orchard where the trees were hung with clusters and festoons of ripe cherries, glistening in the early-evening sun like baubles. Then on, between the lines of olive trees, to the long, low little house in its garden. So lovely, so familiar. It was going to be all right.

Marina was on the terrace, in the sphinx chair. She did not rise to greet him.

'What a silly little car,' she said.

'It's very nippy, pretty good, actually,' he replied, going towards her to embrace her. She avoided him, walking ahead into the house.

'How could you? How *could* you?'

'I owe you an explanation.'

In that instant he decided to be completely honest with her. For honour's sake – Marina's honour and his own, even though he had behaved dishonourably. It would be a relief. Back on track.

But he could not get back on track. He didn't know how to begin to explain.

'Events took over. It's complicated. It had nothing at all to do with us, you and me, with the way we are. It was quite separate. In a way, I couldn't help myself.'

'I don't believe what I'm hearing. That is so pathetic, so

feeble. Try again, Marteau. It's always the woman's fault when something happens, is that what you think?'

'No, of course not.'

They were sitting at the little wooden table in the kitchen, with a bowl of cherries between them. Martagon started eating the cherries, lining up the stones on the table in front of him. Marina had a glass of wine. He shook his head when she offered him one.

He couldn't explain Julie to Marina. That one word kept coming into his mind. Since he was determined to be honest, he had better say it and take the consequences.

'It was because she was – she is – flawless.'

Marina stared. 'I don't understand that word.'

Marina's English was so good that he was always surprised when her vocabulary proved inadequate. He flailed around for a translation.

'*Sans défaut. Sans tâche.*'

'You mean she's a saint, or a nun, or a virgin?'

'None of those things. You know perfectly well she isn't.'

'I don't know perfectly well anything. Who is she? They said I had met her, in your friend Giles's house, that it's his sister. But I don't remember. It's been driving me mad.'

It had not occurred to Martagon that Marina didn't yet know who Julie was. 'She was there at dinner with you, at the millennium time.'

'I said to Billie, "Who is this, what is she like, is she short or tall, dark or fair, is she more pretty than me?"'

'Billie doesn't know her.'

'But she could find out. She asked Nancy to find out.'

'Then you will know already that she is small and thin. Fairish hair. And nowhere near as lovely as you are, Marina.'

'I remember at that dinner, Giles's wife with the Alice

band. It's not her. I remember which one is the wife of the lord who is the friend of the Mulhouses. Not her. I remember one other woman, with a white shirt and glasses and untidy hair. A nothing woman. It's her. How *could* you?'

Martagon thought back. 'That's not her. That's a woman called Mirabel, she's not a nothing woman, she's a water-engineer with Harper Cox.'

'But I don't remember anyone else.'

'Julie was very quiet that evening. She's not really someone you would notice particularly, if you didn't already know her.' He tried to remember what Julie had been wearing, and couldn't.

'Julie. Another nothing woman. A less than nothing woman. So why, Marteau?'

Martagon took some more cherries. Marina poured herself more wine.

Martagon, stripping himself of surface, looked down into a small pool of truth to see what he found there. From now on he had no idea what he would find himself saying. He said, 'She trusts me. She needed me.'

'Do you think that I did not trust you? Do you think that I do not need you?'

'It's quite different. You could have anybody, you are strong, you have a world, you know who you are. Being in love with you is the most magical and extraordinary thing that ever happened to me, you know that. You are in a different category. You are the love of my life.'

'So?'

Martagon arranged his cherry stones in two parallel lines.

'Julie is . . . she is homely, not in the American sense, meaning that she is plain. Though maybe she is that too. I mean, she is like home. She belongs to the world I belong to, or could belong to. With her, I feel, I felt – kind of placed. Which I have never been. I don't know how to express this.'

'What you mean is she's English, and I'm just some sort of foreigner, a *frog*, good for a good time but not serious. Is that how it is?'

'You know it's not that. Don't insult me or yourself . . . Maybe sometimes, when I am tired, I do feel I don't altogether understand you.'

Marina stared at him, unblinking. Then she said, 'I saw a postcard once, that she sent you. At least I suppose now that it was her. It said "J" at the end. It was in an envelope, but you left it around so I read it.'

When he was abroad, Martagon sometimes sent Julie picture postcards. Sometimes he addressed them to Fasil. He sent postcards to lots of people. Sometimes Julie sent a postcard to him, in return. This had been so ever since he first got to know her. The cards never conveyed anything much. They were just a friendly way of keeping in touch.

'If I left one of her postcards around it was because there was absolutely nothing secret or private about it.'

'That's why it frightened me, even then. Because it *wasn't* a love letter. It meant that there was a long, long haul ahead.'

'Haul' was hard for her to pronounce. At first Martagon did not understand. He thought she had said 'hole'. Not that it made much difference. They worked it out.

'But that's just perverse,' he said, thinking about what she meant. 'You might as well be afraid of an electricity bill.'

'Not so perverse,' she replied. 'Because I was right. Anyway, I have been very afraid of electricity bills. That's why I sold Bonplaisir.'

Martagon took a deep breath. 'I haven't lost you, have I?' he asked, looking across the table and into her eyes. 'Can you forgive me?'

'Does she know about you and me, this Julie?'

'No.' And then, remembering her plea of this morning – 'Please don't go to France!' – 'Well, I'm not sure.' What had Tom Scree been saying to her?

'It's still going on, then. Not over at all.'

'I can stop it straight away. Any time I want. I was going to anyway, even if all this hadn't happened. I just wanted to do it gently, so that she was all right about it. I've already told her that I am going to be living in France.'

'You disgust me.'

When, later, he was lying alone in that garden on the day of the airport opening, going over everything that had happened to them all, he thought, I should have been straight with Julie from the beginning. Of course I should. After that extraordinary first evening at her flat. I should have explained to her that Marina and I were a couple, that it was for ever. I should have given Julie the chance to say, 'No more,' at that point. Or to go on, in the full knowledge that it could not last. Not being honest with Julie was perhaps where I stepped off the critical path.

What about not being honest with Marina, though? It was she I betrayed. It's hard to regret the experience of that first time in Julie's bed. There's a grain of truth in that feeble thing I said to Marina, about it having nothing to do with 'us', and about not being able to help myself. Biology, hydraulics, whatever. The engine starts up and everything else is blotted out. And when it's over it can be – though it wasn't with Julie – as if nothing ever happened. That's why you can feel *not* unfaithful when you are unfaithful. If I hadn't been found out – God, what a squalid phrase – if I hadn't been found out, and had brought things to an end with Julie, and gone to live with Marina as we planned, nothing bad would have happened.

But it will not do, thought Martagon, lying in the grass with his eyes closed, looking down into the small pool of truth deep inside him. That is the argument of a deceiver. Of a shallow philanderer. Of a Tom Scree. Worse, it could be the argument of a rapist.

I stepped off the path of my intentions, of my morality, of my love, when I let my mind close down and fucked Julie. I might as well have torn up the map. Yet Julie cannot just be written off as what my parents' church would call 'an occasion of sin'. There is reality in our relationship. An undramatic, everyday reality. I had no right to it. I was greedy. You can't have *this* and *that*.

And now I'm being self-important and portentous. A real piss-artist. If it were not for what has happened, all this would be an everyday story, the sort of a mess everyone gets into at one time or another. A total farce, really.

In the kitchen at the farmhouse it was growing darker. The sun was going down. Down by the bridge, the frogs had started to croak.

'I think I'll have that drink now,' said Martagon to Marina. 'Or do you want me to go straight away?'

She rose, found a clean glass, and poured him some wine. She opened a second bottle, and put it ready. Now the nightingales were starting up as well. Soon it would be time for the owls. It was going to be a long night.

NINE

'I went to see Virginie this morning,' said Marina. 'She always knew how to comfort me. But it's too late. She's too old and ill. I can't tell her my troubles any more.'

'I'm sorry,' said Martagon.

Martagon kept saying he was sorry. Because he was.

He asked Marina where Billie was. Marina said that Billie had gone back to Houston with her aunt Nancy, to look after her. 'Nancy is ill too. She has cancer. She will have the treatment but she is going to die, she knows she is going to die.'

'I'm sorry.'

'She isn't sorry. When I called to say goodbye before they left, she told me. She can't stand her husband. That's why she spent so much time over here. She's always called him Awful Orford, but I'd thought it was a joke. She said that dying was the only way she could get away from him permanently. Drastic, she said, but effective. A last resort. She was actually laughing. I had to laugh too. It was so strange.'

'Why couldn't they just divorce?'

'He wouldn't, and she sort of couldn't. Both their families are very prominent in the community, they're a famous couple, and everyone's very religious, they believe marriage is for ever, and Orford and Nancy fund art shows and head up lots of charities. Divorce was unthinkable. A French person can understand that.'

'She must have been unhappy, then. I'd always imagined her as a sort of superannuated good-time girl. All those parties.'

'That's how it was. She said she thought life was absolute hell for most people but, in the full knowledge of that, you could choose whether to be happy or unhappy. She chose to be happy. Some people, strong people, can do that. I can't.'

Happiness as an orientation. Just what he had thought himself – in the good times. For the first time, Martagon wished he had met Nancy Mulhouse. Now, he never would.

Marina was crying, silently – for Nancy, for herself? She wiped away the tears brusquely with the back of her hand.

'It's like what you once said to me, about one of us having to die before the other,' she said. 'But we meant it so differently.'

'Please stop talking in the past tense,' said Martagon. 'Nothing has changed.'

'Hasn't it? Hasn't it? It's easy for you to say that.'

'I know. I'm so sorry.'

'Please stop saying you are sorry.'

They talked and drank and were silent and talked again. Angers and resentments flared in her, and in him, but only briefly. Neither wanted a conflagration.

'You never told me about the chair,' he said, out of the blue. 'Just why it's so important to you and Jean-Louis.'

Marina shrugged and sighed. 'It will seem nothing to you. You see, it was the only thing in the château which was really our mother's, which belonged to her.'

Papa, she told him, insisted on keeping everything, in every room, exactly as it had been when he was a child. Maman could never move anything, or change anything, or he flew into a rage. She could not reorganize or redecorate her own bedroom, because it had been his mother's. She could not put up a picture or even a photograph.

'When I was about seven, she got out a little wooden ikon she'd always had. She'd brought it from Greece when she married, and hid it in the drawer where she kept her stockings. I knew it was there, I used to go and play with it sometimes. Anyway, she put it up over the *cheminée* in the salon. Papa threw it on the fire.'

'He was a madman.'

'He was as he was . . . She was like a little ghost in her own home. Even her rings were not really her own, they had been her mother-in-law's and belonged to the family, and he never let her forget it. Her great chair was the one and only precious thing of her own – apart from her dog – which he allowed her to have. He respected it, because he knew it was unique and very, very old. She always went to the chair when she was sad, as if she herself were a little dog going to its basket. She spent half the day in the chair, on the terrace, like I told you. When we were little we sat on her knee and played with the sphinx heads on the arms. I used to curl up in it all by myself when she wasn't there, and feel safe.'

'Presumably Jean-Louis wants it because he knows how valuable it is.'

'Not really. It's because the chair is all we have of our mother. It's as if the chair *is* our mother. Jean-Louis and I are children saying to each other, "She loves me much more than she loves you, and I love and understand her better than you do."'

'But you aren't children. It seems absurd. And you've

always told me you couldn't wait to get away from home, from – all that.'

'Yes, yes, Mr Englishman, I know I'm not rational.'

When finally they dragged themselves upstairs, they lay side by side in her big bed, taut and tense, not touching or talking. The contrast with the way they used to be was horrible.

Martagon could not sleep. He thought about the chair story, and about the shape of Marina's life and of his own. They both had a driving need to have and to hold and to belong; to be rooted. They both had an equally strong driving need to get away and fly free. It's the same for everyone. With some people one of these urges predominates, so there's no problem. Some people achieve equilibrium, or a compromise. But lots of people expend emotional energy veering wildly between the two poles and wondering why they aren't happier. This was suddenly so obvious to Martagon that as an insight it seemed banal. It was just that he hadn't formulated it before. He suspected both he and Marina fell into the last category, but he was too stressed, right now, to see anything straight. He wanted to talk to her about it, but it was not the moment.

At about four in the morning Marina got up, put on her dressing-gown, and went downstairs. He heard the terrace door being opened. Looking out of the bedroom window, he saw her lie down in the grass under an olive tree, the white silk of her dressing-gown glimmering in the light from the open door.

He did not go to her. What could he do or say? Perhaps she got some sleep there. He, too, must have slept a little, because he dreamed the stumps dream – with a difference. A variant. Thud-thud, thud-thud on the car window – but it was himself as a child, banging and banging on the glass with arms that had no hands, desperate to be allowed back inside, into safety.

'Maybe I should go,' he said, defeated, in the morning. 'Maybe I really am bad for you. Maybe you should move along.'

'Move along? Move along? Moving along means running through a thick wood in the dark leaving shreds of bleeding flesh dripping from the branches of trees. That's what I dreamed last night.'

So she had slept a little. They did not leave the house all that day. They sat on the terrace. Marina was ashy pale, the sockets of her great eyes blue-black, her mouth dry and flaking. With her fingers, she kept raking her unbrushed hair, hanging in dark strings.

This is how you will look when you are old. I shall be old then too. An inexpressible tenderness for her flooded him. He put his head in his hands.

'I wish my father was still here,' she said.

Martagon was surprised and irritated. He connected her father only with selfishness, overindulgence, and abuse of his wife and daughter. Not to mention the car-crash that had killed Marina's mother as well as himself.

'He used to take me round all the Roman ruins, when I was a child. The theatres at Orange and Nîmes. The remains of the town at Vaison-la-Romaine. He made it all alive. He loved the Romans, it wasn't history to him, he saw continuity, he showed me the way we go on building houses in Provence just like the way the Romans did. What he admired was their respect for order.'

'But from what you told me his own life was completely disordered, apart from his obsession about the house staying the same.'

'He was strong, he could tolerate, he could inhabit – can you say that? – the extremes. I'm like that too. You're always talking about good and bad. My father wasn't good and he wasn't bad. They aren't the only standards. There is ordered and disordered. There is strong and weak.'

'I hate the idea of veering between extremes, though,' said Martagon. 'I'd like to be the same all the way through, like a bar of chocolate. Or a sheet of clear glass. Though I suppose even they are made up of warring molecules held in equilibrium . . . My God, have we have lost our equilibrium, you and I?'

It had to be she who put out a hand first, and she did.

'Don't go, Marteau. We can do it,' she said. 'We can start again. We can get back to where we were, only better and different. If you are sure. Only if you are sure.'

Martagon was sure.

From that moment on they were, tentatively and carefully, with talk and thought, rebuilding – stone upon stone. There was no facile resumption of ecstasy. This was work. When their structure seemed sufficiently stable, they crept into its dark interior and were kind to one another, looking out on to a landscape through which they would soon walk together. The day had moved on and the terrace was already in shade, under an indigo sky. The sun still poured down obliquely on the far end of the garden, spiking the grass into black-green brilliance, every blade casting a shadow.

Marina imposed one condition. He must come permanently to live with her right now, making the farmhouse his home. It didn't matter that Child's Place was not yet sold, it didn't matter that his business and his office were in London, that could all be sorted out afterwards.

Martagon heard what she said. He did not reply at once. He nodded, thinking, working it out.

'Yes,' he said. 'I can do that. I'll do that. But I have to go back to London tomorrow, just for the day.'

'Why?'

At that moment he heard his mobile phone trilling in the kitchen. He went to answer it automatically.

It was Tim Murtagh at Bonplaisir. He didn't want to cause trouble but the men who were moving around the heavy installations in the arrivals hall had felt a bit of sway in the floor. He'd been up there himself and had detected nothing. But he thought he'd better report it.

'Who else knows about this?'

'No one. I tried to speak to Mr Harper in London but he wasn't available, so I was put through to Lord Scree. He told me I'd probably get you at this number. I didn't tell him what it was about.'

'Good man. Give me a moment.'

Martagon put down the phone on the kitchen table. He did not panic. His mind did not race. He did his job and exercised his hard-won professional judgement. He knew the arrangements and specifications for the arrivals hall flooring and its supports intimately, as if it were a street-map he had by heart. He thought it all through, rapidly and, he knew, accurately. Everything – the multiple layering of the glass, the silicon, the seating, the fixings, the specifications for the glass columns – had been tested and retested. The load-bearing was calculated to a factor many times greater than could ever be required. It was all right. He knew it was.

He picked up his phone again. 'I wouldn't worry, Tim. If there was any sway, it was probably minimal, and just a question of settling, under the weight of what you've been putting on it. I'd been meaning to make a flying visit, but I find that's impossible now. But take my word for it, there's not a problem.'

'I just thought I should tell you.'

'You were quite right.'

Not alarmed but fortified, he returned to Marina.

'Why?' she said.

'Why what?'

'Why do you have to go back to London tomorrow?'

He looked her in the eye. 'I have to see Julie.'

She made a despairing gesture.

'Listen, my dear love. Listen carefully. I'm doing a big thing. I'm committing myself to you for ever. It's what I want to do. She knows nothing about all this, she is – innocent. She hasn't done anything wrong. It's I who did wrong. She deserves better. I have to see her, I can't tell her in a letter, or on the telephone, I must do it properly, the difficult and honourable way. It won't be nice, but I have to do it. You must try and understand that.'

'But what if you don't come back?'

'Of course I'll come back.'

'Marteau, I'm so cold.'

Martagon couldn't find any kindling wood or firelighters, though there were big logs in the fireplace. He followed Marina's custom and went around the house, upstairs and downstairs, collecting up from jugs and vases and from hooks on the walls all the bundles of dry, greyish and now scentless lavender from last year. Leaving a trail of dusty shreds in his wake, he carried the lavender over to the hearth and piled it on top of the logs. He found some white household candles in the kitchen and wedged them upright in the lavender, like on a birthday-cake. He lit the candles – and in a few seconds the lavender flared up, regaining fragrance as it burned, filling the room with its healing aroma.

They cooked some pasta, mixed it with garlic softened in plenty of olive oil, and ate it by the roaring fire. They discussed practicalities. He called Julie and left a message on her answering-machine. He booked by telephone a seat on the earliest plane out of Marseille. That would mean he'd have to get up at five o'clock in the morning to be there in time to pick up his ticket. He would return on an afternoon flight.

'So I'll be home in time for a drink before dinner. Don't meet me, I want to find you here at home waiting for me. I'll pick up a car at the airport.'

'That would be better, really. I've said I'll look after George for a bit. Lin's going away, and he's getting Deng – remember that sweet Deng? – to drive over and dump George with me some time during the day.'

'Horrible dog,' said Martagon, not really meaning it this time.

Their mood lightened. They discussed what they would have for dinner tomorrow, the first evening of their new life.

'Do a pigeon, a *pigeon de Bresse*, like you did once before.'

'But it was very plain, I cooked it just with butter and salt, like the man at the market told me.'

'It was pure heaven. And beans, I think beans would be good with it. And tomato salad.'

'I'll leave the tomato salad for you to make, when you come. You do it better than me.'

'There's two bottles of the good Gigondas left, open them during the afternoon. And put some champagne in the fridge.'

'And the day after we'll go to the airport opening, together. I bought a wonderful dress for it, before – before all this.'

They did not make love that night. He kissed her on the lips and sensed that she recoiled. His mouth was viscous with exhaustion. They were both still fragile. Again Marina got up in the small hours and wandered out into the garden.

But she did not lie down in the grass, she returned to the house and to the bedroom, and the bed.

'Your feet are cold,' Martagon said.

She lay on her back and put her hand in his. He held on to it. At last, peace and warmth flooded through his system. They were back together again. The way they were. Christ, the relief. He breathed deeply. He smiled in the darkness and, turning his head, thought she was smiling in the darkness too. Neither of them said anything. He didn't want to sleep, he didn't want to miss one second of being in harmony with Marina, ever again.

But again he must have slept a little, because when the alarm clock shrilled at five he found she had rolled away from him, on to her side. She was sound asleep. The alarm hadn't woken her. Her feet were warm now. He got up, leaving her in the bed.

As the plane began its descent into Gatwick, he began to wish that he had taken the easy way out and stayed on with Marina. He could have left the confrontation with Julie for another time.

No, he could not.

He called Julie at her office as soon as he reached Gatwick. She wasn't in. So he called her home number.

'I've taken the day off work. I don't want you here at the flat,' said Julie. 'I'll meet you somewhere outside. Where we can walk.'

'OK. How about Regent's Park? The rose gardens. There's one or two things I have to do first. Say around twelve.'

Martagon tried to keep his voice normal. This was going to be the hardest thing he had yet had to do. He was about to hurt someone he loved because he loved someone else more.

The first thing he did was to go back to Child's Place. He

unhooked the abstract woodland scene from the wall, and wrapped the painting – still with the photos of Marina stuck on it – in his mother's pashmina and then in newspaper. He secured the rectangular bundle with brown parcel tape. It seemed very important to take something back to France which was his, to put in the farmhouse as a gauge of his permanent residence there. At the last moment, he went to his top drawer and found his mother's engagement ring where he had hidden it, in the toe of a yellow sock that had lost its partner. He put the sock, with the ring in it, in his pocket. All the rest of his stuff, and the files and equipment from his office, could come by carrier later. He quailed at the thought of the administrative complications involved. It would just have to be done.

Then he went into Trailfinders just round the corner in Kensington High Street and confirmed his booking back to Marseille, leaving Gatwick at around three in the afternoon. They printed out his ticket. It had come to £149 for both ways, not bad.

All this to-ing and fro-ing is costing a fortune, though. I can't charge it all up to the firm.

The wrapped painting was awkward to carry. It was just too big to be comfortably tucked under his arm. He had his computer case too. Moving fast was not easy.

He must leave Julie by one o'clock if he was to catch the flight. He would have to try not to keep looking at his watch, while remembering to keep looking at his watch.

Julie was waiting at the ornate gates of the rose gardens when he arrived, by taxi. 'You look a bit rough,' she said.

He did not attempt to kiss her. He touched her awkwardly on the shoulder, and felt her fragile bones. 'I expect I do,' he said. 'I seem to have lost touch with my clean shirts.'

They began to walk around between the beds of roses, not speaking. Martagon was waiting for her to say something.

He thought the roses were hideous. Coarse oranges and reds, brash and fleshy. He wondered whether Julie disliked them too, but it was not the moment to discuss roses. He shifted the wrapped painting to his other side. Julie did not ask what it was. That was perfectly in character. He watched a three-generation Asian family preparing a picnic in a glade just beyond the roses – women in saris spreading out rugs and unpacking food, men in dark trousers and white shirts fooling around with little children. They had hung the children's jackets on the overhanging branches of trees. He would have liked to ask Julie why she thought it was that people from the sub-continent used London's open spaces so much better, and so much more decorously, than anyone else did. He'd often noticed it. But it wasn't the moment to discuss comparative cultures.

'Is it true, then?' she said, after a long time.

Now that the moment had come, Martagon was speechless.

'Everyone knew about it but me,' she said. 'Everyone we know. Except that poor old Giles thought it was all over.'

'What was over? Everyone knew what?' he said, not sure what she did know.

'Don't worry,' she said. 'I'm not going to cry, not like after Tom. I'm not going to make a scene.'

'I didn't think that you were.'

'Didn't you? What exactly *did* you think, all of this time, Martagon?'

'I suppose I thought that things would sort of evolve. Like you yourself said, when we were at the empty house. You and me, it's something real, something else, quite separate, absolutely nothing to do with . . .'

'Go on, you can say her name, can't you?'

'Nothing to do with Marina. With Marina and me.'

'Why didn't you tell me, at the beginning?'

'It was too soon, and then it was too late. And you never asked.'

'That's an absolutely terrible thing to say, you can't get away with that.'

'I'm not trying to get away with anything,' said Martagon.

'I never asked because I trusted you. Of course I assumed that there must have been someone, before. That's normal. But I never imagined . . . until Tom put me wise. Just last week. I didn't want to believe him. When I asked you not to go to France this last time it was like saying, prove to me that it's not true. Didn't you understand that?'

'Not at the time. I did wonder, afterwards. Julie, I am so ashamed, so very sorry.'

'Don't say you're sorry. It doesn't help.'

They walked on again in silence for several minutes. Martagon just had to look at his watch.

'Why don't you say anything?' she asked.

'I don't know what to say.'

'You see, all this time with you, I was getting quite good at being happy,' said Julie. 'It was a new thing for me, ordinary happiness. Not like when I was seeing Tom. That was all over the top. And I found I was happier when I was happy, if you see what I mean. Some people aren't, they're really only happy when they're unhappy. It suits them. It doesn't suit me, not any more. But I keep being pushed right back into being unhappy again.'

'You're very good at being happy,' said Martagon. 'We have been happy together, in our way which is no one else's way.'

He wanted to talk to her about the little unit that they made, she and Fasil and himself, and how precious and comforting it still seemed to him, but could not find the words. He knew he could not expect Julie, at her age, to have Nancy Mulhouse's stoic philosophy.

'You'll be happy again,' he told her. 'You probably think you won't, but you will. You and I can be happy again, too. In time. Differently. We will reconfigure.'

He really meant all that. He didn't say that he was sure she would like Marina when she got to know her. He wasn't at all sure it was true. He wanted to say only what was true. He felt responsible now, and careful, as if he were easing a piece of heavy engineering, fuelled with dangerous emotions, into its casing.

It was not so easy.

'I don't think so,' said Julie, in response to his little speech. 'Because we won't be seeing each other. I never want to set eyes on you again.'

He did not want this at all. Julie was part of the fabric of his life. Fasil too. He took her hand. She did not take it away, but let it lie inertly in his. After a few seconds he let her hand go.

'Remember our deal?' he said. 'That you would always be there for me? That I would always be there for you?'

'There is no deal. There never really was.'

Time was passing.

'Let's just leave it for now. You're coming to the airport opening tomorrow with Giles and Amanda, I'll see you there. We'll find time afterwards, and talk again. Properly.'

'I'm not going. I told them already. And I told them why.'

That hurt. He looked at his watch, quite openly. 'I have to go.'

'Plane to catch, Martagon?'

'Yup . . . What will you do?'

'That's none of your business now.'

'Will you go back to Hailu?'

'That's none of your business either.'

'What will you do right now, after we leave here?'

'None of your business. Though, actually, I'll probably go for a walk. A very long walk.'

She adjusted her little backpack on her shoulders, pulling at the straps.

'Give my love to Fasil.'

'What do you care about Fasil? You've let him down, too, you know.'

'I care a lot about Fasil. I care about you, too. I always will.'

She interrupted him before he finished the sentence. There were tears glittering in her eyes now. 'Just don't say it, Martagon. Don't say it. I don't want to hear it.'

She turned aside and ran from him, lightly and fast, not through the wrought-iron gates but in the opposite direction, back through the rose gardens and towards the wide open area of the park. He watched her disappear, her backpack bobbing behind her.

'I'm sorry,' he said, knowing she could not hear. 'I'm so sorry.'

Martagon just missed one Gatwick Express train at Victoria. It was drawing out as he reached the platform. If he had found a cab two minutes earlier he would have caught it. He had to wait fifteen minutes for the next. No problem. He still had time. Just.

At Gatwick, the electronic sign announced that the next shuttle to the North Terminal would arrive in eight minutes. Eight minutes! So slack, so inefficient. They should be non-stop, one every minute. Thank goodness he had picked up his ticket earlier.

When at last he got to the check-in there was no queue. Thank God again. Phew.

The woman at the desk took his ticket, set it down in

front of her, and worked at her keyboard, looking at the screen. 'I'm sorry, sir, this flight has closed.'

Martagon looked at his watch.

'But it doesn't leave for nearly half an hour. And I've only got hand luggage.'

'I'm sorry, sir, the flight is already closed.'

'The plane's still on the tarmac, isn't it?'

'Yes, it is, sir, but the flight is closed.'

'Then just phone through to the gate and say I'm on my way.'

'I'm sorry, sir, the flight is closed.'

'But I have a ticket. A seat.'

'There were stand-by passengers. We've filled the flight now. I'm sorry, sir, but we have to do that, we do get a lot of no-shows.'

Martagon took a deep breath. He mustn't shout at her. It wasn't her fault, after all. 'OK, OK, so get me on the next one.'

She resumed clicking on her keyboard and looking at the screen. 'I'm sorry, sir, all our flights are fully booked for the rest of today. I could get you on a flight early tomorrow morning.'

'Try the other airlines.'

More clicking. More clicking. Martagon began to sweat.

'There's a Sabena from Heathrow to Brussels at sixteen twenty with a connection to Marseille, but you won't catch that.'

More clicking. More clicking. She found a later Sabena flight via Brussels from Heathrow and he reserved the place. Business class only available. £398. Good God.

It took about an hour by the special bus, once he found the bus and once it started, between Gatwick and Heathrow. Martagon sat through the journey in a stupor.

The Brussels flight took off on time. Martagon had an

aisle seat, next to an English couple – in their late fifties, he judged. The wife, in the window-seat, had a newspaper. She held it over her own lap and her husband's, and the two leaned in to one another, arms and thighs pressed together, so that they could both read it at the same time. They were rather stout. Neither was particularly good-looking. Their clothes were tidy and dull. The easy warmth of their companionship was palpable. It was like sitting next to an old-fashioned double radiator.

No love dramas for them, thought Martagon, no longings to be other than they are, to be rich and famous, to be somewhere else. No betrayals, no anguish other than the anguish endemic to the ordinary trajectory of life. Which for each individual is not ordinary but unique. They had married each other and become more and more married over the years. Perhaps I am getting it wrong, but I don't think so.

Chatting with the couple did not disillusion him. They were going to Brussels to visit their son, who would be meeting them at the airport. He was an MEP. They were travelling business class as a treat. They hadn't had a holiday abroad for years. They were really looking forward to seeing the grandchildren again. They lived in Wantage, and their name was Carter.

'Wantage. Where there's a statue of King Alfred,' said Martagon, remembering the newspaper reports of Arthur's accident.

'That's right. King Alfred was born in Wantage,' Mr Carter said, with pride. 'He was King of Wessex. He drove the Danes out of London in the year eight sixty-eight. He was a great scholar as well. That's why he's called Alfred the Great.'

Martagon thought Mr Carter might be a teacher, or in local government.

'You must know the town, then,' said Mrs Carter, leaning over. 'Do you know the Bear Hotel? On the square, where King Alfred is. We have lovely countryside around too, we do a lot of walking, on the downs. Do you know White Horse Hill?'

Martagon had to confess that he had never even been to Wantage. 'I had a friend who lived near there, but he died.'

'Ah.'

Conversation died too, and Martagon sat back and closed his eyes. The Carters were really nice. Decent, unpretentious, unjudgemental, alert, contented, provincial. Enough money for their needs but not rich. 'Centred', as Tom Scree would say. *English*, like King Alfred and the Berkshire downs. There were millions of English people like them. A true tribe, however mixed genetically with invading Danes, not to mention Normans. His Dorset clients were just examples of the London chattering classes, transposed. The Carters loved their England. It went without saying.

I love England too, but I never really got the chance. Or, rather, I never gave England a chance.

The plane was beginning its descent. The Carters folded away the newspaper and began fussing with their passports.

'Goodbye, goodbye! Have a great time!' He waved to the Carters. Goodbye, England.

Martagon's connection to Marseille was delayed. Technical problems.

He bought *The Economist* and read it mindlessly from cover to cover. Battered and shamed by the past few days, he now had no thoughts, no reactions. Almost, no feelings. Time passed. It struck him that he ought to ring Marina and tell her he would be late for their special dinner. Seriously late.

He tried to call her number on his mobile phone. It didn't work. He hadn't recharged it for days. He found the public phones. The first one he tried was out of order. As he was trying another one he heard his flight being called – the 'final call'. He must have missed the previous announcement. He daren't risk screwing this flight up. She would know he was on his way. He would call her from Marseille.

When the plane touched down at Marignane there was a maddening wait before the cabin doors were opened. Martagon strode fast, almost ran, to the exit hall, struggling with the painting and the computer case.

The first thing to do was to rent a car.

All the car-rental kiosks were closed. Every one of them.

I don't believe it.

An official told him that his flight was the last one in for the evening, and pointed out where he could collect his key and rental documents if he had prebooked.

He hadn't prebooked, he never had before. But, then, maybe he had never flown in at this hour.

He waited for a taxi, and when he reached the top of the queue he clumsily explained his predicament to the driver. He had to rent a car. Any car. Tonight, now. The driver looked dubious, then trundled off, round the airport access roads and into the industrial outskirts of Marseille. It seemed to take an age. The first garage they stopped at was closed. So was the second.

The driver pondered. He then sped off towards the centre of the city, stopping in a back-street. The forecourt of this third garage was dark, but there was a light on in the office. Someone was still there.

With the cab-driver's help Martagon negotiated, for a

silly price, paid in cash, the rental of the garage-owner's nephew's car, left with him while the nephew was *en vacances* with his wife and family in Orlando, Florida.

A digression then ensued while the driver and the garage-man, who were well acquainted, held a lively and well-informed discussion about the respective merits of the Paris Disneyland and the Florida one. Martagon, who had been to neither, and only understood half of what they were saying, stood by.

The nephew's car, parked at the back of the premises, turned out to be an old grey Opel Kadett, which looked as if it had led a hard life. There were rusted dents in the bodywork, and splashes of dried-on mud. But it was a car.

The garage-man went into his office to search for the ignition key. Martagon paid off the cab-driver, and shook hands with him cordially. The taxi disappeared at speed.

The garage-man shunted various other cars out of the way in order to make space for the Opel to get out. The Opel then failed to start. The garage-man sloped off to look for jump-leads. While he was gone, Martagon used the telephone in his office to call Marina. The number was engaged.

The garage-man got the Opel going, and left the engine running. Martagon threw the wrapped painting and his computer case into the passenger seat, shook hands with the garage-man, and drove off.

He had no idea where he was, and it took him a good half-hour to navigate through the maze of streets, and to get on course for the northbound autoroute. But he was, now, at last, on his way. Only about an hour to go.

It was not until he was rattling along the autoroute that he asked himself why on earth he hadn't told the taxi, straight off, to take him all the way to Cabrières d'Aigues.

It was so obvious. It would have been money well spent. The painful session with Julie, and the nightmare of his journey back to Marina, had caused his brain to go into neutral in order to avoid flipping altogether. He hadn't been thinking well. He hadn't been thinking at all. His eyes stung, he felt a bit sick. He hadn't slept properly for about a week, he hadn't eaten for twenty-four hours.

But it was going to be all right now.

He dared to look at the luminous face of his watch. Christ. Half past eleven – could that be right? Of course, French time was an hour ahead of British time, so he had started at a disadvantage. There had still been some light in the western sky when he was in the taxi. But it was midsummer; tomorrow, which was nearly today, was the longest day of the year.

Just then, as he attempted to slacken his speed because of a truck pulling out in front of him to overtake another truck, he realized that something was going wrong with the Opel's brakes. They were not responding properly. His armpits prickled, red alerts flashed in his tired mind. He tried the brake pedal again. This time, nothing at all. With his hand on the handbrake, he veered right, into the slow lane, and proceeded in low gear at thirty kilometres an hour, praying for an exit, any exit, from the autoroute.

Finally there was one. He took a turning at random where the access road forked, and struggled on for half a kilometre, praying for a village. Then, finding himself about to ram the back of a van going even more slowly than himself around a bend, he obeyed an impulse and shot off the road to the right, through an open gate, and into a field of maize – where he turned off the engine, jerked up the handbrake, juddered to a halt, and thanked his lucky stars that he was still alive.

He just had time, before he was overwhelmed by sleepiness, to think: I should have telephoned Marina again. Then, oblivion.

Martagon opened his eyes to morning sunlight, and to the sound of thud-thud, thud-thud, on the window of the car. He thought he was awake; but he must be still asleep and having the dream again. He steeled himself to turn his head. The arms had little fists on the ends of them, and the fists belonged to a small boy with a terrified face. Martagon opened the car door.

The child spoke with such a strong Provençal accent that Martagon understood almost nothing – except that he had thought Martagon was dead. A dead man. No, no, said Martagon, it's all right, I was asleep. He tried to explain about the car and the brakes. The boy pointed across the field to a house half hidden by trees. That was where he and his parents lived. Martagon shouldered his computer case, grasped the painting, left the key in the car, and stumbled after the boy through the maize.

The parents insisted on giving him coffee, and they let him use their telephone. Marina's number was engaged, as before. Perhaps your friend's telephone is out of order, they surmised, taking an interest. The boy's mother, who was pretty and seemingly did not have much to do, offered to drive him to his friend's house. It was not all that far, and she needed to go to the *tabac* anyway. It would be a privilege.

He went into the *tabac* with her. While she chatted to the man behind the counter, he picked up the *Herald Tribune* and started to read it idly. The man looked at him with disapproval. Martagon found coins in his pocket and paid for the paper, which he hadn't wanted. His rescuer was a voluble woman and his conversational French was sorely tested during the remainder of the drive. He asked her to drop him where the track to the farmhouse turned off from the road, and they parted with mutual expressions of pleasure. He knew that she was a little disappointed not to be making the acquaintance of his friend.

When Martagon crossed the bridge over the stream and started up the track towards the farmhouse he stretched his eyes wide, not believing what he saw.

There were two police cars parked in the garden. There were three men walking around, their hands in their pockets. He heard the incoherent crackle of radio communication.

Two of the men detached themselves from the scene when they saw him coming, and walked purposefully towards the spot where he would reach the paved yard, where he and Marina always parked their cars.

Marina's Alfa Romeo was not where it ought to be. It wasn't anywhere.

Martagon's first thought, as he approached the policemen, was: Jean-Louis. Bloody Jean-Louis.

I should have taken all those threats from her crazy brother more seriously. What in hell has been going on?

And then: Where *is* Marina?

A dog came lolloping round the side of the house and started jumping up on him, whining with joy.

'He appears to know you,' said one of the policemen.

'Yes, he knows me,' replied Martagon, pushing George away. 'His name is George.'

I don't understand anything.

'The name of the dog is George,' said the policeman, ironically, taking a note. 'And your name, Monsieur?'

He told them his name. He asked them where Madame was.

Madame is not here. At this moment we do not know where Madame is.

Martagon looked around. Everything looked normal, except that the door to the bicycle shed was hanging open.

Yes, Monsieur, we have already ascertained. There is a gun missing from the shed. But we have found it already.

The policemen spoke to Martagon in a mixture of French and bad English. Martagon spoke to them in a mixture of English and bad French. There were some misunderstandings.

Had Marina been shot? Was she lying wounded, or dead, somewhere in the garden? He would find her, he could make her well, he could bring her alive again. Of course he could.

At that moment Martagon saw a patch of blood, still wet and red, on the paving of the terrace. Beside it, Marina's great chair lay on its side, one arm broken clean off. He picked up the broken arm, and passed his fingers over the sphinx head without touching it.

Please – no fingerprints. Do not distress yourself. Let us go into the house, there are some questions.

George began licking at the patch of blood. Martagon grasped him by the collar and dragged him into the house too, shutting the kitchen door. George went to the dog-bowl and began drinking noisily.

The policemen wrote down everything that Martagon said in their notebooks. When did he last see Marina de Cabrières? When did he last speak to her? What was his relationship with her? What was in that big package he was carrying? Where had he been between dawn and nine o'clock this morning? Could he provide witnesses for that? Did he have a key to the farmhouse? Why had he come? Was he expected?

He answered all their questions truthfully to the best of his ability.

They told him that the old man who leased the vine-fields overlooking the house had seen Madame get into her car with a bag and drive off, very fast, shortly after he came to work, at dawn. The dog chased her car down the avenue, barking, then gave up and wandered back towards the house.

A couple of hours later another car had driven up. It was a taxi. The person who got out of it was Madame's brother. The farmer knew all the family from way back, he used to work for them in the old days.

The farmer said that Jean-Louis paid off the taxi and then walked all round the house, banging at the doors and windows. The dog followed after him, barking. After a while the farmer stopped watching and moved away from his vantage-point to get on with his spraying. He thought of going down to tell Monsieur Jean-Louis that Madame his sister was not there, but it was none of his business. A family matter. One would not wish to intrude.

Half an hour later the farmer heard a gunshot, and then another, and more barking. The sound of guns is not uncommon: hunters from the village taking birds or wild boar, perhaps. But the shots had not come from the woods. He walked back over his field to where he had a good view of the farmhouse and garden. There were two men there now – Madame's brother and another, on the terrace. Madame's brother had fallen on the ground.

'Did he say which one had the gun?'

The other man. The farmer could not or would not say whether he recognized the second man. He was very cautious. But he got on to his tractor immediately, and went home and telephoned the police. He was, quite naturally, afraid, said the policeman.

Afraid – and probably protecting someone he knew, thought Martagon. A neighbour, or a friend or relative.

They showed Martagon a gun, wrapped in transparent plastic. Did he recognize it? Had he ever used it?

Martagon shook his head.

The police had broken into the house and found the telephone off the hook, the receiver lying beside the cradle. Did he know anything about that?

He shook his head.

They found a sealed envelope with his name on it on the kitchen table. Would he recognize Madame's handwriting?

Yes.

The envelope was produced. This, too, was wrapped in transparent plastic.

Yes, that is her handwriting.

The two policemen turned discreetly away as Martagon tore open the envelope. They looked out of the window, both with their hands behind their backs, rocking on their heels.

Martagon stepped outside the door on to the terrace to read Marina's letter.

Afterwards they took the letter back, in its envelope. It would be needed for evidence, if there had been a serious felony. It was his property and would be returned to him, when their investigations were completed and the case closed. They smoothed the ragged top of the envelope and replaced it in the plastic covering. They took down his address and his various contact numbers.

He waited while the answers he had given, and the little that he had said of his own volition, were typed out and printed from a police notebook-computer. He read what constituted a statement, and signed it. He would be recalled, they told him, for further questioning. He should keep himself available.

Of course, he said.

The third policeman was testing the broken chair for fingerprints with powder and brush. When he was satisfied, and had packed up his equipment, he moved away towards the cars. Martagon set the great chair upright and sat down in it, resting his right elbow on the one good arm, nursing the broken one on his knee, his fingers tracing the worn, gilded carving of the sphinx-head. George lay at his feet, his nose on his paws. The two of them watched the police slowly moving off, taking the gun with them. When the sound of their motors had faded away down the track, Martagon went back inside, opened his laptop on the kitchen table, and e-mailed Giles: 'Not coming. Something terrible has happened. Martagon.'

He went back into the garden and stretched out on his back under the olive tree, on the still-flattened patch of grass where Marina had lain during that difficult night.

She had said, in the restaurant in Marseille: 'Pierre would kill Jean-Louis for me.'

Pierre probably did kill Jean-Louis, when he arrived and found Jean-Louis banging about and attempting to carry off Marina's great chair. Then Pierre took the body away in his jeep to dump it in some ditch or thicket. He would know where to hide it. Or maybe Pierre had just wounded Jean-Louis, and had taken him to hospital. If Jean-Louis were lying wounded somewhere on the property, the police – or George – would have found him.

No, not necessarily. Jean-Louis might have been dumped between the two doors in the cavity in the garden wall. The policemen wouldn't have known the space existed.

How had Jean-Louis planned to leave, taking the chair with him, had he not been interrupted? I suppose he had a plan. So many questions. It'll all come out, in time. This story isn't finished yet by any means. But I don't care, actually. I don't give a fuck what happens to either Jean-Louis or Pierre now.

'We are becoming the same person,' she had said. 'Only together are we each complete.'

He tried to recall precisely what she had said in her letter, and couldn't. He had only read it the once. He had been in shock, and shaking. He remembered exactly how it was set out, on a single A4 page, with wide margins, the lines of her familiar handwriting straight and even. She had begun with 'M', and ended with 'M', as she always did. As both of them always did. He remembered, more or less, her first sentences: 'M – just in case you turn up. I don't suppose you will. I waited and waited, and you didn't come and you didn't come and you didn't even call. So I knew you weren't coming. Then the telephone rang and I thought it was you but it was Jean-Louis.'

Jean-Louis had told her he would be over first thing in the morning to take possession of the chair. Martagon couldn't remember what she wrote next, but it must have been then that she contacted Pierre. He remembered the worst part all too well. Her telephone had rung again, very late. Again she thought it must be Martagon. But this time it was Lin.

She thought I had decided to stay with Julie.

I've just been hanging on by a thread, with Marina, all this time. The thread has snapped. It's final.

He remembered more from further down the page, but not word for word. He recalled the gist. Letters putting an end to love affairs have a terrible sameness about them. At the end she said she was getting the first plane to Paris, and was joining Lin. He had been asking her to go and live with him for a long time. For months, she said.

And there was a PS: 'Pierre will come over a little later

and take George home with him. George will be OK with Pierre for the moment.'

Pierre had left George behind, though.

It didn't matter that he couldn't remember everything Marina wrote. She had gone away. She had taken herself away. She was not going to be with him ever any more. It was over.

Martagon lay in the grass where she had lain, for hours, going over and over everything that had happened.

Some time in the late afternoon he thought how all the people would even now be arriving at Bonplaisir. The new structure would be filling up with voices and movement, fulfilling at last its function as a busy, complex working environment.

He opened his eyes and sat up. He should have run over to the airport following Tim Murtagh's call. What if his judgement had been wrong? What if the arrivals hall flooring drifted or cracked or shattered?

There would be panic, horrific injuries, fatalities.

His reputation, for what that was worth in the context of such a disaster, would be ruined for ever. Professionally he would be finished.

Had his decision been based 100 per cent on his professional judgement? Had he been swayed – horrible word – by his intense involvement in the crisis with Marina?

He searched his heart. No, I don't believe so. I really don't. Nevertheless I should have gone over to check it out, if only for Tim's sake.

Martagon had carried the *Herald Tribune* with him when he came out to lie in the grass. He had not opened it all day. Now he riffled through the pages. The report of an architectural conference held earlier in the month in New

York caught his eye. The writer of the article had added his own comments:

> In my view, the main task of architecture today is to mediate between our inner and outer worlds. It is an art of redefining boundaries, of articulating thresholds, bridges, edges, borders and passages. It is an art of transitions – from one place to another, between subjective perception and objective reality, private and public space, and between different ecosystems . . . Floors morph into ramps, spirals into squares; escalators expand space as if through a camera lens. Reason is contorted by desire.

Martagon let the newspaper fall. The art of transitions. Reason is contorted by desire. It surely is, and not only in architecture. Desire is contorted by reason, too. That's the dual tension which keeps the whole show on the road. I wish it were not so. There is no singlehearted purity of being. Except at the moment of birth and the moment of death.

DEPARTURES

Some time in the late afternoon Martagon gets up, a little stiff, and goes back into the house. Marina left everything clean and tidy. There is a bowl of tomatoes on the kitchen table. No sign of the pigeon or of the rest of last night's celebration dinner. She must have eaten it, or binned it, or packed it up like a picnic to take to Paris. She no doubt drank the Gigondas, during that long night.

He opens the fridge, and takes out the bottle of champagne he had told her to put there. He holds his filled glass up against the light and sees the little bubbles rising from the bottom to the top, endlessly, on and on.

I'll tell you now, my darling, why they do that. Perhaps you really did want to know. Listen. There are no bubbles in the bottle at the time when it is corked. Fermentation meanwhile continues. When the bottle is opened the pressure is released and the gases escape in the form of bubbles, bouncing off the inside surfaces, off the invisible imperfections of the glass. You would see, if you stuck something – like chewing-gum – on the inside of the glass, how the bubbles would cluster on it and bounce off.

He hears her husky voice in his head asking, again, 'But

why do the bubbles always fly up, and not round and round like a snowstorm?'

'To find the air.'

Suddenly he is less certain. He has forgotten. He is so tired.

The bubbles in a glass of champagne will always fly upwards, on and on, darling. They just will. Believe me. Until all the gases have escaped, and the wine becomes flat. But we would have finished the bottle, you and I, long before that happened.

He goes back outside again and looks in at the open door of the shed, at the gun-racks on the wall, and the gap, and the bicycles they had never used. Clumsily, he grasps the handlebars of one of the two bicycles and wrenches it out of the embrace of its partner. He pumps up the tyres. It seems OK. He rides shakily off round the house, down the track, over the bridge.

As he comes out of the shade of the wood he hears thunder and feels a few drops of rain. Within seconds, the sky darkens and the drops become a deluge. Martagon plunges on, turning on to the narrow road, which joins the web of similar roads winding between villages, not caring where he is going. The rain pours down, the wind blowing it straight into his face. He is soaked to the skin.

I don't have to go through with this agony. Yes, I do. I do have to go through with it. That is the deal.

He pedals on. He has no option. He passes farm buildings where he could stop and take shelter until the worst of the thunderstorm is over. He notes each one but does not stop, knowing there is no avoidance of grief, and hoping that every particular stab of anguish endured is one that he will not have to bear again, and not realizing that his route through the network of country roads is circular until he recognizes the same hills, the same buildings and groups of trees, feels the jolts of the same potholes and rocks in the road, everything coming round again as the darkening landscape unfolds in front of him. On the horizon he glimpses brightness, as if the weather is about to clear. Then the storm comes down again and he is back where he started, pedalling with no idea of journey's end.

When at last he gets back to the farmhouse the clouds are rolling away and the sun is shining again – not as if nothing has happened, but as if something tremendous has happened. The birds are beginning to sing again, one by one. Every leaf, every blade of grass swells with glossy life. Martagon is not fooled. He is going to have to ride out his misery again, and again, and again. Losing Marina is a bereavement. Only for now, he is part of the grand calm.

He takes a hot shower and smells on his skin the lavender soap, the smell of Marina. He dries himself with Marina's used towels. He notes the absence of her white dressing-gown from its usual hook on the back of the bathroom door.

He wanders out into the garden again and looks back at the house where they were happy. Extraordinary happiness. Perhaps with Lin, who won't ask so much, she will find she can sustain ordinary happiness.

I don't think so. Happiness is not her natural climate. A drama queen. She won't be able to hurt Lin, though, as she has hurt me. She won't be able to *get* him as she got me. They have known each other a long time. She'll have to accommodate his gay tastes, he won't be vulnerable to her. Perhaps because she won't have so much power over him, she will be able to stay with him. She'll enjoy Lin's carry-on, and the entourage – young Deng and all the other aides and assistants, run off their feet fetching and carrying for both of them.

But she won't have *got* him. She *got* me, totally. By saying we would have a child. By asking so much – to give up my kind of life for her kind of life, and making me believe it could work. You did that so well, Marina, like you do everything. You believed it all yourself, at the time. Because you really did love me, I know you did. Loving me was part of the process that was bound to end in – in ending it. You didn't plan it that way. You never were any good at map-reading.

It was I who could not be content with ordinary love, who had to have an extraordinary love. If it hadn't been for Julie, if it hadn't been for the disaster of my return trip, would Marina and I still be together? Maybe. But if it wasn't going to be because of that, there would probably have been something else.

All that stuff that bothered me about being a good person, about what is a good person. It's not really the point, it never was. No wonder I didn't get anywhere with it. It's a vain question, a self-regarding question.

The real point as I see it now is that life has to be *for* something. And if not for God – the universal metaphor – and if not for society as I find it, then for a vision of how the world could be, where we would be both honourable and happy. It's the backward-looking longing for Paradise, for Camelot, the dream of an unspoilt world of integrity and sufficiency, which doesn't even know what dishonour and evil are. Or else, it's the forward-looking millennial vision of a world in which dishonour and evil shall be vanquished in a blaze of redemptive purity.

A vision is a strategy, a solace, an aspiration, a solution even, to things being the way they are. Marina was that vision for me.

For things, the way they are, are not wonderful. Not wonderful at all. But you can embrace the vision and live as if you could bring it about. A vision doesn't grow out of nothing. It corresponds to something understood. I have inhabited a small part of the vision. Different small parts may be all that anyone ever apprehends. I knew it in real life and in real time, through love. Through Marina whom I have lost. Not mild, love-thy-neighbour-as-thyself kind of love, but transforming, consuming love, the creative-destructive kind, neither benign nor malign in itself but the blind cause of perturbation.

Yet I was more aware of being near the still centre of everything, with Marina, than I have ever been in all my life.

Tangling with this kind of love is a risk. Why does something always go wrong? Because risk-taking is not a narrative, it has no critical path. When everything is going wonderfully and you have heaven on earth, you feel you are magically protected and not subject to the rules of everyday. But every roll of the dice is random. The only certainty is a return to the mean. Nothing is for ever. Back to square one.

My father would say, we screw up because of original sin. Put it another way. There is a design fault in us. We are absolutely bound to screw up. I wish my father had not died. He would be seventy now, if he had lived. That's not really old. I should like to have known him better. I should like to have asked him whether there's not perhaps a design fault in his God, since He is said to have created us in His image. That would explain a lot. There's a design fault in you, Marina. There's a design fault in me. All I can do is aim for perfection outside myself in the structures – material or immaterial – that I design. That's my job. Always I fall short.

Except with tomato salad, Marina. That's not nothing, either.

A good person – I can't get away from that formulation now – gets on with it, keeps going, keeps building, holds on to the vision, starting all over again every time.

Martagon shuts George up in the kitchen and wanders off out of the garden and down the track. He crosses the bridge over the stream. He stops on the middle of the bridge, pulls a yellow sock out of his pocket, extracts the small sapphire and diamond ring from its toe, looks at it briefly in the palm of his hand, and drops it into the stream. He puts the sock back in his pocket because he doesn't know what else to do with it. He follows the track through the wood, where it is already dusk. He comes out of the wood into the evening sunlight again, thinking about what has happened, mapping a hinterland.

He strikes up off the track at an angle towards the hills behind the farmhouse, following the rising ground along the edge of the field of vines. From here he can see the farmhouse and the garden. It was from here that the farmer saw Marina drive off, from here that he watched Jean-Louis and Pierre. The farmer has gone home and Martagon is alone on the high ground.

He looks down into Marina's garden. My God. The jeep is driving up to the farmhouse. From here, it looks like a toy. As if he were watching a play from the upper circle of a theatre, Martagon sees Pierre get out, fumble for a key, open the kitchen door and emerge with George on the lead. George is pulling back, bracing his paws on the ground, twisting his squared-off Airedale jaw to escape the lead. He looks as if he is trying to bite. Pierre drags him to the vehicle. George, giving up the struggle, jumps in with the help of a forceful leg-up from Pierre. Pierre goes back to the house, locks up, returns to the jeep and drives away.

Poor old George. Not such a horrible dog, really. Lin

can depend on George the way Marina can depend on Pierre.

She'll end up with Lin in Copenhagen. She's had good times in Scandinavia before. Perhaps she'll contact her old lover Erik Smedius and they'll all get together and have a good laugh about the old days. I wish I were dead.

Martagon turns away from the empty arena of the garden and focuses closely on what is within his range. He notices the blue of copper-sulphate spray on the vine-leaves and sees that the grapes are forming. He looks at the rose bushes planted at the ends of the vine rows. They are there for a purpose. Marina told him that disease in the roses presages disease in the vines. The roses are like miners' canaries. They are modest and functional, not like the gross blooms in Regent's Park. He scrutinizes a particular rose, past its peak, its simple, single, yellow-pink petals distorted and blotched. An ant moves agitatedly among the pistils. He memorizes the rose as he did not memorize Marina's letter.

The sun is going down. Its slanting rays glitter on the stream below and throw into relief the vines dancing across the hill, outlining their sharply angular black stocks, limbs petrified in mid-motion, casting shadows.

Above, the vapour trail of an aeroplane hangs in the sky. There is no wind at all. This is the best time of the day in Provence. Earth, air and water are held in perfect balance. Just for now, because nothing is for ever. Tomorrow the mistral may shake the vines and rattle the poplars.

I wish I were dead. Yes, I may do just that, in the end. To be out of a world where Marina is, somewhere, where I can't be with her. Not now, though, while I am unhinged. To end it all now would be the grand romantic gesture. But when I choose. Maybe never. It would be another failure, a betrayal of life, the dishonourable course.

I already know how to work, and how to love. That's not nothing. It shouldn't go to waste. I'll just keep going.

Martagon walks on towards his unknown destination.

Though Martagon doesn't know it yet, the airport at Bonplaisir is a terrific success. The party is in full swing. Nothing has gone wrong, and nothing will go wrong. It is a triumph.

The mistral will not come tonight. Tomorrow will be a perfect day.

Notes and Acknowledgements

The first line of the poem by George Herbert (1593–1632) from which Julie copies out a stanza is 'Teach Me, My God and King'. The lines about stained glass to which she refers are in Herbert's poem 'The Church Windows'.

Oscar and Lucinda by Peter Carey (1988) is published in paperback by Faber & Faber.

I have taken the liberty of advancing the decision made about the venue for the World Cup 2006 by about six weeks.

The article which Martagon read in the *Herald Tribune* for 24 June 2000 was 'Not Just ANY Philosophy: An Architecture of Ideas' by Herbert Muschamp.

I am grateful to the following for what they have said or written, privately or publicly, formally or informally:

James Carpenter, Sir Jeremy Dixon, Michael Dobbs-Higginson, Dr Ellis Douek, Hugo Glendinning, Professor Paul Glendinning, Bill and Diane Hodgkinson, Tim Macfarlane, Deborah Singmaster.

The following works have also been relevant to the writing of this novel:

William Shakespeare, *Julius Caesar* and *Antony and Cleopatra*.

Sophia and Stefan Behling (eds), *Glass* (1999)
Marcus Binney, *Airport Builders* (1999)
Richard Sennett, *The Conscience of the Eye* (1991), *The Corrosion of Character* (1998).

My first and last thanks are to Kevin O'Sullivan, without whom this book would have been neither conceived nor written.